Long Road Home

Baron Alexander

Wilderwick Press

Forest Row, UK

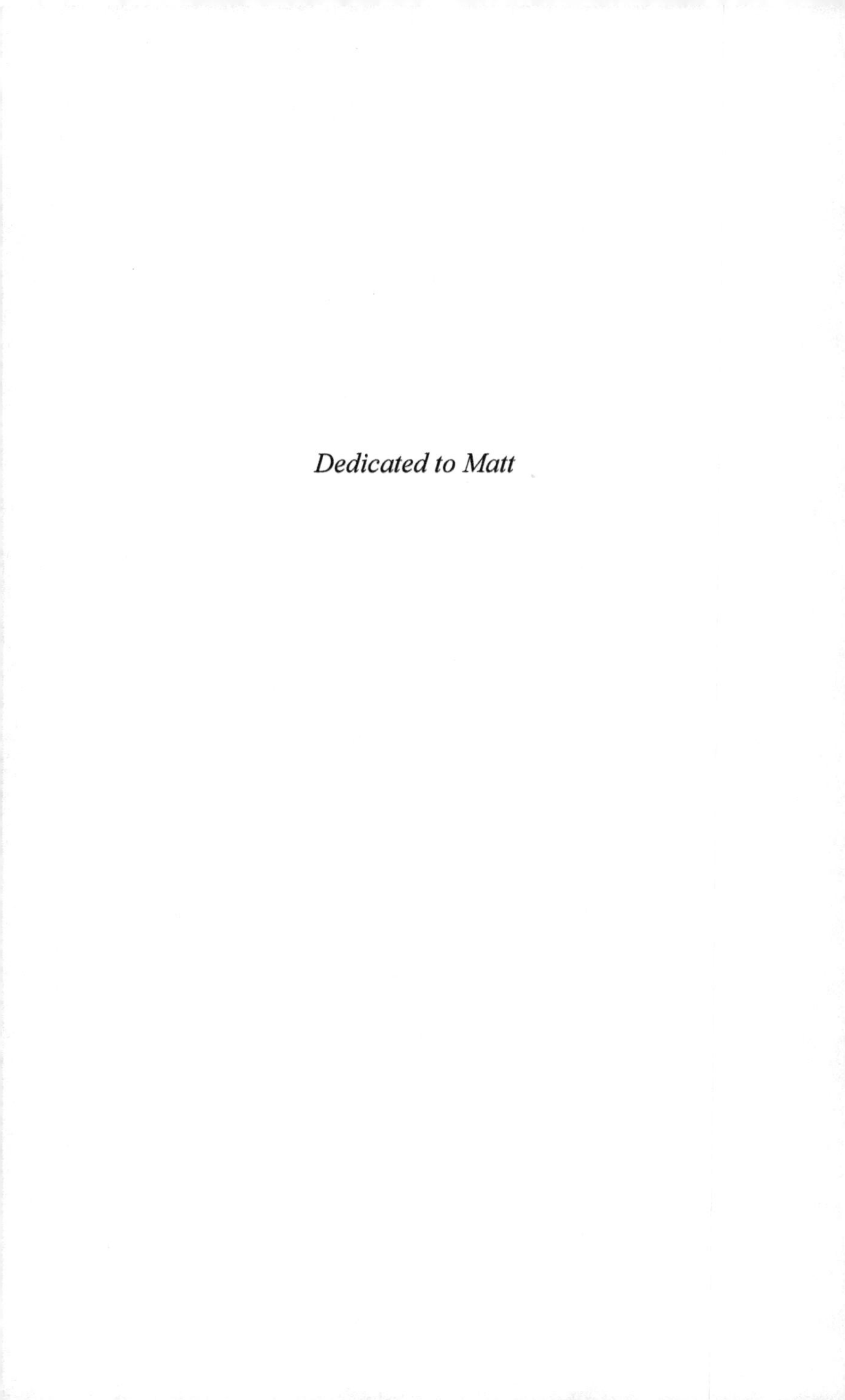

Dedicated to Matt

CONTENTS

CHAPTER ONE

THE GAMBLER

"You!"

Julia turned her head, trying to see who was so rude and so loud. She was surprised to see a large man with blonde hair walking towards her. All heads at the table followed him.

"Me?"

"Yes, you. Don't move."

Thoughts of a poisonous spider on her shoulder flashed through her mind. Then she decided it was a trick by the casino on an unsuspecting guest, so she played along and froze where she stood.

"I need you to stand next to me." The man put his arm around her waist, urging her to join him at the table. More heads turned to watch the spectacle and smiles were on all the faces.

"Sorry?"

"I can't explain now. Just come here."

She allowed him to guide her to the head of the roulette table.

"Let it all ride again, same numbers. Twenty-nine and the neighbours." The man had apparently forgotten about her once she was standing next to him.

The croupier spun the wheel. "No more bets," he said.

The ball bounced and landed on twenty-five. The crowd applauded. The croupier eliminated all of the chips from the felt table top except those on number twenty-five or its borders. The man had bet everything spread over numbers twenty-five to thirty-three. He lost on the other numbers but won thirty-five times the amount placed on number twenty-five.

"See? You bring me luck." He picked up a handful of chips and put them in Julia's hand. "For you."

"What? This is crazy. I'm not lucky. I just lost all of my money."

"You're lucky for me and that's all that matters." He took his entire pile of chips and pushed them towards the croupier. "Everything again on twenty-nine and the neighbours."

A crowd began to form. The croupier turned to a tuxedoed man with an earpiece who had come to ask him something. The man nodded and the croupier took the chips and placed them evenly across the numbers.

"Don't you want to call it a day?" Julia asked. She realised that each pink chip was worth a thousand rand. Each stack looked to be at least twenty high.

The man ignored her and watched as the croupier spun the wheel. This time it was number thirty. Cheers roared and the crowd grew larger. No one else bet as they watched with fascination at the amount of money being wagered. By now, several security staff and the pit boss were standing next to the croupier.

The man's face became purple with excitement. Julia could feel herself strangely drawn to the excitement without knowing why. It was insane. The crowds pushed against her and her body was crushed against his. He didn't seem to notice at first but then put his arm around her waist. She let him. *Nothing and no one would deny this man what he wanted tonight*, she thought. *Not even luck.*

"Everything on twenty-nine," he said.

The whispers whipped through the crowd and they began to cheer and chant, drinks spilling on each other. Julia could only see the whites of their teeth and eyes. Everything else blurred in a suntanned cocktail of gambling fever.

The man returned his hands to grip the edge of the roulette table, Julia forgotten again. She could see the veins on his neck clearly as though he had done heavy lifting. She saw white spittle at the corner of his mouth.

"I'll need to confirm with the house, sir," the croupier said.

"Fuck the house. I'm here to play. Either take the bet or give me my money and I'll go elsewhere."

The crowd cheered louder. He had become their champion.

The croupier looked at the pit boss, who nodded. The man pushed all of his chips towards the croupier, who changed them to purple chips with pink centres, each one worth twenty-five thousand rand. When the mechanics of counting and exchanging chips were over, there was a stack of thirty-two purple chips with pink centres on number twenty-nine.

He spun the wheel and all eyes watched it turn, the white ball whirling in the opposite direction. As soon as the croupier spun the wheel and flicked the ball, the man reached over and moved the stack to number thirteen. It was highly irregular and the pit boss involuntarily lunged forward.

"No further bets," the croupier said, glancing at the pit boss.

The wheel slowed and the ball began to bounce off the ridges. The cheering stopped as people craned their necks to see where it landed. Julia's mouth had gone dry at the sheer magnitude of the bet and recklessness of the man. As the ball did its final dance on the moving numbers, she was pushed hard by a Chinese man beside himself with tension. She heard rather than saw the result. Number thirteen. The crowd went crazy. The man collapsed under congratulations and the pit boss removed the croupier from the table. Random members of the crowd hugged the man and he hugged them back. Women kissed him lustily. It took several minutes for the excitement to die down enough for him to turn and see the pit boss next to him.

"Congratulations, Mr. Smit," he said, shaking his hand. "I didn't think this table had a limit; you just proved us wrong again." He picked up a black cloth and laid it over the table. "Mr. Kerzner has extended his personal congratulations and would like you to take the penthouse villa as your personal residence for as long as you like."

"Tell Sol thanks. If you can have my things moved there, I'll be having a few friends join me to celebrate." The man threw the pit boss a purple and pink chip. To Julia, he picked up a handful of the same chips and put them in her hands. "For you, my lady luck. Thank you."

Julia was too stunned to say anything other than take the chips. The whole process was too surreal. "What's your name?"

"Matthijs. Yours?"

"Julia. Nice to meet you." She had to shout about the crowd.

"Have you had dinner?"

"Not yet."

"Then join me. I just need to cash these in and then we can go and see how we can spend it." He was matter of fact about the win, almost oblivious to the fact he now had enough money to live ten lifetimes in luxury. He almost seemed deflated, as if the whole high of winning was a disappointment.

"I just need to find my friends and let them know where I'm going."

"Have them join us. I have a feeling we're going to have one hell of a party." He had regained his energy, the shadow of disappointment gone, and was preparing to spend his riches.

She went to the craps table to find Jane and Stewart gambling their allotted sums. "How's it going?"

"Stew's just won but I think we're down over half. What's all the commotion about? Were you near enough to see?"

"Apparently, I am the winner's lady luck," she said.

Stewart was in his own world, trying to play the odds the way he had read in his travel book.

"What?"

"I know, it's crazy. He is like a force of nature." Her face was flush. "And he's cute."

"Cute?"

"In a madman kind of way. He grabbed me and put me next to him. There's no other way I can say it. Then he bet everything he had and in three rolls of the wheel, he broke the table. There's a black cloth over it like it's dead."

Jane laughed, the free alcohol flushing her more than her burn. "Then what are you doing here?"

"He's invited us back to his place. He wants you both to come." Julia felt herself tingle at the excitement. This was a gap year for them before they started university. Julia had been accepted at Oxford, to her parents' delight. Jane was going to Bristol, as was Stewart. They had saved enough for three months before they would need to work. South Africa was their destination of choice because their money would go the furthest. Apartheid was finally over, and Mandela had just become president.

"Cute, rich, and old?"

"Cute, rich, young, and generous. Look what he gave me." She showed the handful of chips. "I don't know what each of the colours are worth, but the purple with pink centres are each worth twenty-five thousand rand."

Stewart stopped playing and turned to Julia. "Let me see." He had just lost his final stake and had nothing left to play with. They found a clearing away from the crowds and she pulled out the handfuls of chips.

"He gave me handful of the expensive ones and another of the less expensive ones."

Stewart and Jane looked in stunned silence at their travelling companion's haul. "You truly are lady luck," he said. "I think you have over half a million rand in your hands. That's like a hundred and fifty THOU-SAND pounds sterling!"

"Jules, you're rich!" Jane couldn't contain herself. She was jiggling her whole body in a little dance and began to giggle.

"They say the worst thing that can happen to a person is to win the first time they gamble," Stewart said. "Although, I wouldn't mind having your misfortune!"

"Let's go," Jane said. "What are we waiting for?"

"Do you think I should keep the chips or give them back to him?"

"Don't talk nonsense. This is the best thing that has happened to you. To us." Jane began to feel foolish as soon as she said it. They were Julia's chips, not hers. Definitely not theirs.

"Absolutely," Julia said, suddenly conscious not to create a rift with her friends. "All for one, one for all. I think this means we don't have to find work before uni."

Jane hugged Julia and Stewart joined in reluctantly. The group dynamic had shifted radically and he was trying to understand its consequences.

"You must be Julia's friends," Matt Smit said, appearing next to Julia. "I couldn't help notice the three of you together and I didn't want to lose the most important person of the night." He smiled at Julia and moved close to her. She willed him to put his arm around her and he obliged.

"Guys, this is the person I was talking about. Matt, this is Jane, my best friend from Roedean. And this is Stewart, her boyfriend. Everyone, this is Matt."

"Nice to meet you both. I tried cashing in my chips but apparently, they don't have enough cash and had to issue me with a cheque instead. It'll take some time before they are ready."

The two friends were lost for words and just smiled knowingly, as if it had happened to them on numerous occasions.

"They did give me some cash and I'm a believer that it's worthless unless spent. So, if you don't have any other plans, let's see what trouble we can get up to." He started walking, Julia now fixed to his side. The others followed.

Matt seemed to know everyone in the casino, smiling and accepting handshakes or pats on his back from wait staff, pit bosses, fellow gamblers, and total strangers. If he hadn't known them before, they all knew him now. He was all anyone could talk about. He glided across the floor from the high stakes tables through the great hallways that connected the casino to the high-end shops, restaurants, and hotels.

"What's your favourite colour?"

"Excuse me?" Julia wasn't sure if he was talking to her or some stranger.

"Your favourite colour. Blue, black, purple?"

"Red. Why?"

"I'll show you." He changed course into a jewellery shop attended by three immaculately dressed young women in black, a ridiculously handsome young man in a similar black suit, and an older man Matt seemed to know.

"Matthijs my boy, I hear you've been lucky today."

"I can't complain."

"How can I be of service to you and your friends?"

"I am looking for a coloured stone, red, to match the beauty and luck of this fine woman."

Julia blushed. This was over the top, bordering on farcical. If it hadn't just happened, she wouldn't believe it.

"I have just what you're looking for. A Burmese ruby, finest quality, set in an exquisite bed of diamonds."

"It needs to be just red. Her favourite colour is red, not white or sparkly nonsense."

The man nodded and smiled. "Then I can offer you something even more spectacular, but it is a bit pricey."

"Did I say anything about price?"

"I'll bring it out and see if you like it."

"I'm not the one who needs to like it. Julia must love it."

She stood like a statue waiting to be adorned. Jane and Stewart shuffled like third wheels.

"And you two, what would you like?"

"Nothing, sir. We're fine, thank you."

"Don't sir me. We're not in the army and you're not serving me breakfast. It's Matt and I am going to buy you something. Here. This looks good for you, Stewart. It is Stewart, yes?" He motioned to one of women to bring him a Rolex watch. "Try it on. For you, Jane, I think something a little more elegant. How about a diamond bracelet?" He motioned to another woman to retrieve a string of two-carat diamonds for Jane to try on. "There, that looks spectacular. What do you think?"

They were speechless. "This is too much. We don't know you and you don't need to give this to us."

"I agree. I don't need to give any of this to you. But I want to. You brought Julia into my life and she just won me a fortune. What's a few trinkets between friends?"

Jane stole a glance at Stewart. He made an almost imperceptible shrug in agreement and Jane kissed Matt on the cheek. "Thank you, Matt. It's most kind."

"Thank you, Matt," Stewart said, giving him a firm and appreciative handshake.

The older gentleman returned and placed a necklace on the black velvet in front of Matt. It was a simple gold chain with a thirty-two carat ruby. "I hope that this is simple enough for you, Matthijs?"

"I think it is perfect. What do you think, Julia?"

"I'm speechless. I have never seen anything more beautiful in my life."

"Then it's yours."

"I can't accept this. I don't know you from Adam. I'm not that kind of girl."

"You can and you will and you are, whatever that means. You won me a lot of money and I pay my debts." He picked up the necklace and she turned, holding up her hair to allow him to put it on her. He touched her shoulders and turned her like a doll until she was facing him. "Beautiful."

"Thank you." She leaned in and kissed him on the cheek.

"I hope you are okay with me signing for these? I haven't cashed out yet. Just adjust with the house, if that's okay?"

"Certainly, sir," the man said with gravity. "Enjoy your evening."

The whole detour took fewer than thirty minutes and Matt was walking again, Julia next to him and the other two a step behind. Two men began to tail them a few paces back.

Stewart cautiously tapped Matt's shoulder and leaned in. "Don't look, but I think there are some men following us. I saw them in the reflection of the windows a while back and they are still there."

"Just security, compliments of the casino," Matt said. "They protect their winners."

"Why?"

"Because they know that gamblers gamble and the more we do, the greater the odds the house will win its money back."

"Is that why you do what you do?" Julia asked.

"What's that?"

"Make a few massive bets rather than lots of smaller ones?"

Matt stopped walking and turned to her. "Either you are a natural gambler or you have been reading statistics. That's exactly why, and that's why I value luck when I see it. Everything in life comes down to a bit of luck. We can do the right things, say the right words, and wear the right clothes, but the difference between the herd and the winner is usually luck—of one form or another."

"But why everything on one number?"

"Because I wanted the croupier to know where to throw the ball."

"What? It's rigged?"

"No. Not at all. But a good croupier can spin a ball in a way that it lands on a certain part of the wheel. Thirteen is directly opposite twenty-nine and I knew they would do anything to get the ball to stop on the other side of the wheel. That's why I moved the chips at the last moment. From my thinking, I just reduced my odds significantly down to one in three or four."

"I couldn't believe they allowed that."

"Each house has its own rules. Usually there are no more bets after the ball has gone around the wheel twice. I moved it as soon as the ball was thrown."

"But it was still a big gamble."

"That's why I needed luck. I needed you." He hadn't taken his arm off her since she let him put it on. She moved closer to him, letting his body brush hers.

The four walked in silence, enjoying the moment. Everything seemed possible.

"We're here, just to our right. Best steak you'll have in the world. I hope none of you are vegetarians."

"Not tonight, we're not," said Stewart. His left wrist felt the weight of the yellow gold and he couldn't help swivelling his forearm to catch glimpses of his gift.

The meal was absorbed rather than eaten. It wasn't until desert when something occurred to Julia.

"Are you here alone?"

Matt had taken a large piece of pie into his mouth and needed to finish chewing before replying. "I virtually live here. Everyone here is my friend."

"But you're here with us instead of them." Julia regretted it the moment it left her mouth.

"Yes, exactly. They will be at the party later and at the clubs when we go there, but they weren't standing next to me when I needed them at the table, and they won't be there to pick me up when the money's gone."

"Gone? Why would you ever lose so much money?"

"I won't lose it. I'll spend it. And I'll enjoy every penny. It's my philosophy of life. I don't want to waste a minute or regret anything." Matt paused to drink some wine. "Take you, for example. I only realised you were my lady luck after my third spin with you at the table. I wasn't winning before you came and you were the only thing that had changed. That's why I couldn't let you leave. Once I had you next to me, I let luck do its thing and here we are."

"Sounds superstitious."

"It is and I am. Just try to get me out of my bed on Friday the thirteenth."

They laughed together. He was a whirlwind of energy and they were spectators. He would say something and they would smile. If it was vaguely funny, they would all laugh. When it came time to leave, he paid the bill and they all said thanks. He made sure to push a large bill into the head waiter's hand as it was shaken.

"Next stop, the penthouse."

This was greeted by a general murmur of ascent by the nineteen year olds. Julia had drifted back to walk next to Jane, leaving Matt and Stewart to talk.

"So, what do you think?" Julia ducked a little into a conspiratorial whisper.

"I think he can't be real," Jane said, her head shaking. "But he certainly is generous. I wonder what he'll want in return." She smiled slyly at her friend.

"He could have hired a hooker if that's what he wanted. I think he's genuine and even a little shy."

"Shy? He's about as shy as a raging elephant."

"Yeah, but right now he's flying high. I saw a glimmer of something earlier though. I can't put my finger on it, but there's more to him. I think it's all an act. It's part of who he would like to be or what he needs to do. I think he acts like this because he's expected to.

"Sounds like you've given this some thought."

"I have to. This whole thing is bonkers otherwise. Who in his right mind gives a total stranger a fortune in chips and an insane piece of jewellery?"

"I do like my bracelet," Jane said as she lifted it for Julia to admire.

"And this ruby is something out of an Arabian tale. A ruby? It's so big it looks fake. No one wears something like this." She looked behind her, suddenly conscious of how much money it was worth. She saw the two suited men behind her and felt better. *Not such a crazy idea after all*, she thought.

"So what are you going to do?"

Julia thought about it. She felt as though she was walking three inches above the ground. "I'm single, decent looking, and I'll do what feels right at the time."

"You're gorgeous and you know it. Almost as good looking as me." Jane turned her head and looked sideways at Julia with a playful smile. They linked arms and allowed their hair to flow down their backs.

"Did you just giggle?"

"I thought it was you."

"I know it was you."

"It was, but you did too."

"I did. I can't believe how happy I am. This is crazy!"

Julia skipped ahead and linked her arm in Matt's. Stewart took the hint and dropped back to Jane. They had reached the lift to take them to their villa on the rooftop. A uniformed man opened and closed the doors as they passed. At the lift, another uniformed man pressed the outside button and yet another sat inside the lift to press the button for their floor. He stood when he was told they were going to the penthouse.

"Have a lovely evening, sir. Ladies." He nodded to them in turn.

"This is for you, young man." Matt stuffed a large note into his uniformed pocket. "Make sure my guests are treated well. There should be a fair number arriving over the next few hours." He had also tipped every uniformed employee along the way. When they were alone again, he explained. "That's the only reason I need cash in this place. Everything else I just sign for."

The foyer of the penthouse was decorated in a mock Louis XIV style. It felt both luxurious and ridiculous, like a playground for adults. There wasn't an employee at the door and Matt needed to use his key card. He gave a copy to each of them.

"Welcome to our new home," he proclaimed as he grandly opened the door and they took in the best Sun City had to offer.

"This is unbelievable. How many rooms?"

"I don't know. Check it out."

"Did you look outside? It's got its own pool."

"And hot tub."

"And kitchen."

"And its own home cinema."

"I think I'm moving in," Stewart said. "Jane, what do you think?"

"I agree. This is where I want to spend the rest of my gap year."

"Gap year?" Matt asked.

"It's the year between high school and university," Julia said, trying to be nonchalant about their youth.

Matt paused. "Wait a moment. How old are you?"

"We're all nineteen. How old are you?"

"Twenty-five in November."

"Which day?"

"The twenty-ninth."

"Hence the twenty-nine and neighbours routine. Nice touch."

"And you're a Sagittarius," said Jane.

"Okay, you're all legal and I'd like a drink. The bar should be stocked."

Stewart had already discovered it. "What would you like?"

"Coke please."

"Nothing else?"

"No thanks. But don't let me stop you. Please have whatever you want. There should be champagne, beer, hard stuff, whatever."

Stewart poured the cola into a glass with ice and handed it to Matt.

"Pick your rooms. I'm taking the master suite. I need to shower and put my head down for a few minutes. Make yourself at home and order whatever you want." He went to his room and closed the door.

"Was that weirder than all the weird shit that has happened prior to this?" Jane tried to break the silence.

"I told you he was shy. I'm taking the room next to his. Wait. What about our stuff? I didn't even think this through. We'll have to go back to the apartment."

"It'll be okay," Stewart said. "I can pop over with a taxi and grab it."

"But my stuff is everywhere. I don't want your hands over all my things." Julia was genuinely pouting.

"Don't worry about it. I can go with Stewart and get enough things for a couple of nights. If things work out, we can move the rest over later. Let's take this one step at a time."

"You're the best. This is why I allow you to say you're better looking than me," Julia smiled and then ran away from the water Jane sprayed at her.

"No," said Stewart in a whisper. "We don't know this guy from Jack the Ripper. I'll pop back and pick up our things. Julia, you'll have to suffer me touching your things. Jane, stay here and keep yourselves safe. I'll be back as soon as I can."

When the door clicked shut behind him, Jane smiled conspiratorially at Julia. "I think I'll grab a drink and retire to my room. Holler if you need me, although I have a sneaking suspicion that you'll forget me pretty quickly."

Julia could feel the back of her neck warm. "I don't know what you're talking about." She smiled, her face now as red as her neck.

"Just be careful with him. Stew's right; we really don't have a clue who he is."

"Love you too." Julia kissed her softly on her cheek and watched as her friend took a glass of orange juice with her to her room. Jane blew her a kiss before the door closed and all was quiet again.

Alone, Julia began exploring the villa. She looked out at the pool and slid the door open. Walking along the edge, she took off her shoes and socks and dipped her toe in the water. A little cool but, once inside, it would feel great. There was a mini bar set back from the edge of the pool and a sunken hot tub near the edge of the roof. The floor was a ridged wood of a type she didn't recognise. There were potted palm trees and other greenery strategically placed to provide total privacy, though no one overlooked their space. *I wonder what people get up to here,* she thought. *Or how much this costs. Probably celebrities and Arab sheiks and other international playboys with their women and drugs.* Her mind was reeling with scenarios.

She stepped back inside, still barefooted. The floor was carpeted around the entertainment centre but tiled everywhere else. The ceiling was high and held a massive chandelier. Initially, it seemed out of place with all of the modern conveniences, but it fit in purely by its decadence. There were six rooms and a massive bathroom for guests. She popped her head inside each of the five unoccupied rooms and saw that each one had slight variations. Mirrors on the ceiling in one, mirrors on the wall cabinets in all of them. All with en suite bathrooms. Luxurious. *I can get used to a life like this,* she thought. *A lot better than cleaning toilets and serving food for the next nine months until Oxford.*

She closed each door quietly and walked to the one where Matt was sleeping. She brushed her hair with her hand and did her best to straighten her clothes. She was about to knock but then withdrew her hand. She reached for the doorknob but also stopped, her hand resting on it but not turning. *He's shy*, she thought. *And what the hell am I thinking? I'm not one of those girls.* She took a deep breath and stepped back. She forced herself to walk into another room and closed the door. *What's happening to me? This isn't me. It's only money. It's only jewellery. It doesn't mean I need to do anything.* Her inner voice was a mixture of her mother, her priest, and her friends, but she knew it wasn't the money or the luxuries. *It's the sadness in his eyes, his shyness when he needn't be, and his audacious generosity.*

She leaned against the door for a moment longer and then resolved to act. *Be more like him. Live for the moment. Be impulsive. Don't be a stick in the mud.* She opened her door and went to the bar near the sliding door on the other side of the room. *At least I'll have an excuse if he kicks me out.* She grabbed a coke and poured it into a glass as Stewart had and took a glass of champagne for herself. She started walking across the expanse of the room, a glass in each hand, head erect and picturing herself as someone who does this type of thing all the time. She glanced at Jane's closed door but kept going.

When she reached his door, she had to put down one of the drinks. As she was standing up and reaching for the handle, she heard a knock. It wasn't her and it didn't sound like it came from inside his room. Then again, a knock and a ring of the doorbell. She shook her head, laughing at herself, and went to open the front door.

"Hello, we're here for Matt's party." A man followed by thirteen other women and men just walked inside. "Is he here?" He didn't ask who she was or why she was there. He was looking all around, including the ceiling corners.

"He's just having a quick nap."

"Only Matt could take a nap after a day like this! Tell him Norman is here and that I brought some friends." He nodded to the scantily clad women and some red-faced men who were already at the bar, helping themselves to drinks.

"I will." She walked to Matt's room with a real reason to knock.

"I heard them. I'll be right out," he said. His voice was foggy as if he had really been sleeping.

"Okay," Julia said. "I brought you a Coke if you want."

The door opened and he was in a bathrobe with bare feet. "Thanks, you are a doll." He kissed her on the cheek. She could feel the warmth of his skin and could tell he shaved, the faint smell of the shaving cream lingered on her cheek. He took the drink. "I was thinking of taking a swim. Are you up for it?"

"I don't have a costume."

Norman saw Matt emerge and had come over. "Don't worry, darling. There's only one rule in Matt's pool—the men must keep their bathing costumes on." He had his arm low on her waist and he smelled of alcohol. He must have thought it was funny because he laughed hysterically at his own joke. Matt smiled.

"Don't worry. I'll get them to send up a costume for you. Or you can. Let them know your size and they'll bring a selection."

"Thanks." She grabbed her champagne glass and watched as Matt was pulled into the centre of the room and crowded by his new friends.

The noise increased when one of the new people discovered the sound system. Music erupted and talking turned to shouting. One of the skinny guys with a funny hat designated himself DJ for the night and was moving his head in time to the beat.

"Who's the new girl?" Norman asked when sufficiently far from Julia.

"My good luck charm."

"English?"

"Yaw, and young. Nineteen."

"You devil. I wish I had your luck."

"Is the rest of the gang coming?"

"Tony, Clive, and Ray should be arriving shortly."

"And their wives?"

"With yours in Joburg."

"Is Ma here?"

"Also in Joburg. She'll come when she can." Norman took a swig and put his arm around Matt. "She'd like you to visit her. You haven't seen her in months and she gets worried. You know how she is."

"Yah, yah. Maybe now I've made a few bob I can clear some debts and show my face."

"There are a lot of people waiting to be paid."

"I know." He paused. "What about Maish? Has he said anything?" Matt's voice waivered but he gathered some courage. "They know I'm good for it. If they want to make the juice they charge for their money, they need to share the risk too. Fuck it; it's only money."

"Brother, I love you, but you're fucking crazy. Cheers. Let's enjoy today. Tomorrow will take care of itself, yaw?" He gave him a loose hug and led him towards the pool. "Can I take one of the rooms?"

"What do I look like? They gave me a second villa for you and the rest of the gang. Get yourself settled." He took another set of key cards from his robe's pocket and handed them to Norman.

"You're something else," he said, smiling. He grabbed a girl on his way to his new villa.

Matt shook his head and smiled. *Things never change*, he thought.

More people arrived and it started to feel like a party. A few people jumped into the pool and soon every corner was full of people holding glasses of champagne and eating canapes, which appeared magically along with fruit and other snacks compliments of the house.

Stewart returned from his errand and looked wide-eyed at the crowd.

"Whoa. How long was I gone?"

"I know! This place is turning into a zoo," said Julia.

"Here's your stuff. I think I grabbed everything."

"Thanks. Did you get my swimming costume?"

"Yep, it was flung over the TV in your room."

"Ha! Sorry about that. I appreciate you going to get everything."

"No problem. Are you sure you want to stay here?"

"Are you kidding? Where else are we going to find a party like this?"

"What about your chips? Did you cash them in?"

"Not yet. There's a safe in my room. They're in there."

"Don't leave it too long. Considering how this guy spends money, he may need them back."

"Then he can have them. I'm still not comfortable with all this."

"And the necklace?"

Julia ran her finger along the chain and felt the stone between her fingers. "I'm keeping this no matter what."

"Then pop that into the safe before you put too much of that bubbly down your throat. I'm not sure about some of these characters."

"Let's worry about that later. Jane is in her room, waiting for you. I'm going for a swim." She took her things, went to her room, and locked the door. When she opened it again, she had the same styled robe as Matt's with her costume underneath.

"Take it off!" said a voice over the sound system. She looked over and saw the skinny DJ moving to the music and smiling from ear to ear with his eyebrows raised. He was pointing to her robe.

Smiling at him, she pointed towards the pool and shrugged. He shrugged back good naturedly and carried on dancing by himself. She walked through the sliding doors and found Matt already in the water.

"Come in, it's perfect." His face was round and open. He had a broad chest covered with blonde hair like a carpet. He was smiling and holding his drink in one hand and bouncing slightly.

Julia looked for her friends and saw them arriving in their robes. They looked equally ridiculous. She took hers off and saw both the men and women turn their heads discretely to check her out. She wore a sky blue bikini and wasn't afraid of what they would say. She knew she was a knockout and picked her costume to highlight that. She saw Matt double take out of the corner of her eye. She moved slowly and delicately, claiming a chair next to the pool for her robe. The crowd slowly allowed her to pass as she walked to the pool's steps. As she put her foot in the water, she knew her life would never be the same again.

The Day After the Night Before

He didn't have a chiselled body. In fact, it was quite ordinary and a bit hairy. She woke in a tangle next to him, where she remained until he woke.

"Good morning."

"Hmmm."

He isn't a morning person, she thought. "Last night was like a dream," she said. "In case I didn't thank you, I just want you to know I had a wonderful time. It was like living a fantasy."

"Are you always this talkative first thing?"

"I've been up a while, waiting for you." Another grunt and Matt rolled over, freeing her to get up and shower properly. She wanted to try on a new outfit she ordered sometime between her third and final glass of champagne. He encouraged her to get whatever she wanted and the woman from the shop brought it up to the villa. It sat in its stiff navy blue paper bag with gold lettering surrounded by tissue paper.

Julia walked on tip toes in the morning silence. She could hear the low hum of the lights and the air conditioning she had left on in their room. She picked up her discarded robe and made her way to the bathroom.

In the mirror she could see a tanned face framed with dark blonde hair, the blue colour striking next to the whites of her eyes. She moved her lips to see her teeth, the product of years of braces. She was already flossing as she looked for a toothbrush. *I guess after tonight, I can use his*, she thought. She moved her head left, then right, checking her skin for flaws that may have appeared overnight. Satisfied that all was as it should be, she turned on the shower and waited for the water to reach the right temperature. The head of the shower created a wall of water and her body luxuriated in the warmth and constant touch.

When she finally emerged in her robe, she opened the door to the rest of the villa. All of the bedroom doors were closed and she was pleased to have moved her things into Matt's. The floor was littered with wrappings, streamers, food, and bottles. Boxes of pizza were strewn everywhere, including outside. The fruit was untouched. There was a smell of cigarettes and cigars and she remembered that a few joints had been passed around. She was pleased when Matt refused anything but his Coca-Cola and the occasional sip of champagne.

She went to the fridge to find some bottled water. There was a clink as beer and champagne bottles fell over when the door opened. She found juice and walked outside. It was a glorious morning. The sky was endless as the sun rose and made it even bluer. She had missed the sunrise but could imagine the colours.

"Not bad," said a voice from behind her.

"Jane, you startled me. How long have you been up?"

"Just now. I needed something to drink. I see you had the same idea."

"Yeah, quite the party last night."

"I know. We're a long way from home, Toto."

Julia smiled. "Let's just hope the wicked witch of the east doesn't arrive too soon."

Jane joined her at the edge of the balcony, overlooking the world below. "Just remember that all of this is not real." She put her arm on Julia's shoulder.

"I know. At least it's fun."

"I don't want you to get hurt. These people don't care about us. Yesterday was just another day in their life. Did you see his friends? Tony looks like a criminal and Norman is a sleaze. The gay couple was fun; Thomas' father is a big shot with one of the mining companies and he's spending his inheritance on his partner. Stewart was cool with everything. He surprised me." She took a sip from her drink. "I really think he could be the one."

Julia stopped gazing into the distance and turned to Jane. "He's a nice guy. Strong and steady and smart. And he worships the ground you walk on."

"As he should."

They clinked glasses and found a place to sit.

After a moment, Jane continued. "So?"

"It's early days."

"Day."

"Only one day so far, but so much has happened. This time yesterday, we were down to our last week's money and thinking about finding jobs."

"Or calling home for more."

"Or worse, going home." Julia took a sip of her juice. It tasted like mango but was hard to tell. "Now we have more than enough money to do what we want and return home with the rest."

"But what about Matt?"

"I know. Let's see how it goes. He's dangerous for me. I need to finish my schooling before meeting someone like him. My parents will kill me if I don't go home."

Jane arched her eyebrows. "Not going home? Didn't you just say this was early days?"

"Day. Even worse. It's embarrassing, but I don't know what's up or down. I was just walking from that roulette table when I heard his voice in my ear. Since then, he's been in my head and I can't think of anything else."

"Slow down, Jules. Let's take things one day at a time. What should we do today?"

"Now that we're women of leisure, I'd rather fancy a safari. Everyone talks about Kruger Park and there was no chance of us going there alone before yesterday."

"I like that and I know Stew would love it. Do you think Matt would go for it?"

"All we can do is ask. For all I know, he may have more important business plans arranged."

"We can go by ourselves if need be. We don't need to be escorted by him. It's 1995 and we're liberated, educated women of the world." Jane lifted her head and shook her hair for emphasis. They both laughed softly.

"Let's see how things go," Julia said. She looked into the distance and took a sip from her drink.

It wasn't long before other bodies emerged from their rooms. The morning shuffle of feet, making of coffee, and eventual ordering of room service brought the place to life. It was almost noon before Matt awoke. He emerged freshly shaven, wearing a linen suit and smelling of expensive cologne. When he saw Julia, he kissed her gently and murmured something in her ear that made her giggle. Stewart had settled into reading the *Economist* and Jane was writing in her journal. Everyone else had left.

"I hear you'd like to go on a safari," Matt said to Jane.

"Well, when in Rome. And who knows when we'll have this opportunity again?"

"That sounds like an excellent idea. I've got nothing else planned. Sol is going to be cross that we didn't stay longer but I'm sure he'll be happy when we return." He paused and stepped into the other room. After about ten minutes, he returned with a beaming smile. "I've just been talking to Sol and he's agreed to fly us there in his helicopter and bring us back when we're ready. He'd made all the arrangements. I think you'll love it."

Even Stewart's mouth dropped. "Are you serious? That's amazing."

"They just want us captive so we don't spend our money elsewhere. They still see it as their money that we have. I don't know about any of you, but I've never gone that far in a helicopter. Kruger Park is a full day's drive by car. Not sure how long by helly." He flashed a smile at Julia and looked approvingly at the others.

"You are incredible," Julia said as she embraced him and kissed him on the lips. "Where have you been all this time?"

"Right here in front of you," he said. "And I was thinking the same about you."

The other two looked at each other and rolled their eyes.

They didn't manage to fly that day, but it was arranged for the following day. They enjoyed a live show that evening of magic with an animal thrown in for good measure and some singing afterwards. It was entertaining but not memorable. They had steak at the same restaurant and went to bed early after packing enough for a week's stay in the park.

The helicopter pad was not on the roof of the hotel but set off to the side, away from the complex. They needed to take a buggy to it, escorted by the same uniformed staff who never allowed them to push a button or open a door. They all fit in with a little room to spare. It was the first time any of them, except Matt, had been in a helicopter.

"This is better than going to Disneyland!" Julia said into her mouthpiece. They had earphones on and communicated through the headsets.

"I would hope so," Matt said. "Disneyland is for children. This is the adult version with real flying contraptions and live animals. Wait until you get there. I hope you're not afraid of snakes."

Julia went cold. She hadn't thought about snakes. She envisioned lions, giraffes, and rhinos. Even monkeys and birds would be fine. Snakes, cockroaches, and rodents didn't factor in. "I never thought about it," she said in a diminished voice.

"Don't worry about it. We'll be safe. There are guides and we are staying in the best resort. Just don't walk in the tall grass and try to stay close to me. Us Afrikaners seem to be immune to everything. Even the snakes know they will die if they mess with us." He laughed with pride and took her hand as reassurance.

The helicopter flew tilted forward slightly and the ground was close enough for them to see details of houses and the countryside. The trip took just over two hours and, by the end, they were all thankful it was over. The novelty had worn off after an hour of the noise and congestion.

Kruger Park was indistinguishable from the rest of the countryside except that the animals were supposedly safer inside. Poaching remained a problem. Tourism provided much needed revenues to keep the operation sustainable.

"This is like seeing King Kong's native home," Jane said, wide-eyed as she scanned the horizon. "Mountains, ravines, and everything in between."

"Our lodge is remote but it'll blow your mind. It has all of the modern niceties while still feeling like you're right in the middle of the wilderness." Matt was getting excited. "It is like a religious experience. For some it is like heaven. For others, hell." He was smiling again.

"Will we be able to see the animals?" Stewart asked, his eyes also scanning the horizon.

"Absolutely. As much or as little as you want. You'll be close enough to touch them. We're here for at least five days. You'll have had enough by then."

"Do we drive or are we driven?" Julia asked.

"We'll be put in an open-air jeep and the guide will drive us through the park. You must be careful to keep your hands inside the vehicle. The animals know you are not food if you are inside the vehicle. Outside is another story." He was smiling again. "Don't worry, it's perfectly safe."

The trip to the lodge was uneventful. The building was encased in glass to provide uninterrupted views and was elevated above the tree line. The next few days were full of awe-inspiring sunsets and days full of excitement. They were within a stone's throw of lions, cheetahs, and rhinos. There was only one incident, on their second day, when Julia feared for her life.

They were driving with their guide behind another group of tourists. Matt mumbled occasionally in Afrikaans but no one understood. The driver allowed the other car ahead to get farther away so they weren't nose to tail and turned the engine off so they could marvel at the beauty of their surroundings. He also said something to the man with a gun who sat on a special chair perched on the front of the car.

When he saw Jane and Julia look at the armed man, Matt said, "Don't worry, that poor kefir will satisfy any animal's appetite before it reaches us." He patted a large calibre pistol on his hip. "Just in case he doesn't."

As Jane frowned disapprovingly at the slur, the guide told them to be still and quiet. He turned on the engine but didn't move the car.

Ahead of them, a young bull elephant strolled out of the trees onto the road. The car in front followed too closely and the elephant turned around. Its ears were out to the sides like flared nostrils, and it walked off the path next to the car. All the people were taking pictures, laughing, and pointing.

The elephant ate some leaves off the adjoining tree, looked to be leaving, and then turned towards the car with alarming speed. It lowered its head and rammed the vehicle, flipping it over and trapping its inhabitants underneath. One person dragged himself out, and then pulled a woman out afterwards. The elephant charged again, flipping the vehicle right side up. By this time, the couple were holding each other and crying. The guide looked to be injured and no one else was moving inside the vehicle.

Julia felt herself being pushed back against her seat as Matt jumped out of the car. The man on the seat had also jumped off, running towards the elephant.

"Matt!"

"Stay in the car!"

The elephant looked to be ready to charge the car again when Matt fired his gun twice. The animal stopped and looked in the direction of Julia and the men with the guns. It couldn't have known what they were, but they produced a loud sound.

Matt had fired into the air. The guide had a .458 Winchester Magnum rifle and prepared to fire at the violent elephant.

"No!" Matt's hand pushed the rifle downwards. He turned towards the couple and shouted as loudly as he could manage. "Get out of there. Over here! Move it!" He was waving wildly at the tourists to get to where

Julia was. He fired into the air again but wasn't so foolish as to get any closer to the elephant.

The elephant was now preparing for its final charge. It forgot about the damaged car and the crying couple. It squared itself towards the two men now half way between it and their vehicle. Its ears flapped, its head raised, and it began to walk towards Matt. It went into a run and Matt fired his last remaining bullets at the massive creature's head. It kept coming.

When the single five hundred and ten grain bullet exited the rifle towards the chest of the elephant, the rampage was over. Its aim was true and the mighty beast's front legs crumpled as if it had stumbled. It made a cry that would haunt Julia whenever she saw an elephant's image after that day. It crashed into the dust, dead.

It was not Matt's trusted side arm, but the nameless black man who saved them. He walked, rifle in hand, to the pile of grey flesh on the road. He said nothing but tears flowed freely down his face.

The effect of this incident on Julia was overwhelming. Her initial terror turned to relief as she saw the majestic beast reduced to a lifeless mass. Jane and Stewart sat frozen and unspeaking next to her. For a long while, they watched in disbelief as their host and guide inspected the elephant. The couple had run towards them, their eyes darting between the dead animal and the flipped car with people beneath.

When the tourist couple reached them and Matt turned to signal all was okay, Julia ran towards him. He had already left the carcass to see how the other people were. When she reached him, he was on the citizens' band radio.

"Correct. Man down, need urgent medical attention, over. Send helicopter. Don't worry about the costs, I'll cover it, over. Just send it now, over. Yaw, there are two parties out here. We'll stay until you arrive, over. Great, see you soon, over and out."

She wrapped herself around him as he talked, feeling his damp clothes sweaty from the heat and stress.

"I'll check the driver," she said as she approached the three men in the vehicle. They were in shock but otherwise okay.

"I've called the park services on the CB. They're sending what they can. Hopefully someone will be here within the hour."

"Not sooner?"

"Depends on the pilot. Could be ten minutes if we're lucky."

Matt gently reached for her hand and she found herself crying in his arms. All she would think about was the way he rushed towards the danger and tried to save the elephant despite the danger. She felt his hands against her back and neck and wanted him to watch over her for the rest of their lives.

When they were on the move again, Julia found herself in need of his touch. She stared at his hands and forearms. *Is this the same man I met in the casino? What demons lurk beneath him to be so low one moment and so high the next? And to act with unwavering bravery when called upon?* Her thoughts raced as their car returned them to their lodge. She put her head on his shoulder and closed her eyes.

Matt didn't act as if he had done anything out of the ordinary. He spoke in a low voice to the guide and put his arms around him more than once. *How can he call him kefir in one breath and embrace him in the next?* Julia watched in silent amazement. *South Africans*, she thought. *It's as complicated as an old married couple.*

Joan and Stewart were silent, holding hands and trying to act as though nothing happened. When they reached their lodge, they had some wine and eventually managed to laugh at the day's adventures. The next day, the third of their safari, Jane and Stewart discreetly decided to leave Matt and Julia to spend time alone.

"There's a gathering of all the tourists in the main campground. They're having a Braai and celebrating the guide's bravery. They want you to come as well."

Matt shook his head. "Let the poor bastard get his reward. Life's hard enough for these poor kefirs. I don't need the glory."

Stewart shrugged and left with Jane. Julia took advantage of their time alone to ask Matt some questions.

"I've been having the best time of my life," she said. "But I don't understand something."

"What's that?"

"Don't you work?"

Matt just about fell over laughing. "Don't swear at me with that four-letter word."

"You mean you don't do anything except gamble?"

"Not exactly. My family is involved with property management in Joburg. I put part of my winnings into that so I'll have an income later when my luck runs out." He smirked. "But hopefully you don't run out on me just yet." He reached over and pulled her to him. She squirmed playfully, trying to keep the conversation going.

"Don't you want to do anything more with your talents?"

"Why? How many people have you heard on their deathbeds say they wished they spent more time in the office? Most people work for money. They work their entire lives, too tired or restricted to take more than a few days holiday now and then. When they finally have time, their bodies are decrepit or, worse, their minds begin to slip. Not having prepared for retirement, they don't have any skills to live. They just know how to sit in front of the TV or play some senseless game. They were born to die, not live. I was born to live."

"All this sounds great, but how did you get to be so good or so lucky? Why not stocks and bonds?"

"I do those as well. There are a handful of us who keep our minds busy with floating companies and another handful figuring out how to sink them."

"I don't understand."

"It's all a game. You just need to decide whether you are going to be a sucker or a winner."

"Isn't that illegal?"

Matt shrugged. "So far we haven't had any problems." He smiled. "Besides, it's no different than anywhere else in the world. The game is fixed and we just happen to be the ones doing the fixing."

"But that's what the mafia does." She said it before thinking.

Matt's smile was toothless but broad. "That's nonsense, but there are a small handful of people who call the shots. Luckily, I know enough of them to keep my life interesting. So far, I make them money so they tolerate me."

"And when you don't?"

"I can't think like that. It's unlucky." He tickled her until she let him kiss her. "And I can't have my lucky charm thinking unlucky thoughts."

∞

The rest of their trip was perfect. The weather was unrelenting sunshine and clear skies. The animals were usually found near the watering holes, drinking, eating, and in one instance, mating. Matt was right that after five days, it was enough. The helicopter was called and they returned to their penthouse villa.

"Finally, civilisation." Matt dropped into the big armchair in the middle of the room as Julia got him a Coke and herself a water.

"Guys?" Jane came forward awkwardly, sitting across from Matt and Julia.

"Yaw?" When he was tired, his Afrikaans' accent became more pronounced.

"First, I wanted to thank you for everything. It's been fantastic. But I think it's time for Stew and me to get going."

Matt sat up. "What happened? Is it something I did?"

"No, not at all. In fact, the opposite. It's just that I can see the two of you want to be alone with each other and I'm feeling a bit like a third wheel."

"Nonsense."

"Thanks but I think it's for the best. I'll call you every so often to get updates. Stew and I wanted to check out Cape Town next, maybe find some work."

Julia felt terrible. She didn't want Jane to leave but she also wanted Matt to herself. He had become irre-sistible to her. "You're welcome to stay," she said. As she said it, she realised how it sounded. It was her and Matt on one side and Jane and Stew on the other. *We're the providers*, she thought. *They're dependents. That's what's bothering them.*

"Thanks." She was beginning to cry. "But it's been a blast and I don't think we'll ever replicate this last week. I just want to check out on a high, that's all." She made a motion with her arms and Julia came over to hug her.

"What are these? No tears allowed. Enjoy Cape Town and give me a call. We'll see what's happening and maybe pop over. Who knows, maybe I'll have been kicked out by then." She glanced at Matt and winked. He was shaking his head while smiling.

"What type of work are you looking for?" Matt asked. "I've got a lot of friends out there."

"Anything, really. Something in a nice hotel? Or perhaps in a vineyard? I hear there are some great wines down there."

"When you go, I'll give you the name of the manager of the best hotel in Cape Town. You call him and tell him that Matthijs Smit told him to give you a proper job and he'll sort you out. If that isn't your style, I've got an old friend from school who owns one of the largest vineyards in the area. I'll give you his details and see how things go. It's hard work, those vineyards. Better let the kefirs do the heavy stuff and leave the drinking to yourselves."

Jane winced at his casual use of the word. "Thanks," she said. "Much appreciated."

"Okay, so that's settled. You're not leaving straight away. Tonight we've got some A-list performers. Could be Cher, I don't know. Something big, so stick around. We'll have a nice steak beforehand and there'll be a party here afterwards. You can leave tomorrow or next week, but stay tonight. Promise me."

Jane laughed at his sales pitch. "Okay, we'll be here. Thanks again."

Matt was right. It was Cher and the crowd acted as one in response to her over-the-top outfits and dated lyrics. She was a large personality and they loved her. Jane managed to get an autograph and photo with her, but Julia wasn't as big a fan. The party continued and, this time, they found it in full swing by the time they arrived.

"There are people in the pool in their suits," Julia said to Matt.

He smiled. "Yes, yes. Absolutely mental. Let's get changed and join them!" His smile froze briefly when he saw Maish next to the pool. Maish raised his glass to Matt when they made eye contact. "On second thought, you get ready. I need to talk to someone first."

Jane saw more drugs being passed around and consumed this time, but most of the people were simply enjoying the freedom of doing whatever they wanted. Women went topless, one man streaked. Most looked away, half laughing to themselves. Matt seemed both oblivious to and aware of everything. When it was something funny, he saw and acknowledged it. When it was embarrassing or foolish, he ignored it. He seemed determined to be in a good mood. Julia was always in his arms or within a finger's breadth of him. Jane found herself in her room with Stewart waiting for the time to pass. They were beginning to feel the age difference.

"Everyone's older than us. I feel like we are annoying them with our presence," Stewart said.

"It's only because she looks older, with that figure and face," Jane said.

"She's Jules. She won't change. She wants the world and is going for it. She's been going for it as long as you've known her. That's why we came here in the first place. It was her idea. Don't compare yourself to her. Thank god you're not her. I'm in love with you because of who you are."

Jane couldn't pout or be miserable with Stewart saying all of those nice things. She squirmed a little, allowing him to sit closer to her on the bed. "You're just saying that."

"I'm not and you know it. She's fun, yes, but you're the real deal. That's why I can't wait to leave this mad-house and spend the rest of our time together somewhere else. Let's start in Cape Town and go where our noses lead us."

"How come you're so perfect?"

"Why are you so beautiful?"

Jane was smiling again and turned to kiss him. She turned her head briefly to see if their door was closed, then returned to Stewart. *Tomorrow, we're outta here,* she thought.

Chapter Three

Matt and Julia

It is a truth universally acknowledged that the sexiest part of a woman is her brain, and Matt excited Julia's. The following weeks were spent not partying but talking, dreaming, and scheming. Her entire perception of the world was challenged. Matt didn't work and only played, yet was rich and happy. Her parents worked non-stop and were moderately comfortable and miserable.

"That can't be real," she said, her hand covering her laugh. "Why isn't he in jail?"

"That's just the way Tony is. He is one of the smartest barristers in South Africa but is crooked as a dog's hind leg. But it's all legal."

"And Moshe? He pretended to be an investment banker and optioned a hundred million pounds without having to even prove he had a cent?"

"He just called all the big firms in London and placed the order. He had thirty days to settle. He knew if he couldn't pay at the end of thirty days, he'd be bust or go to jail. As it happened, the gamble paid off and he made money. The banks all ended up paying him."

"That couldn't happen today, could it?"

"No. That was back in the seventies when firms trusted each other more. Computers weren't around yet and brokers did the deals and let the back office sort things out. He took advantage of that and it paid off for him big time."

"Isn't that dangerous? Illegal?"

"I'm not sure if it was legal, but he got away with it. As far as the banks were concerned, he was another broker placing orders on behalf of his clients. They didn't suspect anything."

"Imagine that." She sat back in her chair and looked into the pale blue of the pool, the mosaic moving with the surface reflections. "All you need to do is find out where there is trust in the system and then take advantage of it."

"I'm saying that trust exists where regulation is lacking and regulation is lacking because everyone assumes a certain code of conduct. Trust. It's fundamental to every aspect of our lives, from our cultural makeup to why we believe pieces of paper are worth something. Money is all about trust, confidence in the country that prints it. If you look at the endless regulation of everything from property to consumer credit legislation, it is the result of governments trying to rectify a fraud previously perpetrated against someone. I look at what we do as helping society regulate itself."

Julia couldn't help herself laughing. "You are a founding father of modern regulatory legislation."

Matt liked that. "In the flesh."

"So what's your next move? Are you going to do something with all that money you made or just wile away in five star hotels the rest of your life?"

"That sounds pretty good to me," he said, not taking the bait. "I lived in Hotel de Paris for six months. It's a stone throw from Monaco's main casino and I had some of the best times of my life there."

"When was that?"

"Two years ago. The grand prix race goes by under your nose from there. The noise was unbearable."

"How have you done so much when you are still so young?"

Matt blushed, but it could have been the champagne. It was one of the rare times he enjoyed a glass. Tonight they were enjoying foie gras and Beluga caviar, the latter in portions he ate like most people ate ice cream, with a spoon. "Let me tell you a story. It's all true."

"Go on," she wiggled in her seat to get comfortable and leaned in.

"When I was young, about four years old, I was in London with my mother. We went onto a bus and ended up sitting next to an old woman who now I believe was a gypsy. The woman started talking to us when she noticed the top of my head, pointing to the double crown that my hair made. She asked my mother's permission and then took my hand and looked deeply into my eyes. She told my mother I would be very lucky in money matters and would travel a lot. I was to be smart but naughty and would have many wives. My mother thanked her and gave her some money, but never forgot about it. She repeated it to me each time I got into trouble, so much so that I eventually believed it. I expected myself to think outside of the box. Some people call this naughty, but I called it being smart.

"It all came together when I was seventeen. My parents went travelling to America and I was left at home. I had been begging them for something, I can't remember what. They had a parcel of land they didn't know what to do with, something like twenty acres. They told me if I could sell the land, they would give me a commission. I asked them how much they wanted for it and they agreed to give me anything above that price as my commission. When they left, I took surveyors and had the land subdivided on paper and then planned to hold an auction with a braai on a weekend. I took out a full-page ad in the three best newspapers announcing the opening of a spectacular piece of land just past the outskirts of Johannesburg and a free braai for anyone who attended, provided they bring the voucher from the advertisement. I divided the land into fifty parcels and received my parents' asking price after only selling five pieces. The rest was profit for me. After that, I had the bug. I knew I was a speculator, and some said a gambler, but I won more than I lost and here I am today."

Julia was shaking her head with a faraway smile. "You mean you never had a normal job?"

"I studied law and even got an articling position, but by then I was making more money on my schemes and I decided not to be a solicitor. Time magazine had me on the cover of their magazine as one to watch. I became a millionaire when I was twenty-one and lost most of it shortly after. I have made and lost millions since then."

"And then this most recent win," she added.

"Yes. I don't think they will be advertising that. I think it must be the largest win ever in roulette. I imagine they'll be changing the limits per table after this; I can't see them ever allowing themselves to be that vulnerable again."

"So, what next?"

"I plan to live happily ever after," he said with a smirk.

Julia threw a pillow at him. "Seriously. What does a person do who has everything they want?"

Matt paused. "I don't know what I want, so even if I had it, I wouldn't know."

"Well, I have exactly what I want." She got up and sat in his lap.

At that moment, they turned their heads as a person walked through their sliding doors to where they were sitting. Matt stood up, causing Julia to fall.

"Matthijs! What's going on here?"

"Matt, who is this person?" Julia asked. She rubbed her arm where it banged the floor.

"This person? Who the hell is she?" the woman almost roared. "Tell your trollop to pack her bags."

Matt just stood there, all bravado gone. "Hello, Mother."

"Mother?" Julia pulled herself off the floor and extended her hand. "Nice to meet…"

"Never mind that," she said, not looking at her. "I want to talk to my son in private."

The silence that followed weighed on Julia until her ears began to ring. It was no more than a moment, but felt like an eternity as she tried to take in what was happening. In the end, she quietly slipped past the formidable woman in front of her, eyes down, and went inside. She closed the glass doors behind her.

When safely inside, she dared to glance over her shoulder to see the older woman animated and Matt deflated. She could only guess what was going on. Obviously, she wasn't what his mother wanted for her son. Too young? Not rich enough? Her mind was trying to digest this new twist as she went to the kitchen to get some water and put on some coffee.

She took a sip of water and prepared the grounds in the filter and pushed the button on the coffee machine. It took a few moments before the trickle of black began to pool at the bottom of the glass carafe, but that was longer than his mother planned to stay. She heard the patio door open and the tail end of the conversation.

"And you're just going to walk out on your responsibilities?"

She did not hear what Matt said in reply. It could not have been the right thing because the next thing Julia saw was a blur of fabric and hair as she strode past and then out the front door.

"Was it something I said?"

"No. She's a complicated woman."

"I would have liked to meet her. Parents like me."

"She will love you but she needs to get to know you. All in good time."

"She looks pretty serious and plenty mad. What did you do?"

"It's complicated. I'll tell you later. Now, let's have some of that coffee and maybe find a movie on the idiot box." He came next to her, kissing her neck and putting his arm around her waist. He smelled of caviar and champagne, salty and sweet.

He said nothing else on the subject for the rest of the evening or even the next morning.

"I need to pop out today and run some errands. Can you occupy yourself?"

"Sure. Anything I can do or perhaps come along?"

"Not this time. I'll call you if there are any delays."

The day went and she received a call around five at night saying he wouldn't be able to make it back but would definitely get home the following day. It was almost midnight the next day before he returned. Again, not a word was said other than his usual casual banter.

"Is this anything to do with what happened with your mother the other night?" Julia said eventually, feeling the need to raise the subject herself.

"A little. Some housekeeping issues back in Joburg. Nothing too serious."

"You were gone two days."

"I know and I'm sorry. Won't happen again. Go to sleep and we'll talk in the morning."

The next morning started around noon for Matt and, instead of talking, he decided to pop into the casino for some fun.

"How long are you going to go for?"

"Not long. Just to see the guys and show my face. We can't stay here without playing."

He closed the door and she opened a book next to the pool. The place felt empty without him. She missed the frenetic energy of people calling and asking his advice or just stopping by to chat. It filled the days with colourful people with varied backgrounds. Matt received them all equally, enjoying being the centre of attention.

The day passed slowly and Julia found herself looking towards the front door, waiting for it to burst open.

Or a phone call to say that he wanted her to join him. Anything would have been better than the muffled silence as the day wore on.

Day turned to evening and she hadn't heard from him. She decided to go find him, searching through the smoke-filled rooms of well-dressed men and women. She hadn't spent much time in the casino area since meeting Matt so people didn't recognise her. She sought out the pit boss, visible because of his wide stance and the impact he made on her that first day.

"Excuse me, sir? Would you happen to know where Matt Smit is? He told me he would be here."

The man had a perfectly bald head, shiny as if waxed. His neck's skin folded over his white shirt collar. "Sorry, Miss, but I haven't seen him all day. I would have noticed if he was here." He smiled. "He's quite the character and everyone knows him. He's well liked."

"Thank you for that. Perhaps he's elsewhere. I'll keep looking." She felt strangely alone, the tables cold and foreign. Even the smoke seemed invasive.

She decided to get a telephone directory and see if she could find his name. There weren't any directories for Johannesburg. She called the operator but there were too many M. Smits to choose from. She realised that she had spent almost three weeks with a man and she didn't know the first thing about him—except that he made her feel wanted and special. Without him, the villa seemed crass and showy, devoid of any life. She would have preferred an intimate apartment or a place away from all the activity of the resort. The clean rooms, perfectly manicured grounds, and sterile halls all became grating on her. Nothing was real; everything was manufactured or managed for the guests. Even the smiles of the uniformed men and women annoyed her. All she could see was their poverty next to the riches they were forced to work in. *Everything is fake in this place*, she thought.

When she returned to the penthouse villa, she found him sitting in the lounge next to a beautiful woman. His eyes were hollowed when he turned to look at her and she froze, the door unclosed behind her.

"So this is the whore you've been shacked up with?" The woman spoke with a sneer.

"It's not what you think."

"What else could it be? You've got three children who haven't seen their father for three months. Then you show up out of nowhere as though nothing happened. I thought you were dead. I wished you were dead."

Julia hadn't moved a muscle, eyes fixed on this woman. She found herself looking at her from the corners of her eyes.

Matt got up and walked towards Julia. "Julia, this is Alicia. She's my wife."

Julia felt a jolt of burning through her body as the adrenaline spread, causing her to shake mildly. Her muscles began to fill with blood and she was torn between punching Matt, running away, or just collapsing in tears. Instead, she walked calmly towards Alicia and extended her hand. "Nice to meet you."

"Nice to meet me? Are you fucking stupid as well as a whore? Get the hell out of here before I beat your skinny ass back to England." Alicia had stood up and looked capable of throwing the first punch.

Matt put himself between them. "Settle down, the two of you. This is my fault and not either of yours. I thought it would be good to put you both in a room and see if we can resolve things."

"Resolve? What are you trying to say? Do you want a divorce?"

"No, but I don't want to give up Julia either."

Julia had heard enough. "I'm sorry, Alicia. I didn't know." She walked as calmly as she could to her room. She pulled out her large backpack and began putting her things inside. As she looked down, the tears blurred her vision and she let them fall, trying not to make a sound. She remembered her necklace and casino chips and pushed them inside as well. There was no sound from the lounge where her lover and his wife sat. It was only a few minutes before she returned to see them both looking at her.

"Julia, you don't have to go," Matt said.

Alicia didn't say anything.

Julia didn't say anything either and closed the door as she left.

Chapter Four

Shock

"What a bunch of messed up people," Jane said as Julia recounted her misadventures. "What was Matt thinking? To make you his concubine? Add you to his harem? And what was Alicia thinking unless this has happened before? Do you think she likes it or just needs him to keep up appearances?"

Julia was silent, sipping her wine as she spread out on the bed next to Jane. The tears had all been cried out and the anger had passed. All that remained was exhaustion. "I thought he was the one," she said. "I was falling in love with him. He was smart, good looking, and rich. What more can a girl want?"

"To wake up. You were living a fairy tale and all fairy tales come to an end. At least you didn't get pregnant or killed by one of his psycho friends. Did you notice that his friends weren't all hoity-toity? Some looked like they were pretty rough guys."

"He's not a bad guy. Everything was perfect and then wasn't." She couldn't get her head around the abruptness of everything. It was as though everyone tolerated his flings and outrageous behaviour but then reeled him back in when they thought he had had enough.

"Look, Jules, you've had a great run. It was crazy and ended as quickly as it started. No harm, no foul. Relax with us for a bit and then begin building your life. Uni starts in six months and I don't want to regret wasting my time."

"I think I've got enough thrills to last me some time. Thanks for letting me hang with you and Stew, but maybe I should cut this year short and head back home. There's nothing for me here and all I'll do is be reminded of him everywhere I turn."

Jane nodded and put her arm around Julia. "Give it a week. If you still feel the same, head home and I'll see you when I get back."

"You're a good friend but I have an even more serious question." She paused for effect. "Do you have any chocolate?"

They laughed and got off the bed to hunt for some snacks.

When he arrived, it wasn't totally unexpected; they were staying at his friend's hotel. Julia had taken her own suite and heard the soft knock on her door mid-morning. When she opened it, he was standing with flowers and a face that couldn't look more contrite.

"I'm sorry," he said. She took the flowers and laid them on her dressing table.

"I think we're past sorry. What I saw was bordering on bat-shit crazy. Is this a regular thing where you introduce your wife to your mistress, hoping everyone will be friends?"

"Let me explain. If you want nothing to do with me after I'm finished, I'll leave you alone."

Julia slowly rubbed her fingertips together, feeling sweat forming in the small ridges. She lowered her eyes to her hands and stood still, not saying a thing. Matt, seeing her not disagree, began his story.

"Four months ago, my luck ran out and I found myself owing a lot of money to the wrong type of people. I tried to negotiate terms but they weren't interested. You need to understand that I was a big deal in everyone's eyes but these people didn't care. They didn't care about the front cover of *Time* magazine or the millions I had made them along the way. They didn't care that I had a mansion in Houghton or three kids in private school to pay for. They didn't care that people still knew me as a rich man. They didn't care that as soon as they came after me, every chance of me succeeding in the future would be over. No one gives money to a poor man, however good his idea. They give rich people more money because they feel they don't need it. Success breeds success and failure breeds failure. Them coming after me would mean ruin to my family and me.

"You've seen my mother. She still acts as though nothing has happened so she can keep up appearances. That's why she forced me to return to my family and to treat you as she did. But she didn't know what I had been through these last few months and what you mean to me." He tried to reach out to her but she pulled away, still staring at her hands.

"My mother loves me unconditionally. She could never see any wrong with anything I did. People would say that if I told her I was going out to rob a bank, she would reply that I should take a scarf so I wouldn't catch a cold. She was there when the bullets ripped through my home while my wife and children were sleeping. She knew it was a warning. She was there when Tony came to collect on the debt. Yeah, the same Tony from the party that first night. He brought Ray, a convicted rapist, to guard the home from any future attacks. She knew and I knew and my wife knew what was going on. We were being held hostage by Ray to ensure we didn't do a runner." Julia had moved to the chair next to the dressing table, sitting erect and listening but not turning to look at Matt. He followed and sat on the edge of the bed.

"One night, I was out and Alicia heard something in the back garden. She grabbed her gun—yes, I know, it's difficult for you Brits but we all have guns here— and opened the back door and yelled a warning before emptying the clip randomly into the night air. Tensions were high and all the blame was on me. During this time, we were forced to act to the outside world as though nothing had changed. I can handle threats from bad people. I can handle a lot of things—but I couldn't handle the pure hatred that came from Alicia's eyes and tongue. Even my mother carried a disappointed look when she wasn't fearing for her life.

"The pressure eventually got to me and I no longer wanted to be part of it. I sunk into a depression. I didn't get out of bed, didn't scheme a way out of our mess, didn't talk at all. I began to believe that the best way forward for me was to end my life. It was a shock to think about it at first; I never said it out loud for fear of making it more real. But the thought kept coming back into my head and soon thoughts of how I could achieve it followed.

Julia turned her body towards him, but remained silent. He sat up a little taller and was about to reach out and touch her leg. A further look from her returned his hands to his own lap.

"It started as I watched the pool boy doing his thing. I saw the bottled acid being poured into the water and imagined it being poured down my throat. I could feel the cap on the plastic bottle in my fingers, the crystallised salts gritty as I unscrewed it. I could feel the weight of its contents shift as I would lift it to my lips and pour it in as quickly as possible, knowing that the result would be the disintegration of mouth and innards. I would withstand incredible pain but I would surely die. I wanted to feel pain because I was so numb with the situation I was in.

"I also thought about hanging myself. I could do it anywhere, even off the handle of my bedroom door if I was desperate enough. I decided against this in the end because it wasn't cool." Julia looked up at that. Her eyes were angry but glassy. Matt was no longer looking at her. It had become his confession and his gaze was lifted into a point where two of the room's walls met.

"The next day, I was lying in my bath and I thought about simply slicing my wrists and waiting for death in the hot water. I would drift away and wouldn't feel a thing. In the end, my ego got in the way as I felt this was too prosaic a way for the great Matthijs Smit to die."

Despite the morbidity, Julia found the corner of her mouth turning up briefly at his self-deprecation.

"Walking in front of a bus or jumping off a cliff seemed just stupid and I dismissed it. Then I found myself slapping a fly and the idea struck me. I wondered at its bad luck. What were the odds, I thought, that it would be killed by me. Then I knew what I would do. Chance had defined my existence until that point in my life and I decided that luck would decide my fate going forward." He stood up and began pacing, wanting to get the story out.

Julia followed him with her head and eyes as he paced.

"I had a revolver, a .38, among my guns at home. I loaded one bullet into the cylinder and went into my study. I sat behind my desk and wrote a note to my family explaining how I couldn't go on. Then I spun the cylinder, put the barrel to my head, and pulled the trigger. As you can see, I am standing here before you. It didn't blow my head off. At the time, I was amazed I wasn't shaking or sweating or anything you would expect. I was resigned to what fate had in store for me. I did it again, willing it to blow the side of my head open. I did it five times in total before I put down the gun. I removed the bullet and put the gun away. I decided in a fevered state that fate wasn't done with me yet." He was working himself up, shaking his head as he talked and pacing the length of her room. Julia was now fully engaged with his story. Her face mirrored the emotions of each sentence.

"I packed my things and left my home, family, and everything I had cared for in the past. It was as though I was reborn that day, like I was meant for something more. I went back to those same bad people and borrowed a relatively small amount compared to what was owing. I promised them five percent per day interest and they, for some reason, accepted. I went to the casino to try my luck. I was convinced that if I could survive five spins of the cylinder, I would try five spins of the table. And that was when I met you."

Matt stopped pacing and looked at Julia. He could hear his own heart pumping in his chest. She said nothing.

"I left my wife and then I met you. You saved me. I am alive and debt free with loads left over. And I am pretty sure that I love you."

"You made that pretty clear in front of your wife," Julia said, snapping back to life. She also stood up and had become flush with the anger that was growing inside her as she listened. "We were living a paradise of romance, only to have you slap me in the face with your wife—with you not defending me and sitting meekly by. I feel sorry for you but I think you're full of bullshit."

"Jules…"

"Don't call me that. I'm sorry you lost your money. I'm sorry you almost killed yourself. I'm happy it all worked out for you. But you shit all over me and I'm not going to forgive you that easily." She opened the door and walked out, leaving Matt staring after her.

"Julia," he said, following her. "I never told that to anyone. Please, stop. Listen to me."

She stopped at the top of the staircase, portraits of solemn faces looked down on them from their gilded frames.

"I have no more tricks. No more secrets. I am a man who has met the woman he wants to spend his life with. Please, don't be angry with me." He softly placed his hand on hers.

She let him. She could still feel the raw loss and imagined herself picking up a knife or a gun to ease the pain, the indifferent steel awaiting her will. She felt the shudder as her mind and soul rejected the thought. When she then looked into his eyes, she realised he had been telling the truth. His eyes spoke of shame and desperation yet when they looked back at her, they held out hope of a new beginning.

Julia linked her fingers in his and moved closer to him. His other arm instinctively found its way around her waist, pulling her gently towards him. *Why does he smell so good, so manly?* she thought. Her perfume mixed with his as she pressed herself next to his body, head slightly turned towards his. His eyes were locked on hers, waiting for her to allow him to kiss her.

∞

When Jane saw the two of them enter the dining area, she shook her head and sighed in resignation. *It's her life*, she thought. *All I can do is support my friend, even if her boyfriend is a creep.*

"Hi Jane," Matt said as though they had just seen each other earlier that day. There was no hint of anything that had gone before.

"Hi Matt. I'm surprised to see you but glad you were able to make it for Jules." She would be polite but not welcoming.

"I know it hasn't been the easiest for Jules or any of you. My life has been complicated these last few months. But Jules has been my saviour."

And you're still with your wife, you slime bag, Jane thought. Outwardly, she did a little eyebrow lift and smile and went to find Stewart, leaving the two alone.

"I think your friends are upset with me."

"You hurt me and they're protecting me."

"I hope you can forgive me."

"I'm here, aren't I?"

He smiled and put his hands around hers, kissing them tenderly. "Yes, you are."

They sat in silence, hand in hand, looking at Table Mountain and the waves that rolled relentlessly along the ocean's surface, the Indian and the Atlantic vying for their influence over the inert land mass. At some point, Julia fell asleep against Matt and they relaxed for the first time since his mother burst into their lives. Matt, gently erasing the life he was tired of, and Julia constructing a life for them both in her dreams. It was only thirty minutes but they both awoke as new-borns, startled that they had fallen asleep at all. Exhausted, they both carefully made their way upstairs to her room and fell asleep until the next morning.

Chapter Five

End of the Beginning

"I love my children but I can't be married to her any longer."

Julia stroked his hair as his head lay in her lap, the waves lapping against the small fishing boat they had hired. The three months since Cape Town had been the happiest time in her life as they grew closer each day. Most of the time was spent wondering at the beauty of everything around them, nature at its rawest and most unrestrained. They talked about her future at Oxford and his interest in taking some courses to sharpen his brain. They talked more of philosophy, religion, and politics than business and power, but they always came back to the simple fact that he was still married with young children.

"You can't change the fact that you have children and I wouldn't want to drag you away from them." *What kind of father leaves his children for six months without seeing them?* she thought. It was something that bothered her about him. Somehow, he could turn off a part of his life without any regret or sorrow. He either starved or showered you with his attention. *And what about me? Are there children in our future? Are you going to tire of me and leave me too?*

"You aren't dragging me anywhere. This is between Alicia and me. I want to be here with you. I can't remember when I have wanted to wake up in the morning or go to sleep in the evening. You make the food taste better, the air cleaner and the sun brighter. I can't imagine a life without you."

He didn't address the children, she thought. *He never addresses the children.* "Let's change the subject. Where do you want to live?"

"Here, with you."

"No, seriously. Which town, which country?"

"Cape Town is nice but I'm from Joburg and that's where I'd like to live. You'll love it."

"With your children and hopefully ex-wife?"

Matt blushed. "It's more than that. Joburg is where the action is. It's like New York City for all of Africa. I'm too young to retire to Cape Town and grow grapes."

"Just asking."

"You? Where would you like to live?"

"London. Paris. New York. I don't know, all of them. None of them. I want more from life. I want to make a difference, an impact on others. I want to look back on my life and say I've made a difference."

"And do I factor in on your plans?"

She bent down to kiss him. "Yes, you stupid man. I just figured you can live anywhere on Earth. Why not in Europe or the US? We can visit here but I think I'd get tired of living in paradise without international courts, corporate takeovers, and political intrigue."

"We have all of that here, you know."

"Yes, but it's like comparing a Ford to a Ferrari. Both are cars and both ride well, but one is truly glorious."

"I had a Ferrari; didn't like it especially." He was smiling.

"Don't be cheeky. You know what I mean."

"I do. You want the catwalk, the fancy cars, and fame. You can have all that here."

Julia paused, thinking about the options. She had been on school trips to Paris and had fallen in love with the dirty chic roads and its history. The architecture was spellbinding and she could spend days just walking along the Seine. She hadn't been to New York but wanted to feel the chaos and power of its money and people, tall buildings, and unstoppable ambition. She wanted to have lunch at the top of the World Trade Centre and discuss deals with diplomats at the UN. Realising she was silent too long, she replied, "I want more."

Matt sat up and checked the poles for any movement. *No bites, no dinner*, he thought. *Maybe this wasn't such a great idea. We'll be eating canned sardines if we don't catch something soon.* "Want a beer?"

Realising he didn't like the direction of the conversation, she let him change it. "Sure, but only if it's cold."

"Animals prefer to stay in the pack or herd because it's safe. The leader exerts the most energy and is the most vulnerable. When birds are migrating, the lead bird changes constantly as it takes the brunt of the air. Cyclists desperately hold behind the leader's slipstream, trying to conserve their energy for the final push. Buffaloes look like they're running rampant but there's order. We tend to see wolves before seeing the leader. The alpha is undisputed—until he isn't. Then it is a fight to the death, his successor assuming the mantle. People are no different. Leaders take the glory and approbation but true trailblazers take the full impact of headwinds. Up until just before I met you, I willingly took the leader's place. Then my luck changed and I just about ceased to be. Are you sure you want that type of pressure?"

Julia snapped open the beer and took a long slug, allowing the time to think. "Yes. I want it all. The stress, aggravation, as well as the fame." Her jaw jut out against the sky as she took another long drink.

"That's what I love about you. You're fearless."

"And so are you. I saw you that day with the elephant."

"That was desperation."

"Courage is fear overcome, not reckless or suicidal behaviour." She regretted the word as soon as she uttered it. She hadn't meant to say it; she was just repeating what she had heard before.

His head lowered and was silent for a moment. "You give me too much credit." His mind drifted to the real reasons he hadn't left Alicia—her family and the power they exerted. Julia was strong. He had seen that. But was she strong enough for the truth? Could he ever tell her about Alicia's uncle Maish or her father? Or how everything he had he owed to them?

Julia didn't want Matt to feel sorry for himself. He was supposed to be her hero, not some injured soldier for her to nurse back to health. He was her elephant slayer, casino crushing superman. She went next to him and held him close. "You're my hero. That's all that matters."

She's lying, he thought. *I saw the flicker, the hesitation in her eyes. She's tolerating me.* "I love you," he said, kissing her deeply. They both tasted of beer and salty sweat.

∞

They went to Johannesburg to look for a house together. They would stay in Houghton, as it was the best and safest area.

"Prices are good," Matt said. "Everyone is getting out of South Africa now that the kefirs are in charge. They feel it's just a matter of time before they bash our white brains in." He was grinning at the image.

"Then maybe we shouldn't stay here. Let's go. There's nothing holding us here."

"Africa's in my blood," he said. "I love its weather, people, and energy."

"But you hate the blacks."

"I don't hate 'em. I love them and they love me. Just ask anyone I deal with." He was serious and she knew why. He paid them exorbitantly and treated them as men, albeit slightly less than whites.

"You are probably the exception and you still call them names."

"I can't help it," he was grinning again. "It'll take a generation to wash those words out." It sounded enlightened but also lazy.

"Still, maybe we should look at moving to England."

"With all that rain and cold? It would be hell."

"Then where?"

He froze and she followed his eyes. Driving slowly up the road towards them was Alicia and their children in a red Mercedes. In the passenger seat sat Maish. She watched the woman who called her a whore four months ago. As they drove past, Matt's eyes followed and watched the brake lights disappear around the corner.

"Sorry?" He hadn't replied for a moment after the car turned the corner.

Julia looked at him, eyes pinching at the corners. "Is there something I should know? We're talking about buying homes, living in places around the world and then she drives past and you shut down."

Matt swallowed forcibly, mouth opening twice before words came out. "It was a shock, that's all. I haven't seen my children for so long I didn't think the sight of them would have such an effect on me." He had begun to sweat and he took out a handkerchief to wipe his brow. She had always thought that an elegant accessory for a man but now looked at it with disgust.

"I think you have some real thinking to do," she said, her anger beginning to boil up inside her. "I'm giving you my life but it seems you are giving me your spare time. When it comes down to it, you're married and will stay that way. I'm just some distraction you convinced yourself was important. Some lucky charm."

"You've got it all wrong, sweetheart. I was just surprised, that's all. I love you and I need you."

"You need self-confidence, not me. I didn't want to say anything before, but I can't help it now. You need to get your shit together or you can't be with me. I love you and always will but your heart is with another. Or, if it isn't, you're too afraid to leave her. Whatever the case, you're not mine, and I need my own man." Tears were filling her eyes and she was determined not to cry.

Her face was red with the hurt and adrenaline. She stood as dignified as possible, trying not to create a scene in front of the houses they planned to move into; hoping he did the right thing next, fearing he wouldn't.

Instead, Matt was silent. His eyes dropped and head began looking at the grass and the cracks in the pavement and then upwards as a plane made a sound in the sky as it passed. He couldn't look at her. *She sees through me*, he thought. *She's too smart not to have. She knows I'm a coward.* His heart beat faster and he began to panic. "Don't leave me," he finally said. "I love you, Jules. Just don't leave me. I'm with you, honest to God. I was just surprised."

Julia's tears began to fall silently down her cheeks and splash against her shirt. She let them fall freely. "I thought you were the one. I was ready to sacrifice everything. Oxford, Paris, New York, the world. All I needed you to do was one thing." Her nose began to run and she ran her sleeve along it. "I think I know what I need to do." He handed her his handkerchief and she blew her nose and wiped her eyes. "Thank you." He waved it away when she tried to hand it back to him.

"Don't leave me, Jules. We'll be fine."

"We won't be fine. I'm not a fool. Today you weren't ready. Next time, you'll be able to mask your feelings and sneak behind my back. I am pleased I was able to see such an honest emotion and reaction from you. I'm just crushed at what that emotion was." She began walking back to their car.

"I'm leaving for England on the next flight. My classes start in three weeks and I don't want to miss it. Figure out what you want to do and let me know." She got in the car and drove off, leaving him a solitary figure amidst the gates and gardens of the most exclusive homes of Johannesburg.

What the hell just happened? he thought. *One second, I'm on top of the world, a beautiful and intelligent woman on my arm. The next, everything turns to shit.*

He stood for a few moments absorbing the cards luck had dealt him. Nodding to himself, he began walking in the direction of the red brake lights.

Later that evening, sitting in the South African Airways' first class lounge, Julia watched her boarding gate with one eye and the door to the lounge with the other. *Just come through that door,* she thought, *and everything's forgiven. Just fight for me. Let me have one tenth of the connection you have with Alicia.* She didn't want to feel like his mistress but his actions spoke louder than any words. She feared she was what Alicia said she was.

When the final boarding call came, she stood up and clutched her small handbag. She thought about the ruby necklace or her share of the winnings inside it. That much he couldn't take from her.

Chapter Six

Hard Graft

Daniel Stone pulled up his white Iveco van in front of the old school. It was now twenty-six flats and he was its proud owner, as of four months ago. He bought it from a local rugby coach who had bought it from a retired major and his son who, in turn, bought it from the council in a sweet inside deal. Daniel didn't mind as it still turned a tidy profit. *Thirty percent return*, he told his brother. *Come in with me. It's full of asylum seekers and housing benefit, guaranteed payers.*

But no one joined him. It was 1996. The last property crash was fresh in everyone's minds, and another was expected soon. His grandfather had recently died and left him fifty thousand pounds in his will. His brother bought a car and paid off his credit card debt. Dan took out a personal loan from the bank to add to his inheritance and used it as the deposit to purchase the old school. If all went well, it would be free and clear in five years.

"What is it you want the money for?" The bank manager still wore a three piece suit and was looking forward to his retirement. He was pleasant and professional and smelled of tobacco and breath mints.

"It's a solid Victorian brick and stone structure with high ceilings and a Welsh slate roof. The income is strong and I am buying it for less than ten percent of its replacement value, according to the insurance company."

The manager looked up, eyebrows raised. "Does this concern you? Repairs still cost money. Your rent is good but it may not be sufficient to maintain such a large structure."

Daniel was speechless. He thought it meant he bought well. "I will be on site every day. I'll make sure things don't get out of hand. And the market is rising. A new casino is being built next door and I may be able to sell off each flat individually."

"Margate has taken some knocks lately, hasn't it?" The manager was poking holes in Daniel's plan.

"Yes. The cheap flights have killed it as a holiday destination. Brits prefer to go to Majorca or Ibiza. They don't care that Dickens' home was in nearby Broadstairs or that he drank in the local pub. Maybe that'll change over time."

"Are you worried? Who's going to rent your flats?"

"The government has been encouraging welfare recipients to relocate to seaside resorts. People are relocating and finding life better in places like Margate."

What Daniel didn't explain was the arrival of the asylum seekers. It was a two-edged benefit for landlords. On one hand, they received higher rents and the money was paid directly from the government. The downside was the wear and tear on the properties. Cultural clashes and absent landlords meant deterioration of housing stock. Soon, Margate began to deteriorate and holiday makers stopped coming. Tourists became fearful of the gangs of hungry looking men with nothing to do. EasyJet or Ryanair could whisk people to Greece or Italy just as easily.

In the end, the bank approved his loan and he bought the property. Dan didn't mind that his building was full of asylum seekers and those on housing benefit. He did mind that the type of welfare families he had were of the lowest class. They were mean, dirty, and unpredictable. As part of his business model, he required tenants to top up their rent. The council would only pay fifty pounds per week in rent and he wanted another tenner.

Today was rent collection day. The council paid by cheque directly but he had to collect the cash himself. He carried a small crowbar just in case.

"Hi Dennis," he said, sitting down on the picnic table outside the pub. It was less than fifty paces from the building's front door. "How're things?"

"Everything's fine, boss. I fixed a leak on flat twelve two days ago. There was a broken window on the door to the landing and I put some wood on it until you decide what to do with it."

"Is it one of those windows with wire in it?"

"Yeah. Expensive."

"Can we just take the door off?"

"I think we need it for fire regs."

He's not a stupid as he looks, Dan thought. *Even though he's a cross-eyed motherfucking liar.* "Do you know who did it?"

"Nope."

"How much do I owe you for this last week?"

Dennis took a sip of his beer and rubbed the stubble on his head, the fat spilling out from where his t-shirt lifted around his waist. "A fiver for fixing the leak, same for the window, as I found the wood, and the usual tenner for me being on call. So a score in total."

Dan handed him twenty pounds in four, five pound notes.

"Anything else you need, boss?"

"No. I just need to collect the top-ups. Anyone do a runner since last week?"

"Not that I know of. The Albanians don't open their door. I think they're afraid of us."

That's because you are all a bunch of dirty slobs. At least the Albanians keep their flat neat, he thought. "Okay, I'll check them out. They'll answer the door to me."

Daniel got up and walked to the front door, his receipt book in one hand, crowbar in the other. No-one commented on the crowbar, partly because it was only half the normal size and could have been something he had just been using on a job. When he opened the front door, the familiar smell hit him. A combination of unwashed laundry, human sweat, and cheap cooking ingredients wafted towards him. It was the smell of poverty. Too often he would receive a call from the council saying that they needed desperately to house a person. He never said no with the result that he housed the most desperate, down-and-out people in Margate. It impacted on his idea of humanity and fair play, prejudicing him against the smells and condition of poverty. *I think I'd kill myself before giving up like this*, he thought. Then he realised much of this was beyond these people's control. *They simply don't have the tools to escape this hell.*

As he walked up the stairs, he could smell the urine and see the lack of cleaning, despite paying Dennis. The first thing he did when he purchased the building was bring the fire regulations up to date. The council served notice on him and then gave him three months to bring everything up to code. It cost him a small fortune but he did it out of cash flow. The building brought in eighty thousand pounds a year gross. He didn't pay for heating or electricity in the flats, but he was responsible for a working fire alarm and safe exits.

Today, the hallways were clear and the exit signs and emergency lighting all looked as they should. He was feeling good about things. He anticipated increasing his sixty thousand per year profit on this building by eventually getting rid of the current tenants and making the flats luxurious and marketed to the working class. The market was moving and perhaps in five years, he could double or triple his money by selling them individually.

When he saw the water in the hallway, it took him a moment to register what he was seeing. He looked at the direction of the flow and realised someone had ripped the main water pipe off the wall. All the flats below would flood. *There goes my profit for the year*, he thought.

He ran outside to find Dennis sitting exactly where he left him. "Come on, it's an emergency. Water everywhere. I need to turn off the stop cock." Dan was yelling across the parking lot and he saw Dennis getting up slowly. He continued to rummage through his tools in the back of his van. He needed to find something to stop the water. He decided to crimp the copper water line while Dennis found the stop cock.

"Where is it?"

Dan found himself suspecting Dennis. "Upstairs. Water main torn off the wall. Lots of damage. I hope you're ready for some extra work."

Dennis smiled slightly. "Sure thing, boss. Stop cock is outside. It'll kill the water to the whole building."

"Are you one hundred percent sure?"

"One hundred percent."

"Okay, then let's go. I won't damage the pipe further by crimping it. Let's stop it at the source."

That was the day Daniel decided to sell the building. He realised he would never make any money. The certainty came when the insurance paid out and then cancelled the insurance policy. They deemed the building uninsurable, as though it was in a warzone.

He put an ad in the classified section of the Estates Gazette and had twenty calls before noon. Everyone was keen on the high returns. Daniel had marketed it at four hundred thousand pounds and found a buyer within the week. He had owned it for less than six months when it sold and parlayed his inheritance into a two hundred thousand pound profit in less than a year. He was hooked on property.

He took the entire amount and bought more flats in the area, accumulating more than a hundred before he was done. He refused to repeat his experience with the old school and instead bought based on location, focusing on future conversion to flats to sell and create an income stream. Nothing less than fifteen percent return was acceptable. It took less than a year and he had become a significant landlord, albeit at the lower end of the spectrum.

The following months saw him working every hour of every day. The vibrations of his van forced him to listen to the radio at full blast. It made his ears ring when he shut off the engine.

It was early Sunday, 31 August, 1997 and he had just returned home to his flat in London. His body was sore and all he wanted to do was crawl into bed. Just before he turned off the engine, he heard the news. Diana was dead.

The radio voice was sombre and Daniel was shocked at the accident. *They probably killed her,* he thought. Many in the pubs would later agree with him, citing the royal family's dislike of the headstrong woman. The public poured out their grief and the newspapers filled their pages with the event that was capitalised by the recently elected prime minister, dragging the queen out of her castles onto the streets. Diana was proclaimed the people's princess and a new hope filled the air for the future prosperity of the country. However sad the day, the country came together as few events could have done.

Daniel was so effected by the death that he took the advice of some friends and tried to work less. He was working hard and driving tired. *That could have been me tangled in this van,* he thought. He even agreed to be set up on a blind date.

"I am not looking to be the richest man in the graveyard," he said. "I just need enough to satisfy my personal needs so I can pursue my artistic and intellectual interests." *I'm sounding like a right prat*, he thought. *Just calm down. If you try too hard, you'll just chase her away.*

"But don't you think it's too easy to get caught in the trap of wealth? To forget about the destination and get carried away with the ride?" Her eyes sparkled as she spoke, her beer hardly drunk but her fingers traced the condensation of the glass absentmindedly.

"I think too many people assume they are rich or wealthy before they actually are. They start spending money before their wealth is sustainable. Before they realise their mistake, they create a lifestyle that requires them to chase money instead of enjoying the fruits of their efforts. In short, they live outside of their means. That is the essential element in the wealth trap." Dan was pleased with his reply.

"You sound so sure of yourself."

"I think about it a lot because I don't want to get caught up in it. I work hard now so eventually my money will work for me, not the other way around." He didn't want to talk about himself and they had talked enough about money. "So what about you? What's your story?"

"No story. Just a student."

"Where you going?"

"Oxford."

"Nice. Which college?"

"Balliol." She wound her hair around her finger.

"Any subject in particular?"

"Just finishing my undergrad in history and English literature but I am thinking about an MBA at LSE next."

"I did my MBA at LSE as well," he said. His time at the London School of Economics was the most fun he had in his life, but difficult academically.

"So we're a power couple in the making," she said playfully. "Business degrees, making money, and talking about everything but."

"I talk about money, but it's not my goal. It's the means to my end."

"And what end is that?"

"My personal enlightenment." As he said it, he could have slapped himself. *Personal enlightenment? Are you crazy? You're making yourself into a weirdo.*

"That's admirable," she said. Her long blonde hair reached to the middle of her back. She wore a thin wool sweater with little frayed fingers of thread that stood out like underwater coral.

"Sorry for saying something stupid like that. It sounds ridiculous. Anyway, I think it's because I'm a bit nervous. I've never been on a blind date before."

"Me neither. My friends felt I needed to get out."

"Worried about you?"

"Yeah. Same with you?"

"Them, my mother, and even my tenants. Why can't they understand?"

"That's what I tell them. I'm not interested."

Daniel took a sip of his diminishing beer and tried not to stare at her. She was confident, relaxed, and had the type of looks you expect on a billboard or chiselled into a Grecian statue. She didn't wear glasses and her skin was milky, almost like porcelain. Her fingers were long and elegant, tapered and finished in an expensive manicure. *She looks like an heiress to a great fortune and not an earnest student*, he thought. "But we're both here, despite ourselves," he said.

She laughed. "I think we protest too much. Maybe we're human after all."

"I'm twenty-five years old and I work every hour of the week. My passion is to create a portfolio of rental properties to allow me to retire by the time I'm thirty. I may dabble after that, but not too seriously. I want to eventually find the right woman, have a family, and live happily ever after. Just not now." Daniel decided being honest was his best hope. "But at the same time, I'm terribly lonely and wouldn't mind having someone in my life."

"So you're looking for a good time, not a long time?" Her smile was from ear to ear.

"Not like that," he stammered. "I'm looking for a friend."

"Have you tried a dog?"

"Too much work."

"So you're looking for a friend whom you don't have any attachments to who is less trouble than a dog. Oh, and you probably would like to have sex with this friend?"

Daniel blushed. "You make me sound like a mercenary. I'm just trying to be honest. I'm sorry if I offended you." He started to get up to leave and reached into his pocket to find a note to pay the bill. He felt her hand on his arm.

"Don't go. Please. I'm just being honest as well. I don't know how or if this will go anywhere, but I'd like to be your friend if you'll let me." Her smile would have melted the chains on any heart.

"Okay, I'd like that very much. Let me introduce myself, friend. My name is Daniel. Daniel Stone."

"Julia. Julia Frist." She shook his hand, blushing slightly. *This is ridiculous*, she thought. *But fun.*

Love

"I think I may really like Daniel," Julia said. "It's only been a few weeks but I find myself thinking about the feeling of his jacket on my skin or the smell of his cologne as he comes close to me."

"That's wonderful. I'm so happy for you, especially after the last couple of years. You haven't had the best of luck with men." Jane was visiting from Bristol and the two sat cross legged on Julia's bed in her dorm room. She was lucky enough to have the room to herself.

"We haven't even kissed, not really. Just a peck and a minor snog."

"That doesn't matter. Do you think he likes you?"

"He shows up and seems to like me."

"He'd be crazy not to. You are more gorgeous each time I see you. If you weren't my best friend, I'd hate you."

Julia smiled appreciatively. "Thanks. You always know what to say."

"Seriously, he wouldn't be meeting up with you and going to shows or hanging out talking nonsense if he didn't want to spend time with you."

"But I told him I didn't want anything more than friendship, and he more or less said the same thing. I don't know if I was being honest or hoping he'd just leave."

Jane put her socked foot against Julia's leg, stretching her back and leg muscles as she talked. "All guys want more, you know that. You're no babe in the woods either. Just take control of the situation and decide what you want to do. He'll follow your lead."

"But I want a man to lead."

"He will eventually, but men need guidance. First, you have to let him know you are open to suggestion. Then, guide him to make the first move and the rest follows."

"You're too cynical."

"It's because I've been with the same man for so many years."

"How's Stew?"

"He's perfect." Jane adjusted herself a little before continuing. "I think he's going to ask me to marry him." She said it in an excited whisper.

"That's excellent news," Julia said, leaning over and hugging her friend. "I assume you'll say yes?"

"I can't imagine living my life with someone else." Jane took on a faraway look in her eyes. "I just wish you could experience the same thing."

"I thought I had with Matt."

"Have you heard from him recently?"

"No, and I don't want to."

"You don't have any feelings for him?"

"Of course I do but he's an asshole and a coward. One second, he's telling me that he loves me and we'll live happily ever after as we shop for houses. The next second, he freezes at the mere sight of his family. He will never leave them."

"You haven't spoken to him for over two years?"

"He called a few times shortly afterwards. He was in London more than once and even came to Oxford. But I wouldn't see him. He left a note and I burned it."

"Dramatic."

"I'm realising I'm that type of person."

"Hmmm… In better news, if Stew asks, will you be my maid of honour?"

Julia melted, her face relaxing from the previous tension and tears began to well in her eyes. She hugged Jane for a long moment before saying, "Yes. A thousand times yes."

The engagement was announced within a fortnight with a wedding three months after that. They planned to host it in Bristol just before Christmas.

"Will you come?" Julia was holding the invitation as she looked into Daniel's eyes. He had grown more attractive each time she saw him, and she loved the intensity of his gaze and the strength of his hands. She liked her hands in his and the gentle strength of him next to her. He felt like the perfect complement to her.

"Of course, if you'll have me."

"Of course I'll have you. I've wanted you since the moment you stumbled into that pub on our first blind date. I liked the way you had to duck to avoid the low beams, brushing the dried hops out of your head as you rubbed against it. I tried not to smile at the time, as I wasn't in the mood to really meet someone. Then you sat down and I could feel the air of your slipstream waft over you and…" she couldn't speak anymore because he was kissing her.

"Has anyone told you that you talk too much?" He was smiling as he held her head gently between his hands. He kissed her lightly, allowing her body to fall into his open jacket. The outer part was wet and she wanted to feel his warmth and be next to him.

"I'm a little afraid at how much I want to be with you," she said.

"A little ahead of schedule?" he smiled.

"Yes. Definitely."

"Shall we pause and book our next date in five years?"

She feigned thinking but then shook her head. "But I was thinking of us stopping dating."

Daniel felt a shock run through his body and he stood erect, pulling himself away from her so that he could see her face. She was smiling. He was confused.

"I don't want to date you anymore, Dan. I want you to move in with me. Or me with you. I don't care. I'm ready to take another step if you are."

Suddenly Daniel didn't know what day it was. He didn't realise the bond he had with Julia. The thought of losing her broke something inside of him. The thought of living with her was beyond his wildest hopes. *I wish she would give me some indication of what she planned,* he thought. *I'm falling in love with her but I don't feel in control. And it's happening so fast. It's not what I was planning for.* His mind raced but he knew what his answer would be the moment she asked.

"I'd like that more than I can express in words."

"Do you think life will allow us to be happy?"

"Life has made us happy," he said. He had forgotten about the wedding invitation and his business and only wanted to continue having Julia look at him like she was. "Maybe we should rent a flat somewhere in London so we both move in and it becomes our place from day one."

Julia liked the way he was considerate like that. She had known many people struggle with their relationships because they were the person who moved into another's space. This way, the space was neutral and they would make it theirs. "I like that. Perhaps we can get a place close to LSE?"

"I was thinking the same thing. You can catch the train to Oxford until you're done your degree and then walk to LSE. I also think we should buy rather than rent. The property market is only going one way and rent is wasted money. Besides, even in the worst case scenario and we split, the investment can be sold and split as well."

Julia didn't like how much that reminded her of Matt, but she kept silent. "I think that's a good idea. I've heard similar things. We can probably get a first time buyer's mortgage." She didn't want to say she could pay for it with cash.

"Excellent. I'll take a look at things. Just in case I get carried away, would you be offended if we bought a strip instead of a flat?"

"A strip?"

"It's the whole freehold, so we can be our own bosses. It may be a large home or many flats. We can live in one and rent out the rest, giving us extra income."

"How would we fund it?"

"I'm working on that. I think it's doable. Banks are finally lending again. They must have recovered from the last crash. If we can, we should try. Even if we move out and buy something bigger later on, we can still rent out the property forever—to students, professors, whomever."

Julia laughed. "I just asked you to move in together and you are building us a portfolio and moving us into a larger home elsewhere?"

"Just thinking ahead. I like compressing life to maximise our options."

"That's what I love about you."

∞

The wedding was spectacular. The sandstone of Bristol's architecture provided the perfect background to the brilliant white silk dress Jane wore and the snow that fell lightly around her. It didn't stay on the ground but it provided a lovely backdrop for pictures with their fluffy flakes drifting silently to the ground. The wedding was held at Christ Church in Clifton, a part of Bristol not far from where they studied.

"I never noticed the spire before today," Jane said to Julia. "It actually looks as I feel, reaching into an endless sky." She looked like she was going to start crying and Julia handed her a tissue.

"It's a beautiful venue, Jane. Couldn't be nicer and couldn't be happening to nicer people."

"Is everything ready?"

"Everything's done. The people are in the church, waiting on you. You look beautiful, radiant, and ready. If there's nothing else, I think we should go and get you hitched." She smiled as she gave her hand and helped Jane up. She followed and gathered the train. When they reached the horse-drawn carriage, they had to negotiate the step up but it passed without incidence. Julia joined Jane inside.

"No going back," Jane said.

"There's always going back," Julia said. "But I don't think you're having second thoughts."

"No. Just saying it because I think everyone says it." She looked like a little face with arms encased in a sloppy meringue. "I look hilarious, I know, but I can't stop loving it." She was smiling as she watched the cityscape pass, safe from the falling snow by the enclosed carriage.

"You look as I hope to one day feel," Julia said. It made Jane start crying again and they were both careful to not smear her makeup.

"You're not allowed to talk to me anymore. I can't walk down the aisle like a character out of the *Rocky Horror Picture Show*, eyeliner and mascara running down my cheeks." The image made her smile. She thought her cheeks would break from smiling. The two smiled and held hands until the carriage came to a halt outside Christ Church.

The site of the church was fifteen hundred years old with its current structure built in 1841. Neither Jane nor Stewart were religious but they wanted their union to be sacred and the church represented stability, age, and continuity. It was also beautiful, with its carved stone and wood and stained glass windows creating the perfect ambiance. It was full with over two hundred guests and the priest at the alter awaiting the bride, the groom at his left. The groom had his best man and four groomsmen with an equal number for the bride. Julia had taken her place near the altar and waited with the congregation for the music, the bride, and her father, who was to give her away.

From the second row, Daniel could only see Julia. The bride came, got married, and left in grand fashion. All the while, he looked at the profile of his love, dressed in a colour somewhere between red and pink, as were the rest of the bridesmaids. He caught the glitter of light off some diamonds in her necklace and the pronounced ruby, which sat tantalisingly on her chest. He had never seen her so beautiful or wanted her so much.

"How are you enjoying it?" Julia was in his arms, dancing as the evening drew to a close.

"Everything was perfect. I've never enjoyed a wedding so much. The service wasn't too long. The meal was tasty and the speeches were fun. All in all, it was a great day." He was warm from the champagne and could feel her perspiration through the elaborate dress as he held her lower back.

"Heating was on a bit high, but better than being too cold this time of year." She was more clinical in her observations than he expected.

"I didn't notice it."

"Me neither until just now. Do you feel like getting out of here?"

"Are you allowed?"

"The bride and groom have left. My duties are over." She smiled and leaned in for a kiss. Her nose was sweaty and left a damp place on his face. He didn't wipe it away.

"Then let's go."

The outside was slushy wet from the snow so they took a taxi instead of walking back to their hotel. Inside their cab, Julia put her head against his shoulder and drifted to sleep without a word, her hand in his. *I'm going to marry her*, he thought. *She's perfect.*

Chapter Eight

Reality

"What are you doing for millennium eve?" The architect put his work away and was ready to leave the meeting, trying to engage with Daniel and hoping that a friendship might lead to more business.

"I need to check with my wife. We hadn't planned anything but you know how it goes. I'm sure she'll get invited somewhere and I'll tag along."

"It doesn't happen often. And back up your computer files. They're saying this millennium bug'll crash everything we have. If it's really important, print it out. That's what I'm doing."

"I bought a new computer a few months ago with the dates sorted out. I updated all of my software so hopefully I'm okay. Who would've thought something as simple as date format would cause such chaos?"

"You get one of those colourful new Macs?"

"No. I'm a PC guy. Cheaper and easier to replace. I got an IBM clone. I think it's pretty good. Even upgraded to a laser printer. It's like a miracle. So much better than my old dot matrix."

"Soon the computers will be telling us what to do."

"I'm not so sure. I'm just happy when they don't crash. I do daily backups and weekly backups, waiting for everything to be lost. All I use them for is the management of my properties."

"For me, all my drawings are on them. I'm becoming increasingly dependent on them. Anyway, enjoy your holidays and see you in the New Year."

"Thanks Alex. Have a good one."

When he left, Daniel got up to make himself coffee. Everyone had gone and he was planning on shutting the office for the Christmas holidays, opening on the fifth of January. *Now, if only I could find a present for Julia*, he thought, *my life would be complete. I can't believe it's been two and half years since we met, a year and a half since we married. Twenty seven and married. Who would have thought?*

He closed the shop they bought together two years ago. It was part of a strip with flats above, close to the London School of Economics. They had since moved to a house in Belsize Square but kept the west end property as a rental income and their office address. *Better than working from home,* he thought.

"We're going to Jane's for a Christmas party," Julia said as he opened the door. "We're supposed to be there by seven. Dinner party, so don't eat anything." She kissed him as a dervish kisses the air, rushing to her next task, which was finding some wine as a gift and some chocolates to pop in her mouth.

"Sounds good. Can I wear this?" He looked at her and realised not. She wore her favourite necklace with a black velvet dress that hugged her body. He still found himself jolted when he saw her like that.

In reply, she looked at him with a smirk and began to slowly shake her head. "I think you need to try a bit harder." She kissed him again and patted him on the bum to get him up the stairs to change.

When he emerged, he wore a dark navy blazer with an expensive shirt but no tie. His trousers were an expensive cotton and wool mix in a cream colour. His shoes were the ones he wore to work. He shaved and splashed on some cologne, feeling he should have showered with all the effort he was putting in. He was rewarded with more kisses and coos from Julia and then they whisked themselves into a waiting cab. *Married life is good*, he thought.

That evening was just one of a dozen parties he had to endure prior to the New Year's party. The actual New Year's Eve party was to be held at Winfield House, the official residence of the American Ambassador.

"Wow," Daniel said when he found out. "Pretty fancy stuff."

Julia did something with her shoulder to make her look like a little girl and batted her eyelashes at him. "I'm not just a pretty face, you know." They both giggled with excitement at the prospect of the invitation.

On the day, Daniel took extra care with his personal hygiene, dressing in a tuxedo, as it was listed as a black tie event. Julia wore a new dress that complemented her waspy waist and full bosom, falling away across her athletic hips and legs into a pool of fabric that hovered above the floor. To finish her glam, as she called it, she put on her ruby necklace.

"You look like a goddess," he said. It had the desired effect and he could see her become gooey inside.

"Don't touch me or you'll ruin it," she said between giggles. She deftly applied her finishing makeup and considered herself in front of the mirror. "That'll do." *Damn*, she thought. *How do I freeze this moment in time? It's all downhill from here.*

Daniel softly touched her waist and kissed her neck. Her hair was lifted in an elaborate braid that exposed her back. He found himself stirred by the sight of her neck and flawless skin. He touched the base of her neck and allowed his fingertips to trace her spine until his hand was resting on her hips. "I can't believe you married me. You are the best thing that has ever happened to me."

"I know," she said, smiling.

He smiled but would have preferred a different reply. "Shall we?" He indicated with his hand that it was time to go.

As they entered Regent's Park, the cab turned right and Daniel could see joggers along the adjoining canal. He saw what he assumed to be plain clothes police walking on the pavement and shortly saw the police vehicles and heavily armed officers as they approached the entrance gate to Winfield House. There was a high steel fence encased with rhododendrons and other evergreen bushes. They were searched once inside the outside gate. No one could see the ambassador's house from the road. The entire complex was within the larger Regent's Park, which was open to everyone, and it made security tricky at times.

Their hosts made the process as painless as possible but the reality was there were a lot of high value targets attending the party and many terrorists would have loved to orchestrate that type of strike. Once inside, their earlier ordeals were forgotten as they luxuriated in the mansion and tried not to stare at the guests.

They entered the main ballroom, which wasn't as grand as Daniel had dreamed about, but was impressive nonetheless. "There must be a hundred penguin suits here already," he said.

"And a hundred expensive gowns," she replied, her eyes taking in the women and their frocks.

"Do you think we arrived too early?"

"It's ten o'clock. I think it's enough. I'm glad not to be eating in this."

"Did I tell you how lovely you look tonight?"

"No," she pouted.

"You do."

She smiled. "Champagne?"

"Certainly. Coming right up." He found a table with glasses already filled and took two. As he walked back, he could see her talking to a tall, athletic black man in a very expensive tuxedo. *How is it possible*, he thought, *for some people to always look better than others, even when we're all dressed the same?* The tuxedo looked tailored and the white collar was crisp. *He looks like James Bond*, he thought.

"I got you something, sweetheart," he said as he passed the glass to Julia. He ensured that this man heard him and tried to hand it to her left hand to emphasise her wedding ring.

"Thank you. Dan, I want you to meet Jeff, my mentor at LSE. He's the reason we were invited. Jeff, Dan."

"Nice to finally meet you, Dan."

He's got a grip like a vice. Who is he? Superman? "And you, Jeff. I knew Jules had a mentor but I didn't expect him to be so… impressive." He found the word and hoped he wasn't making a fool of himself. *Where is this jealousy coming from?*

"Sorry to not have met under different circumstances. I'm rarely in the UK and most of our interaction is via phone and, increasingly, email. I would have preferred fish and chips and a pint myself."

"I can see why after having to put up with this hardship," Julia said, smiling. She was enjoying the evening and had let her guard down. Jeff was a brilliant Wall Street raider who allowed her an hour of access each week. She found it invaluable and prepared questions for him to ensure she squeezed the most out of their time together.

"This is my first time here as well," he said. "I'm over on some business and my client received the invitation for himself and his advisors as a gesture by the ambassador. It is a nice perk when Americans are dealing with other Americans. But enough about business, tonight is about welcoming in the New Year. I have to circulate but I'll see you two later. Nice to meet you, Dan."

"He's like a force of nature," Daniel said when he was gone.

"He's quite something. Do you know what his full name is? Jefferson Washington Money. How funny is that?"

"Funny funny and funny ha ha," Daniel said. "How'd that happen and what does he do, exactly? Everything about him seems better, stronger, and nicer."

"I know," she said. "I noticed the same thing. "It's as though his skin was painted by an artist. It's flawless."

"It was the first thing I noticed. He must be an athlete. I thought he may have been a soldier or security at first."

"Now that's racist," she said, a touch of anger in her voice.

"How? He's got a body that most guys would kill for and looks better in his tux than anyone else here. How is that racist?"

"Maybe not."

"I'm sure that doesn't hurt his business either. What did you say his fund is worth? Two hundred million?"

"That's just what he started with when he broke away from the bigger firms. It's up to a billion now."

"Wow. What does he charge?"

"The usual, two and twenty. He's been in business for himself for only three years and has already earned over hundred million for himself. He is trying to increase his fund to ten billion. Apparently the pension funds are waiting on the side-lines to see if he implodes. So far, all the indications are looking good."

"I feel inadequate with my slum flats and handful of London properties."

"Different type of person. You're happy in your skin. He must have some fire in him to keep going. He doesn't work for money or power... it's something else." Her eyes had a faraway look in them Daniel hadn't seen before. He felt a twinge of uneasiness but then reassured himself that there was always someone richer, better looking, and younger than you, wherever you went in life.

"Here's to your mentorship," Daniel said, trying to stay positive. "Let's hope some of his success rubs off on you."

"To us." She clinked glasses and tilted it back. As she righted her sight on Daniel, she began to ask for another when she saw something that caused the blood to drain from her face and muscles to go slack. Her whole body seemed to shrink with the shock.

"What is it?" he said, noticing her sudden change of appearance. He followed her frozen gaze and saw Jeff coming towards them with his arm around a man's shoulders. The man was smiling and laughing, red faced, with what looked like glass of Coca Cola instead of champagne. He noticed his face change as well.

"Julia, Dan, I wanted you to meet our mutual bene-factor. This is Mr. Matthijs Smit of Johannesburg. He's the client I was talking to you about."

Julia's mouth went dry and noticed the room move slightly but she stayed on her feet. Her hands were at her sides and she didn't move. She noticed Matt staring at her ruby necklace and saw his face drop. Time slowed down and she looked for an exit like a cornered animal. Then panic passed and she took a deep breath.

"Nice to meet you, Mr. Smit," she said. "Jeff, I thought you said your clients were Americans?"

"More or less. Mr. Smit is a major investor in an alternative venture we are pursuing. We can't talk about it due to take-over regulations but I can assure you that it is an American company taking over another American company. Of interest to Mr. Smit are its assets within the UK."

"Sounds fascinating, Mr. Smit," Daniel said. "What field of work do you focus on?"

"Please, call me Matt. Nothing too risky, I'm afraid. I look across all fields and try to find the arbitrage and then call people like Jeff to help me execute the inefficiency in the marketplace."

Julia was silent, the smile gone. She was shocked into nodding along with the men. Her mind was racing as she felt the strong reaction to Matt. *Am I still in love with that asshole? It can't be. It's probably just some unresolved anger brought to the surface*, she thought. The men were talking but their voices faded into the increasing noise of the crowd. It was thirty minutes to midnight and soon the party would be either just beginning or end abruptly. If she had her way, she would end it now, but not before punching Matt in the face.

She could see them laughing and patting each other on the shoulders. Even Matt's face lifted as he tore his eyes from the ruby that now burned on her chest. Her breath was difficult and her primary objective was to stay standing and not run out the door.

"How can you say no to a guy named Mr. Money?" Matt said. "When I first heard his name, I started laughing, thinking it was a joke, but Jeff is the smartest guy on Wall Street and will probably be one of the richest men in the world someday, mark my words." He finished his cola and handed the empty glass to a passing waiter. He grabbed four fresh glasses of champagne and handed them out. "I think we're getting close to the appointed time. I need to find my wife before she bawls me out for talking business at a party. Nice to meet you Dan, Julia. See you around, Jeff."

"Sorry to leave you both," Jeff said, watching Matt merge with the crowd, "but I need to find my date or I won't have one tomorrow." He flashed a smile and leaned in to kiss Julia on the cheek. He shook Dan's hand and disappeared.

"I like him," Dan said. "Even that South African bloke seemed okay. Full of life and… what's wrong?"

"Nothing. Maybe it was something I ate. I'm not feeling particularly well."

"Okay, we'll go. But let's wait until after midnight."

∞

"Who do you think is going to win? Gore or Bush?" Julia wanted to talk about something other than the research strewn on the table in front of her. "My eyes are going square and I need a break." The phone was on hands free, but she picked up the handset and leaned back on her chair, feeling the tension of the cord as it stretched to its maximum length.

"What, tired of drilling into the numbers?" The voice on the other end was strong and confident, teasing her when she drifted off her assignment.

"Sorry Jeff, I just need to take a break and talk rather than analyse. When I got into this, I was expecting a different sort of life. This world you live in is all about risk analysis and nothing to do with gambling. I'm not sure I'm cut out for this."

"You are or I wouldn't be spending my time with you. We all need a little encouragement once in a while. I hit the same wall but you'll find that it falls away and everything becomes easier."

"Yeah, but you did that when you were eighteen in your spare time while getting your MBA from Harvard."

There was a pause on the other end of the line. "Maybe you just need a change of scenery. Grab your husband and fly over, my treat. Come and see how we do it on this side of the pond. Maybe that'll give some perspective to your frustration."

Julia smiled at the thought. "I'd like that, thanks. I'll ask Dan. But you haven't answered my question. Who do you think'll win?"

"Gore, hands down. Bush looks good on paper but I don't think he'll get over the line."

"Who is better for the firm?"

"Bush, hands down."

"Funny," she said. "How much of a difference will it make?"

"Hard to say," he said slowly. "I've met them both. Gore is smarter, no question about that, but Bush is a team player. He'll help us more. In the end, we'll make money or not based on our analysis."

"Like what I'm doing?"

"You'll see. There are different levels to it. You are doing the grunt work right now but each level requires the same diligence. It is like a chain; if any link is weak, it breaks. All of our business is based on the work you and other analysts do."

Julia was silent for a moment. "Then why aren't we paid more?"

There was a small laugh on the other end of the phone. "Because there are so many of you smart young things. If you want to join the top ranks, you need to find a way to distinguish yourself from the crowd."

"And you'll help me do that?"

"I'll try, but I'm not about to jeopardise my job just yet." There was mirth in his voice. He enjoyed talking to her.

"I'm not looking to take over the world, just to leave my mark on it."

"Then you need to find your own deal and make money for your bosses. You need to get out of the world of analysis and into the world of decision making. This only happens when you make money for your superiors."

"I'm still in school."

"You're finished next year. I've been meaning to talk to you about this at some point, hoping to do it in person. I'd like you to work with our firm when you're done. No promises, but you've got what it takes."

She felt a warmth fill her torso and spread to her arms and legs. "Jeff, I'd like that very much."

"Let's start with a short visit when you can in the next few months and then see how things develop."

"Thank you."

"My pleasure. Now get back to work!" She could feel the smile in the words before the phone went dead.

That evening, she broached the subject to Daniel. "We can go for a week. If we include the weekends, it makes it long enough to be both a holiday and a work trip." She took a bite of her prawn toast, eying the shredded duck.

"I'm okay with it. I've never been to New York and all's quiet on the rental front. I'm just so pleased we were in property rather than stocks. You'll know better, but it looks like the party is over on the internet stocks."

She took a deep breath and exhaled. "I know. Depressing. I thought we'd find some bullshit dot-com business and make our millions. We missed it by an inch."

"That's why I always say you need to look at cash flow."

Julia had heard this too many times and was getting annoyed by it. "Cash flow is important to pay the bills, yes. But it doesn't make you rich. Every cash flow has been arbitraged to the point where huge wealth cannot be achieved through that path."

"Maybe," he said, "but look at Buffett. Every business he buys is based on cash flow and old fashioned common sense."

"Buffett doesn't get tech stocks. He's more interested in Coca Cola or carpet manufacturers," she said. "That's fine if you have the mind of a computer and endless sums of money to invest. I need to find a way to create wealth."

Daniel kissed her, lips greasy from their Chinese takeaway. "You'll find it."

New York City

They landed at JFK airport shortly after George W. Bush was voted in as president. It was busy like Heathrow, but different in a way they couldn't put their fingers on. The taxi ride to the World Trade Center was uneventful.

"Which floor?" Daniel's hand was poised by the elevator.

"One hundred six or seven, one of the two. We're having lunch at Windows on the World."

"I'm starting to like it here," he said as the elevator began its ascent.

"If they're trying to impress, it's working. One of the things I dreamed about growing up was having lunch at the top of the World Trade Center and meeting with the world's rich and famous."

Daniel reached for Julia's hand. She squeezed his and smiled.

They exited at the hundred and seventh floor and looked in awe at the view. The sense of perspective was overwhelming and they stood silently taking it in until a waiter approached them.

"Can I help you?"

"Yes, we have an appointment."

"Name?"

"Stone."

"Ah, yes, Mr. Money is already here." He said the name without a flicker of a smile.

I love that name, Daniel thought. He squeezed Julia's hand as they walked towards the round table with three chairs set next to the window. Its white table cloth gleamed in the morning sun.

"Glad you could make it." Jeff shook Daniel's hand and then gently touched Julia's waist as he leaned in to kiss her on each cheek. "Nice view, huh?"

"Unbelievable. I could sit here all day."

"I know. Our offices aren't far below this so your desk will enjoy a similar view."

Julia looked at Daniel. "I like that—but I thought I would work from London."

"You can, but the real money is here."

"I thought you work a lot from your Hampton home," Daniel asked.

"I do, but our staff are here, London, and Hong Kong. We are thinking about opening an office in Singapore but that's further down the line."

"And what about living arrangements?"

"We'd give you an allowance. You can either rent or buy as you wish. I understand you're a property man, Dan. New York is a great place to play monopoly." He waved to the waiter. "I assume we're eating here and not just having coffee? The food is almost as good as the view."

"I was thinking that this trip was going to be a holiday," Daniel said. "Now, it has become fun. I'll start looking for a new home after lunch."

Afterwards, Julia could barely contain herself. She could not wait until they reached the ground floor. "Are you sure you are okay with this? It's a big move." She was looking at him with her big eyes.

"Of course. That's the reason I do what I do. I want the property to work for me, not me for it. If we can't leave to pursue our dreams, then I've failed."

She wrapped her arms around him, holding him close. "Thank you." Daniel stroked her hair.

"I think it'll be a good opportunity for us to build a US portfolio. I've always wanted to have income streams in two currencies."

"You'll be a star," she said, slowly allowing her body to separate from his. "This is a big move. I can't believe it's happening."

"Why? You're top of your class, dedicated to your subject, and married to the best person in the world. I'm just surprised it didn't happen sooner." He was smirking and took a friendly punch to his shoulder. *Everything'll be fine*, he thought.

∞

Her final year went like lightning and she was back in New York by September 2001. They had found a brownstone within walking distance of work but she still used a taxi. Despite the air travel, expense of moving, and the stress of final exams, the greatest trauma was the cutting of her hair. *I've got to look the part*, she thought.

On Tuesday morning, Julia woke early. *Damn jet lag*, she thought. *It's been over a week already. What am I going to do at five a.m.?* She decided to get up and get dressed. She wore an Armani pantsuit, black with high heels to reassert her femininity. It was a difficult balance; men had a uniform, women had a wardrobe. *I'll get the hang of this eventually.*

Her taxi delivered her to the front of the World Trade Center's north tower. Jeff's office was on the seventy-second floor. "Not the best location," he admitted at the time, "but not bad." She went to her desk and grabbed a coffee. Half the staff were already there; they usually got in by six to ensure their bosses were armed with the latest analysis of how their portfolios were performing. Recommendations such as 'buy', 'sell', or 'hold' were stamped in bold red across the top of the report just in case their superiors didn't care to read the reasoning inside.

The office noise receded as Julia focussed on her computer screen. It was a skill she had since a child. She was able to focus on the tasks at hand, allowing her to complete them in much less time and with fewer errors. When in the zone, she didn't feel stress, anxiety, or fear. Numbers were even less fearsome than the literature of her undergrad. Mathematics didn't allow for many interpretations, and she liked having answers to problems. It was why she felt refreshed at the end of her work day when her colleagues looked drained. It was this talent that Jefferson Money saw when he agreed to mentor her, and the reason she was sitting in his offices.

As she reached for her cup, the room moved, and her coffee slid off her desk. It wasn't just hers. All of the computers, books, and snacks slid off desks. Everyone swore or sounded surprised.

She heard a deafening sound above her, like fifty books being slammed shut next to her ears at the same time. It rumbled and crossed from her left to her right. She looked at the ceiling as the lights went out. She looked outside and saw what looked like flames, then smoke, then papers and other debris falling past her window.

"It's a bomb!" Cheryl from accounts screamed. "It's just like before in '93."

"Everyone stay calm." A red haired man in red suspenders tried to take control of the room. He was head of bonds, Julia knew, and people turned to him. "I don't know what the fuck has happened but I don't like it. We're going to stay put until we hear something further. I don't want us to stop someone else getting help by clogging up the exits."

There were murmurs as most agreed with him. The rest agreed because they didn't like the idea of walking down seventy-two flights of stairs. Julia noticed that everyone had a phone to their ear when hers rang too. She looked at it in disbelief, her body numb from sensory overload. She reached into her bag.

"Hello?"

"Jules. Dan. You're okay, thank god!"

The moment became real at that point and she felt the tears begin. "I'm okay but there's something wrong. The building moved and the power is off. I think there was a bomb higher up in the building."

She heard silence before he spoke. "Just get out of there."

"They said to stay still. They don't want us to block the exits."

"Fuck what they say. Get out of there. Get forgiveness later. Promise me."

"I'm scared." She didn't want to say it but the smoke outside was blocking her windows. It was close.

"I love you Jules. Get out. Now."

"I love you too. I'll call when I'm safe."

She saw a dog race past her, aggravated, trying to get his master to walk down. It was the Seeing Eye dog for one of the senior analysts. *How does a blind guy do this shit? I guess he must be really good to be running with the big dogs*, she thought. Then she laughed at the stupid expression. She took her phone and some money and was wishing she wore more sensible shoes. She decided to start walking.

"You going?" Corinne was watching her, trying to decide which way to go.

"Yep. I'll take my chances."

"I'm going with you." They went to the fire escape stairs. "I never thought I'd ever go through this door," Corinne said.

"Me either."

The emergency lights had kicked in and all those who decided to leave began to trickle towards the stairs. As they entered the stairwell, Julia looked up and thought she could see movement. *Impossible*, she thought. *It's concrete and steel. This building isn't going anywhere.*

Her heel made a click against the steel and concrete parts of the stairs. She put her arm on the rail and foot on the next stair. "How long do you think before we hit the bottom?"

"I don't know. Forever?"

"I'm taking off my shoes." She tied them and slung them over her shoulder, walking barefoot. Corrine did the same. She noticed the dog and his master behind them, the man gripping the harness and finding the edge of the steps. *Good boy*, she thought.

They walked in silence, as if in a cheap amusement ride where you walked into a dark room and strangers shook the walls and made mechanical noises to scare you. No one joked, no one pushed. Just one step in front of the other.

Julia looked down at her watch and saw the big hand point just past the twelve. She knew it was a little slow. At that moment, she heard doors to stairwells open and people screaming that a plane hit the south tower. Their pace increased but then slowed as more people joined the long downward march. She looked at the large number fifty-two on the back of the stairwell door.

Then everyone stopped. It was 9:16 according to her watch.

"What's going on?"

"I don't know. I think it's the firemen. They're coming up."

"We're blocking the exit." *Are we causing all those people to die because we're too cowardly to stay put?* she thought. "Everyone push to the side," she said. Give them room."

"They aren't here yet. It'll take them some time."

"Then why aren't we moving?" At that moment, whatever blockage was ahead of them must have cleared, and the line started up again. *One step, slowly, OK, another. You'll be* OK. *One step at a time.* All she could think about was Daniel and being in his arms. She could feel the nose of the guide dog touch her leg on occasion. She found it reassuring.

People wore blank looks on their faces. Captains of football teams, heads of chess teams, and the best and brightest in the country all had to walk one step at a time. There was no way to rush, no way to cut the line. They just passed the fortieth floor and it was taking a long time.

"Make a hole." The voice was firm, exhausted, and determined. Julia heard them before seeing them. Their black helmets with yellow reflective strips bobbed ever upwards, their oxygen strapped to their backs. All of the office workers pushed themselves tight to the wall and allowed the men to use the rail.

Time slowed further and the air began to be less breathable. Or maybe that was her perception. She was part of an endless centipede of people, required to put one foot in front of the other. *This shouldn't have taken more than twenty minutes*, she thought. *But I'm still here*. She looked and saw nineteen on the back of the next door. *I'm close.*

There were more firemen going up now, causing the pace to slow. Her feet were stepped on numerous times. She barely made a sound. All she needed to do was survive.

When she reached the last landing and saw the open doors to the outside air, she almost wept. *Just keep moving*, a voice inside her said. When she was finally in the street, her shoes back on, she looked up and became still again. Flames and black smoke billowed from both buildings. She stood like that for a long moment until she felt a kindly hand touch her shoulder.

"Please ma'am. You need to keep moving. Follow the others." It was a police officer with a kind face. She would never forget it. He had freckles on his cheeks and looked used to smiling. She wondered if he would ever truly smile again.

She flipped open her phone and called Daniel. *I need to talk to you, sweetheart, more than ever,* she thought. *Busy?* She tried again. *No service? What the hell?* She decided to follow the crowd away from the burning inferno, but first she needed to sit down and rest her feet. They were killing her. She saw the guide dog pass her as well as Corinne and the rest of the people from her floor. She nodded absentmindedly and others did the same. They looked like zombies, with eyes glazed and shuffling feet. It reminded her of when she attacked an anthill as a child and most ants streamed out in every direction while some stayed to protect their home. She watched as the emergency services men and women streamed towards the inferno and couldn't help but make the connection. They would sacrifice themselves if need be, like those ants.

But they aren't ants, and I need to get out of here, she thought. She forced herself to stand on her feet and began to walk again. *How long has it been? Half an hour? An hour? Those stairs took forever. And my feet.*

I need to sit for a second. I think I see blood. She felt the warm liquid rather than seeing it and found a post to lean against. There wasn't a bench or edge to sit on. She felt her body go weak as it relaxed, knowing it was safe. She looked at both burning towers, surreal in the smoke. *It's like a terrible movie.* People were walking as fast as they could past her.

"Ma'am, it's not safe here. You need to keep moving. Just follow the people." Another police officer called to her and pointed. She nodded numbly, watching how people simply obeyed. There weren't arguments and any disputes that may have existed earlier ceased to matter. Someone, somewhere, wanted to hurt them and they were succeeding.

She pushed against the post and started walking again. She could see papers floating down around her and continued walking as though it was as normal as rain. When the rumbling began, she knew she was in trouble.

Chapter Nine

The Others

"Goddamn it to hell. Can't you drive this any faster?" Jefferson Money banged on the barrier separating him from the driver.

"If you hit that again, I'm going to throw you out."

"I'm sorry. I just need to get to this meeting. It's a matter of life and death."

"I'm going as fast as possible."

"Holy shit. Did you just see that?"

"What?"

"Something hit the north tower."

The driver continued talking but Jeff didn't hear anything. He called his office but couldn't get through to Steven, the broker who could have handled the order. Instead, he called London and placed aggressive positions across a dozen named stocks. When he finished the call, it was almost nine o'clock. *This is amazing luck*, he thought. *How many people get to see something in real time and are able to capitalise on it?* He began dialling another number and had just gone through the pleasantries when the next plane struck. He knew everyone across the world would be watching this soon and his window was closing fast. He gave instructions and put his phone in his pocket. He couldn't do any more. *A once in a lifetime opportunity.*

"I can't get any closer, sir. Everything's closed. Is there anywhere else I can take you?"

"That's fine. I'll get out here." He doubled the fare as a tip and started walking towards his office. There was only one way in or out from where his taxi dropped him. *Those buildings have withstood bombs before. They'll withstand this. I just need to get everything back online before we lose our advantage.* His walk was determined, like a Titan bestriding the world. He hoped to make a killing today and needed to reassure his troops.

He walked for over thirty minutes before he saw the sea of people coming towards him. His last conversation replayed in his mind as he realised the plane that hit the north tower could have wiped out his company. *Is that why they're not answering?* He couldn't walk any faster and running was not an option with all the people coming the other direction. When he looked up, all he could see was flames and black smoke, smouldering like badly lit cigars. Soon, he was too close to see anything but the surrounding buildings and the people coming relentlessly towards him. He thought he could see Brian, the kid from the copy room, but the face disappeared into the sea of others before he could be sure.

The next moment he felt the earth move.

In front of him, straight out of a bad horror movie, the south tower began to fall. He stopped walking and just stared. It was beautiful and horrific in equal measures. He marvelled at the vertical disintegration of hundreds of millions of dollars and the culmination of human knowledge on construction. *It is as if God is pushing down the building with his finger*, he thought. *As simple as me stepping on an aluminium can.*

A cloud of dust was spreading, slowly at first, but relentlessly outwards. It masked the south tower's position and observers seemed uncertain if it was there or not. Jeff knew it was down and he was watching its constituent parts rain on its surroundings with the fury of an ancient god.

He dropped his eyes from the heavens and looked around him. The cloud would reach them all. It was approaching faster than they could run. He was rooted to the spot, full of guilt at his first instinct. Full of self-loathing at his glee as he dialled that number in London and then Zurich. His head continued to drop until he looked at his shoes and the pavement beneath him.

"Jeff!"

He didn't look up. The drive that made him Mr. Money suddenly abandoned him and he resigned himself to be submitted to the gods' will.

"Jeff!" The voice was near. It was familiar, not the rumbling that would haunt him all his remaining days, or the cries of strangers. He raised his head slightly as arms grabbed him. "We need to move now!"

"Wha--?"

"We need to walk. There, turn around. Good. Now walk. Forget about everything and just walk."

He found himself putting one foot in front of the other, following the crowd of people he had just watched pass him. "Julia? What are you doing here?"

"Getting out. I don't think we should be talking." She looked over her shoulder, the cloud looming like the monster in a child's dream.

He turned as though he was about to speak but then swivelled and continued walking. She took his hand and held tight. Her head was tilted forward, as though walking against a strong headwind, and she was almost pulling him. *Speed up*, he thought. *You're embarrassing yourself. Pull yourself together.* He increased his pace and noticed she was doing it in high heels. *That must hurt like hell.*

Some part of his brain caused him to take off his shirt and rip it in two. He gave her one half. He discarded his jacket.

"Hold your breath," she yelled as she looked over her shoulder. She crouched next to a car, putting the car between them and the approaching cloud. Just before it enveloped them, she scanned the area for any shop or building to find shelter. "Unless we break the windows, we're stuck here," she yelled.

And then it came. And came. Julia held Jeff's hand tighter than she had anticipated. They put their heads just below the bumper of the car, hoping to salvage an additional breath. They breathed through his shirt when the cloud covered them. The sounds of sizzling pieces of something were all around, the dust itself super fine like talcum powder.

Their eyes were closed for the first thirty seconds, thankful to have someone to share the moment with. Neither talked as the ash that followed lay on them like a grey dusting of fresh snow.

Jeff regained his senses and stood up after the initial scare had passed. His bare chest was grey, as was his head, face, and the rest of his body. Julia was the same, barely a distinguishing mark between where her clothes started and skin began. They were two sentient forms in grey, now walking again.

With each step, they returned to the land of the living. Emergency response teams and shop owners brought water and even masks out to cleanse their faces and replace the shredded shirt they held to their mouths. Soon even those sights passed and they continued walking over the Brooklyn Bridge and back to a world now traumatized.

"My place isn't far from here."

"Thanks, but I think I should go home."

"Is there anyone there waiting for you?" her voice was concerned.

He hesitated. "No, but I should call my parents. They'll be worried."

"You can call them from my place."

Jeff struggled with something inside and then nodded. "Nice area."

"We committed to the job. We bought a brownstone. Daniel's very excited." Their conversation seemed forced, clipped, and unnatural after living through the last hour together.

"You can't go wrong with New York property."

"Unless someone decides to attack your city." Her head was shaking, trying to make light of the situation. "I don't even care. All I want is to shower this shit off me and change into something comfortable."

When they arrived, she pulled out her key, thanking herself for wearing something with a pocket, and opened the door. "Welcome, JW."

"What'd you call me?"

Julia pretended not to hear him and started walking inside, kicking off her bloodied shoes and heading to her bedroom. "There's a shower in the spare bedroom. Help yourself. It's just over there. I need to clean up and I'll meet you in the kitchen after. I need a hell of a big glass of wine.

"I'd like that." He was removing his shoes. JW. *I like that too.* "Julia? You wouldn't have a spare shirt, would you?"

There was no response and he could see the powdered remains on the floor in front of him, her shoes kicked towards the wall. The grey dust fell sporadically but with enough substance up the stairs to create a trail for him to follow. He removed his shoes. His bare chest was covered in burns from the embers. When he reached the top, he could see a bathroom with its door open to his right. *That must be mine*, he thought. To his left, he saw what must have been the master bedroom. The door was slightly ajar.

The exhaustion he felt was complete. He had experienced more adrenaline, fear, and shock than he had his entire life. Still on the landing, he felt his breathing become shallow. His back hunched and he began to take off his remaining clothes. His wallet weighed unevenly as his pants fell to the ground, the belt making a little rattle. There were no coins to fall to the hard wood floor. He remained standing in the same spot, wearing only his socks and underwear, white but stained from the same hellish dust that rained down on him from his office. He took off his socks and felt the cool oak floor beneath his soles. He looked once more at the slightly ajar door, pivoted, and walked right towards the spare bath.

He closed the door and locked it, turning on the water in the shower to get it going. He watched himself in the mirror as the shower's heat fogged the glass and his eyes stared at nothing more than condensation. He found a towel and put it on the floor and then stepped into the shower. It felt like being reborn, his scales from the outside world washed away. He washed his hair twice and then scrubbed his face, ears, and body like he just woke up in a coffin. The eerie grey-white substance settled around his feet. He began to cry.

∞

Julia was surprised to see the dirty clothes at the top of the stairs. *I'm not going to judge*, she thought. *I'll kick it over there and he can deal with it later. Right now, I'm going to have a glass of wine and see if I can get Dan on the phone.* She began walking down the stairs and paused, realising that her boss was naked in the shower on the other side of the wall. *Who would've thought?* She laughed and continued towards the kitchen.

The fridge had champagne but that seemed disrespectful. She pulled out a bottle of prosecco and two glasses. She poured herself a glass and drank it, then poured another one and turned on the television. The images caused her to feel nauseated and she turned it off. *I won't be missing anything*, she thought. *We'll be forced to relive this horror forever.*

She opened the fridge again and looked for something to eat or at least put on the table but found only pears and leftover pizza. She pulled them out and did her best to make it look presentable on the table. The shower was still going upstairs, so she decided to call Dan.

"Dan?"

"Jules," the relief was palpable and there was a delay before he continued. "I was so worried. Your mobile wasn't working and the images were horrific. I'm so glad you called. I love you."

"I love you too. It's been intense and crazy and scary but I'm okay. I'm back home."

"I wish I was there, sweetheart."

"Me too."

"People are talking war. Markets are tanking and I can't get to you." He laughed. "That was in the wrong order. I am so stressed because I can't hold you right now. I want to hold you next to me and tell you how much I love you."

"Me too, baby. It's great to hear your voice. I just need to unwind and I'll call you later, okay?"

"Okay, darling. I'm here waiting for you. Love you."

"Love you." As she hung up, she realised she forgot to tell him about Jeff.

She had finished her second glass and decided to put on some coffee. *Dangerous to get drunk before your boss even shows up*, she thought.

"That smells good." Jeff walked in looking like he didn't have a care in the world. "I borrowed what looked like Dan's clothes. I hope it's okay." He wore jeans and a t-shirt. The jeans were fine but the t-shirt was tight and showed off his six-pack and pecs. He was bare footed.

"Coffee or prosecco? For food, I've only got some leftovers or some fruit."

Jeff walked like a panther, heel to toe, every muscle working. Julia was leaning next to the counter as he approached and reached behind her for the prosecco. "I think I'll start with something refreshing before I hit the java." She wasn't sure whether it was the heat from the shower or his natural smell but it began to make Julia dizzy.

"If you need to call anyone, the landline is working. I know my cell wasn't working earlier."

"Thanks." His voice was deep and relaxed. She became self-conscious in her robe and covered her legs.

"Do you want anything?"

He hesitated before answering and then turned to face her. He put his hand to her face in the most gentle of gestures. "It's been quite the day."

Julia felt herself gravitate towards him. The next thing she realised, she was within inches of his body. It glowed with a heat that her heightened senses wanted more than air. She became conscious of her mouth and lips and her hands rested on his waist, fingers hooked into his jeans. *Dan's jeans*, she corrected herself. She barely heard herself say, "Yeah."

He leaned in and kissed her on the lips and then pulled back to look at her, waiting to see what she would do. She was breathing, weaving in the sensory overload, and then leaned towards him and kissed him back. It was soft at first, becoming more desperate as their bodies yearned for an outlet from the day's events.

He put his hand in her wet hair and then onto her robe. Her hands felt for his shirt, forcing her to glance down and realise what she was doing. *Stop*, she thought. He kissed her. *Stop*. She kissed him. "Stop," she finally said aloud.

He pulled back and lowered his hands. "I'm sorry."

"No, I'm sorry. I just can't do this. I'm married, JW."

JW *again*, he thought. *I could get used to hearing that, especially with her accent.* "No, it's my fault. There was no excuse. I just got caught up in the moment. I think I should leave."

"No," she said, grabbing his hand. "Stay. It's batshit crazy out there. Let's see if there's some takeaway we can order and watch some shitty movies. Unless you want to play catatonic out there." She nodded towards the outside world.

"You know that we'll probably be at war by the end of today," he said, confused by her attitude.

"And this is going to change today how?"

He smiled and nodded as he finished his drink. "Do you have anything stronger than this chick drink?"

"Dan's scotch is over there, by the pasta." She pointed to the cupboard highest up on the wall.

"That's more like it. Do you mind?"

"I have survived two falling skyscrapers and some very enticing divorce bait. I can handle you drinking some of Dan's booze."

"Julia, I think we're going to be good friends."

"Jules. All my friends call me Jules."

"Call me JW. Wait, you already do."

"Sorry about that."

"I'm kidding. I love it. No one calls me that, but from today on, I'll be known as JW."

"To a new life."

"A new life."

Chapter Ten

JW

"Our next candidate is a young African-American man from Colorado, case file 3255A." Paula Jacobs opened the brown folder to see a picture of the applicant clipped to the top right corner. The folder was thicker than the others and was full of news clippings, testimonials, and even a letter from his state's governor.

"Don't we already have our quota of Negros?"

"Yes, but this young man may be worth a second look." She ignored the out-dated term and began scanning the pages in the folder.

"Why? Is he some exceptional athlete? Our athletics department is a joke."

"No, he's a serious student. In fact, he's a little younger than most of the applicants."

"A black wunderkind? Let me see that file." Eric Smith's gout was playing up and his irritability increased proportionately. "Can you hand me that ashtray at the same time? Thanks."

"He interned with Bell Labs while still in High School. There's a letter of recommendation from Ian Ross."

"*The* Ian Ross?" Eric forgot his gout and sat up straighter, the mere thought of such a powerful man forced him to be on his best behaviour.

"The one and only."

"Maybe this young man is Cornell material after all."

You're such a stuck up asshole, she thought. *At first glance, he's a nigger who graduates to being a Negro, and then a black man. Your highest compliment is to call him what he is: a young man. I wish you'd hear yourself.* Out loud she said, "Yes sir. I have been reviewing his file and he is one of the best applicants."

"Not bad. He can stay in Ujamma with the rest of them. Is he fee paying or scholarship?"

"Both. His parents enrolled him and were about to pay but Bell Labs put up a scholarship for him."

"I'm beginning to like this young gentleman. Make sure you manage to get him to see me when he's settled in." He lit another cigarette and closed the file. Paula picked it up and placed it on the pile marked 'accepted'.

Jefferson Washington Money was sixteen years old when he first walked on campus, born in 1965 to Bill and Vera Money of Denver, Colorado. Both of his parents had PhDs, his mother's in literature and his father's in chemistry. He knew he was different but that was as much to do with his brain as the colour of his skin. He was mediocre in sports, primarily because his parents never allowed him to have a spare moment to himself.

"You will continue practicing your lessons until you get it right," his mother said.

"But I don't like the piano."

"You will play the piano whether you like it or not." Vera Money stood erect and proud, rarely lowering her head and never lowering her standards. "We are not like other people, Jefferson. You will learn that one day. We are better." She turned on the metronome and pointed to the sheet music.

While music and sports did not come easily to young Jefferson, everything else did. He was reading by the age of two and writing fluently by five. His father challenged him to read the entire Encyclopaedia Britannica, testing him on occasion to ensure he didn't cheat. Not only did he read, he remembered everything. When his parents realised the gifts bestowed on their eldest, they redoubled their efforts to give him the tools he would need in life.

"You will spend as much time as required with Aunt Vivian until you learn to dance."

"But I don't like dancing."

"You will learn to dance whether you like it or not." The refrain was identical and resistance was futile. Jefferson learned what was needed to be the gentleman his parents envisioned.

High school was too easy for him and he challenged the tests to advance faster. His interest in engineering and chemistry caused him to contact Bell Labs directly. His parents were unaware of his interest and only realised it when they saw the long distance calls on their phone bills. The director humoured him and allowed him to visit, thinking the child would get tired and leave. Instead, he found himself offering the child a position as an intern during his summer holidays.

The wonderment and smiles that attended Jefferson was normal for him and he expected the same at his new university at Cornell.

"Hey kid."

Jefferson turned around to a sea of white faces. He had taken a seat where he usually did, up front and centre.

"What are you doing here? This isn't high school."

"I'm not in high school. I'm a student here." It was obvious and he didn't understand why they asked the question.

"Just don't start crying like a baby on us."

Jefferson stood up. He was almost full height, despite his age. "I'm not a baby." He hadn't felt this emotion before back home in Denver. His blood was pumping and his body tensed.

"Relax brother, we're just jiving with you." There were more laughs as the bully gave his neighbour a high five and lost interest in Jefferson.

"Don't worry about him. He's a jerk."

Jefferson couldn't see who was talking as he was still glaring at the person three rows back. The lecturing room was stepped to allow for all students to see and hear the professor. He turned to see a woman arranging her things next to his seat. "Sorry about that. I'm not usually like this."

"I can imagine. Kyle does that to people. He comes across as a jerk but he's okay once you get to know him. By the way, I'm Irene." She put her hand out.

"Jefferson. Nice to meet you." He liked the gentleness of her hands and the soft perfume she wore. It was summer and she wore shorts, her one leg bouncing on the other when crossed. He tried to tear his eyes away but couldn't.

"You seem younger than the other students. How's that?"

He snapped his eyes to hers. "I dunno. Studying comes easy for me, I guess." He found himself becoming shy, not sure how to answer even the most simple questions.

"Maybe you can help me study sometimes." She smiled and he melted.

"Yeah, that sounds good. Let me know."

The professor arrived and the class began. *I'm going to like being a university student*, he thought.

Only a week later, she kissed him gently under the harsh campus lights. "I need to go back. See you in class tomorrow?"

He was shaking from adrenaline and nodded. He smiled and waved as she turned the corner. *I'm definitely liking being a university student.* He swivelled on his toes, did a little tap dance routine his Aunt forced into him, and began walking back to his dorm.

By the time he saw the movement out of the corner of his eye, something hit the side of his head. An explosion of lights erupted behind his eyes and the ground rushed towards him. His hand stopped him from receiving more damage from the earth but wasn't able to stop the boots that rained on him from heaven. He curled himself into a ball as the beating was fast and then stopped. They ran away without saying a word and he lay where they left him.

When he went to class the next morning, he sat in the back of the class. Irene saw and ran up the stairs, hand in front of her mouth.

"It looks worse than it is."

"It looks pretty bad," she said. She touched the side of his swollen eye with her fingertips.

"I got jumped shortly after you left last night."

Her face darkened and she turned to scan the heads in front of her. No one looked back. She didn't say a word and put her hands in his, then kissed the swelling ugliness next to his eye.

"I want to join the gym," he said, face set. The pain had gone when she kissed him but he didn't want this to happen again.

She squeezed his hand when the professor came in. "Let's talk later."

Jefferson began to eat more meat and spend time in the gym. His studies were just as easy as high school and his grades didn't suffer. He put on twenty pounds of muscle, cut his hair the way jocks did, and dressed like an athlete instead of a geek.

"Looks like my boy is all grown up." Kyle's voice cut across the green as Jefferson was walking one day.

"You talking to me, boy?" Jefferson said it with his jaw out. He stopped and let Kyle walk up to him. He didn't break his stare.

"Take that back."

"What? Boy?"

"Yeah."

"Who's going to make me, boy?" Jefferson dropped the books he was carrying and began to ready himself.

"Me."

"And who's army?"

As he readied himself for a punch from Kyle, Jefferson felt a side tackle that sent him flying to the ground. Again. The perpetrator was one of Kyle's friends, six foot tall, two hundred pounds.

"Pretty funny stuff for a coward. Let me stand up and we'll see what you've got."

"Lenny, leave him alone. Let's see what the nigger's got."

He had never heard that word ascribed to him before. It felt odd, like a throwback to the days of Martin

Luther King Junior and the marches of the sixties. He took a deep breath and stood up. He had just turned sixteen and was almost six foot two inches. His muscles made him weigh over two hundred pounds and he felt ready for Kyle.

"Are you waiting for a bell or can I whoop your black ass back to the cotton fields?"

Jeff swung, his arm longer than Kyle's, and missed. In return, he felt a foot in his gut, just below the sternum. He collapsed onto his knees. He looked up just in time to feel Kyle's fist smash into the same side of his head as the time three months earlier. When he came to, he saw the others disappearing and felt the snow against his face. *Merry Christmas*, he thought, and then started to laugh. *I just hope this heals before I go home. I can't have my parents see this.*

Luckily, his brain was mightier than his brawn and he was plucked from his undergraduate courses after the first term.

"Your aptitude for mathematics and analysis is being wasted in those first year courses," Dean Eric Smith said across his desk. "I want Cornell to challenge you, make you the best person you can be."

"Yes, sir. I want that as well, but..." his voice trailed off.

"But what?"

"Nothing, sir. I just want to do well, that's all."

"Good. I have talked to Professors Teunissen and Gold and they have agreed to put together a special programme of studies for you. You will take their advanced applied math courses and see how that suits you."

"Thank you, sir. I don't want to be any trouble."

"None whatsoever. You are special and we want you to push your brain to see what it can do. All we are here for is to provide you with the tools. It's then up to you to do something with it."

Those words echoed in Jefferson's ears throughout his four years at Cornell and MBA at Harvard. He kept going to the gym, eventually creating the body of an Olympic water polo player. He learned to wear blazers and tailor his clothes to accent his athleticism. He found it made him more attractive to women but, at the same time, more credible to professors and employers. When he interviewed for jobs, Goldman Sachs snapped him up as the archetypal employee—smart, well dressed, and ambitious.

"Money, people like you."

"Thank you, sir."

"But you need to leverage your skills. You've got the looks and the brains, but you need to hone your killer instinct."

"Sir?"

"You need to close the deals."

"I thought I was."

"Which is why we are having this conversation. I want to put you with David in the Hi-tech M&A. That's where the money will be in the next decade or so. If you want to make a mark, that's where to do it. And we need that brain of yours. It's hard to know what is real and what is just some pimply teen's wet dream."

"Thank you, sir. I'll do my best."

"I know you will. And Money?"

"Yes, sir?"

"Don't forget that you are a nice guy. You are the iron fist in the velvet glove. Let them massage the velvet but make sure you get them in your iron grip."

"Yes, sir." He was smiling to himself. The great-great-grandson of slaves was now the hottest commodity of the most powerful firm on Wall Street.

October 19, 1987—Black Monday—came and went and Jefferson survived. He learned his trade and made friends in an industry without sympathy. Within ten years, he had overseen and was part of over one hundred billion dollars of mergers. He was a player and decided to go out on his own.

"Thank you, everyone, for making this a reality. I couldn't have done it without you. Today, I can announce that Global View Equities Ltd. is now fully funded with two billion dollars under management." He waited for the applause to end. "I want to reiterate my commitment to the hi-tech sector by focussing on viable start-ups and ensuring aggressive returns for investors. If we don't achieve at least twenty percent on your money, I'm not doing my job."

The crowd of employees and press raised their champagne glasses to the wunderkind who seemed unable to make a misstep.

"Mr. Money, a word if you can? Freya Dunn from the FT."

"Anything for our friends in the press." He was all confidence, his smile wide and hands spread.

"Your rise to the top of the world of finance has been swift. How do you explain that?"

"Good investments and straight talking to our investors. I don't try to hide from poor decisions and I point out their risks on good ones. They are co-pilots with me."

"I am hearing rumours that your clients have followed you from Goldman's."

"I have been very fortunate to work with the best minds in the world of finance at my old firm. Some of the investors agreed that I was one of those and followed me here. Goldman Sachs was aware of every party who followed."

"And they invested in you as well?"

Jefferson paused. "Where did you hear that?"

"A little bird." The reporter smiled.

"Yes, they believe in me and have seeded GVE with two hundred million dollars of their own money. I didn't want to advertise that but I believe it is the greatest indicator of confidence in my ability as captain of this ship to steer us through the unknown waters ahead."

"One more…"

"I'm sorry, Ms. Dunn, but I need to be in a meeting. We'll continue this another time." He made his way past and through the crowds to an investor who was waiting patiently for him in his private office.

"Mr. Smit, I'm sorry to have kept you waiting."

"Not a problem. Please, call me Matt."

"Okay, Matt."

"I've been enjoying everyone singing your praises. If you are half as good as everyone is saying, we should be good friends." His South African accent sounded out of place in the steel and glass of the seventy-second floor of the World Trade Center's north tower. All of New York lay before them like a battle map in front of Napoleon.

"I understand you were thinking of investing something with us."

"Yes, but I'd like to be part of the management structure."

"Sorry, but we're not looking for that type of money."

"I am happy with the returns you seem to be getting for your investors," Matt said, "but I would rather share the risk of your position. I know you charge a two percent management fee on my money just to turn the lights on. Then you charge me twenty percent of any profits you make me above ten percent. Fair enough. I would like to know if I could convince you to let me join you as an equity partner in your firm."

Jefferson pursed his lips. "I don't know why I would do that. I'm fully staffed, capitalised, and I have two billion to manage. There is no risk."

Matt reconsidered. "Okay. No harm in me asking. I have a hundred million dollars to invest with you. It's all I have so please don't lose it."

"I doubt that, Mr. Smit."

"Matt, please."

"I doubt that, Matt, but I'll do my best to turn that into something even more impressive. Is there any sector in particular you want to go with?"

"I don't know anything about this stuff. I just know that people say you are the best. I'm investing in you, not whatever trinket is paying the bills. I would also like to be considered if you decide to open up shares in management at some point."

"I'll consider it." He extended his hand and they shook. "We'll be in touch."

"Quick question: What about starting up another fund to operate in parallel to your hi-tech operation? I could then invest my hundred million in that. It wouldn't cost you anything to take that type of risk. It could then invest in non-tech companies or mixed, whatever you feel is best. We could ensure there is no conflict in the mandate. That should keep your existing investors happy."

"I like that. Much better than tapping onto this fund. Besides, it may be better to run multiple funds. I think you may have something there. Let me run some numbers. Are you staying in town for a while?"

"I'm here as long as you need me."

"Then let's grab dinner this Thursday and see what we've come up with by then."

"That's a deal."

Anglo-American Trade Limited grew from that simple meeting into a ten billion dollar fund. Matt was a silent partner with forty-nine percent of the management company and fifty-five percent of the revenues as a compromise for lack of control. His investment came from Alicia's family. He knew it was mob money but he was so far in he couldn't change course. The fund invested in boring companies like Staples, Whole Foods, Express Scripts, and Starbucks but also in some conventional hi-tech firms such as Amazon and Cisco. It made the two men paper billionaires and best friends.

That was before the Millennium Eve party at the American Ambassador's residence in London.

Chapter Eleven

A New World

The clean-up of Ground Zero was complete and the lawsuits were just getting going. Memories became ghosts to haunt and inspire. Jefferson looked over the mass of concrete from his new office space before turning away and stepping onto the podium. In front of him were over a hundred pairs of eyes looking back. They stood amidst the raw concrete pillars and floor, clean but bare. There were no walls and people adjusted themselves to have a clear line of sight to the podium. All around them was the city, muted behind the triple glazed glass windows that filled the space from floor to ceiling.

When JW stood in front of them, he wore a sombre face and dark suit but his words were defiant. "We're still here." He paused to let the words ripple through the room. People nodded, also sombre. "We're here because we were lucky enough to be on the seventy-second floor and not higher." There was a sniffle from someone in the crowd. "We lost a lot of friends that day and our country lost something more. We lost our ability to ignore the rest of the world, thinking that we are isolated from the violence and terror." His voice began to rise and he forced himself to lower it. "But I am not speaking about that today. I am here to say that we are back. Back to where we were before that day. Back to a position where the future looks better than the past. Back to a position of making ourselves and America great again."

There was an applause but the memories of that day a year before were still raw. It seemed wrong to feel good amidst all that grief and loss.

"You stand today in what will become our new offices. No more temporary offices. No more guilt about being alive. Today is a new beginning for me, for you, and for the company. I wanted you here today so that you can imprint this moment as the beginning of a new world."

He's laying it on a bit thick, Julia thought. *But he's the boss*. To Leonie next to her, she said, "I wonder when all of this will be a reality. I only see a shell."

"I know, but at least the company is doing well. It shouldn't be more than a couple of months."

"I've heard talk about him bringing the two funds together. I've only been working with GVE. Do you know anything about AAT?"

"Just that it makes a shit load of money. Can't be bad for us."

"I just wish I could be part of that. I'm itching to do something other than analysis and money placement. I want to do some deals."

Leonie turned to Julia. "Then ask him. He's pretty cool with things. Just make sure you can perform." She said it with a tone that Julia couldn't place. Jealous? Condescending?

"I think I will, thanks." She tuned out the negativity and left after the speech.

∞

Back home, Daniel was pacing. "I know you've just had the worst few years imaginable but I think we should be taking a big position in property. It's never been easier to get money. Banks are virtually throwing money at us."

"Do what you think is best. Ask me about IPO values and net present values of credit swaps and I'll give you an answer. Ask me about property and I fall asleep. It just seems so slow."

"Granted, while I'm not dealing with the hundreds of millions that you do. At least it's our money and what we earn we keep. I can get a hundred percent mortgage, even more to cover the transaction costs. All I have to do is sign and buy. I started with almost nothing so this really is a walk in the park for me."

"I believe in you. Whatever you want to do, I'm in." She was thinking about her meeting with Wallace from RABO bank and wasn't listening.

"I want to buy residential and commercial to balance out the risk. I've talked to my financial adviser and he feels we could go on a fifty million dollar spending spree."

Julia stopped thinking and started listening. "How much? That's insane. We barely have a million in equity in our home."

"I know. But there it is. I think things will change but we should grab this opportunity."

"Could we lose the house?"

Daniel paused. "Yes, but the chances are so low it is almost impossible. Property always goes up, especially residential. The risk is on the commercial but I want that to increase our returns."

"I guess if we don't spin the wheel we can't win." As she said it, she jolted as those memories from Sun City washed over her, sending a cool chill through her body. *Why does he still affect me after all this time?*

"You're the best." He kissed her and bounced out of the kitchen towards his study. He needed to call Simon and see what the terms of the facility would be.

I know. She wiped the countertop and remembered that kiss from JW there a year ago. *I should have told Dan but it was nothing. Better to let sleeping dogs lie.*

The next day, she asked JW for a promotion.

"Why now?"

"Because I'm worth it." She stood straight-backed and looked him in the eye. He was six inches taller than her, so her head tilted slightly upwards.

"Perhaps. What do you want to do?" He took a sip of water. His mouth still went dry when he was alone with her in a room, especially with her looking at him like this.

"I'd like to join the acquisitions team at Anglo-American Trade. They have the most money to spend and aren't restricted to hi-tech stocks like GVE. I think I could add value."

"AAT? Where has this come from?"

"Your speech. It's a new world." She smiled but didn't flinch. In the wild and in the office, the one who blinks first loses.

He took another sip and sat down. "Let me think about it. Tom is about to step down. Perhaps you can second his replacement." He leaned back in his chair. "I can get you there but no promises after that. You either sink or swim."

Julia was bubbling inside and almost burst. "You won't regret this, JW. Thank you." She wanted to hug him but was conscious of their physicality since that day. She extended her hand and shook his. His was warm and peaceful. "I've got to get back to my station. Let me know!" She left, the office door closing gently behind her.

I love it when she says JW, he thought. *That accent, those lips*. He shook his head. "And the rest of her," he said aloud.

∞

"So what you're saying is that if I want to borrow ten million dollars, I can't, but if I borrow fifty million, I can." Daniel was sitting in the bank president's office on the thirty-fifth floor along with his head of credit. It was a relatively small bank and they wanted to impress on him that credit and senior management were of one mind. He fiddled with the complimentary pen and tapped the notepad with his other hand. He could see the other bank employees passing through the vertical window next to the door, but otherwise all he could see were the two men, the table, and various framed certificates on the wall.

"It's not as simple as that, but yes," Graham Westfield said. "You don't qualify for a conventional loan, so that is why we can't lend you ten million. But if you issue paper from your company, we would be happy to underwrite it."

"And the minimum issue is fifty million," Daniel added.

"Yes."

"It can be more," the credit man said. "Subject to the lending criteria."

"How is that possible? Don't get me wrong, I love this proposal and I want to build a significant property portfolio, but it sounds too good to be true."

"Not at all. The market is hungry for debt. We help you issue this commercial paper and then sell it into the marketplace. It is bundled with other debt and under-written so the risk to the end user is minimal."

"A win-win," Graham added.

Daniel was trying to absorb this. "So what do I do next?"

"Find your properties and secure them by way of option or something similar. Come back here and let us help you make money. We'll raise the debt for you and the rest is up to you."

"Gentlemen, I am beginning to like New York better than London. This would not be possible there."

"It might be, but you need to go big; their minimum lot size is larger. We may be able to help you over there once we have a track record over here."

Daniel shook both of their hands. "I think we'll be doing a lot of business. I'll be in touch."

When he left the office, he was floating on air. He looked around and could imagine owning every building in his vision. *All I need to do is find someone to sell to me*, he thought.

During the coming weeks and months, he spent every waking moment with agents. Most of the large superstructures were beyond his ability to fund. Things like bridges and infrastructure projects were, first, not for sale and, second, in the hundreds of millions each. He wanted a mixed portfolio of commercial and residential, but he found quality commercial too difficult to source. Residential, however, was much easier—and it always went up in value. What it lacked in rental returns, it made up for in equity increases.

"Ms. Patel, I'm interested in rental returns. I don't know New York and I need some guidance. I'm not afraid of working hard or being in rough neighbourhoods. In the UK, I made my money in the lower end of the market."

"Then you may want to look at Harlem. I know it has a scary name but, from what we can tell, it has the greatest potential."

"Am I going to get gunned down or stabbed in a gang war?"

The agent laughed. "Not at all. That's just Hollywood trying to sell movies. You'd be surprised at how things have improved. There are multi-million dollar apartments and reasonably priced ones too. As with anywhere, there are streets to avoid."

"And that's where you come in?"

"Exactly. Just tell me what you want and I'll do my best to get it for you." She dressed professionally but her skirt was tight and showed off her legs, calf muscles toned in their high heels. She stood close to Daniel as she spoke.

Within four months, he was back at the bank signing the paperwork. He had purchased one hundred sixty apartments, mainly in blocks, with a rental return that comfortably serviced the debt.

The excitement lasted just over a month before the itch was back and he was looking for more properties to buy.

"Who would have thought we'd be where we are today only five years ago?" Daniel said, red wine poised at his lips.

"I only met you five years ago," Julia said with a wink. "Before you, I didn't think I would find anyone I could love."

Daniel never understood that about Julia. *She's so beautiful and smart*, he thought. *Men would line up around the block to spend time with her. And she doesn't think she could find love?* "I'm just glad you came into my life," he said. "I don't need much. You make me want more so I can give you more."

She put her glass down and took his hands. "I don't need any more. Just you. Don't do this just to impress me."

"I'm not. I'm doing it because they're giving me the money." He laughed and she joined him. "It's the craziest thing. I always read about issuing debt and buying up everything you could see, but I never thought it could be a reality. It wouldn't be possible in the UK."

"No, you're right. I'm seeing the same thing at work. I've been put in charge of a new division dealing purely with mortgages on homes. They are calling it sub-primes and making shit into peanut butter by wrapping it with an insurance policy."

"Is it something I can tap into?"

"Not sure. I'm just dealing with packaging the debt and selling it to pension funds and investors around the world, mainly European funds."

"Maybe you'll end up buying the paper that I'm creating."

"Maybe. I think your paper would be considered too good for the tranches I work with. I can have a word with JW and see if we can scratch each other's back."

"I don't want to put you in an awkward position."

"Not at all." She took a long sip of wine. "It's all about money. As long as we are up front and record any possible conflicts of interest, we'll be fine. As long as the firm makes money, no one really cares too much about the details."

"God bless America." They clinked glasses.

∞

"Have you ensured that Deutsche Capital is happy with their purchases? Good. Now, more importantly, it has just been announced that HSBC has bought up Household International. This means sub-prime is here to stay, folks. I want you to get your hands on everything you can. There's a window of opportunity that should last a few years and I don't want Bear Stearns and Household International monopolising this." JW's heads of departments were sitting around their boardroom table, the absentees present via a speaker phone in the middle of the table. He was standing, fingers pressed against the Cherrywood and leather table top. "Any questions?"

"Are we looking to buy and hold?"

"We are in the business of making money. We buy, repackage, and sell. I don't want to be holding anything longer than six weeks. Keep buying, keep selling. We're not trying to make a killing on any one deal. This is about volume, folks."

"What about the more exotic sub-primes?" Julia asked.

"What do you mean?"

"Ones where paper is being written by mortgage companies and the borrowers have no equity in the house, no proven income, and could just as easily be a junkie as a junior executive."

JW laughed. "We'll buy everything provided AIG or one of the other major firms underwrites it. Try to chisel the price the best you can."

"Will do, boss," she said with a mock salute.

"Our objective is to increase our stock of these mortgages to at least twenty billion dollars. It is the best money making arbitrage in the marketplace and currently accounts for seventy percent of our profits, despite us having twelve billion under management."

"I have a contact at a couple of the originators. If you give me the green light, I can be more aggressive in our bidding for their product. I could probably get us fifty billion in paper just from those two sources." Julia had been researching this and was sceptical about the whole process. But she did her job and what was expected of her.

"That's what I like to see." JW slapped the table. "Yes, talk to them and see what we can do. I think we should consider opening up another dedicated fund just for these investments. What are your thoughts?" There was general agreement around the table. *Why do I even have these meetings if all they do is agree with me?* he thought.

When the meeting was over, JW took Julia aside.

"What do you think, Jules? Are we being too aggressive?"

"I think these are shitty products made good with insurance wrappers. It works for now. We need to monitor the situation and make sure we don't get caught with our pants down."

"That sounds conservative. No one else in the market is talking like that."

"The heads of the top five investment banks have said something similar but then continue playing the game because their shareholders would crucify them if they didn't take advantage of this opportunity. I guess we're in the same boat."

Smart girl, JW thought. "Just get us bulked up on those notes and then watch this space like a hawk. No one ever said making shit loads of money was easy." He smiled and patted Julia on the back. "Good luck."

"Thank you, JW."

He watched her leave and imagined her saying good night instead. Since her start two years ago, she had become more confident in her trades and dealings with her predominantly male counterparts. She never allowed herself to be too long in a room with him, or anyone else for that matter. She was professional and hard working. *Most maddening, she seems happy with that husband of hers. How can she settle for a two-bit property dealer?*

∞

Johannesburg, South Africa

Matthijs Smit hung up the phone and smiled. "That was New York. We just got our quarterly payment. Things couldn't be better."

"Any problem with the currency issues?"

"None that I can see."

"You managed to get your winnings out six years ago. I never thought you had it in you."

"At a steep cost. Your guys gouged me fifteen percent."

"But look at what you have now."

"Not just me. Us. We're tied at the hip on this."

"OK, not so loud. But things look good?"

"We own forty-nine percent of a management company that runs a ten billion dollar fund. JW has invested wisely and we have a strong portfolio."

"Maybe we should get out while we're ahead?"

"I wouldn't. JW is too smart to get caught behind the curve. We're investing heavily in the latest fad. Something to do with funding home mortgages. Bush wants to see everyone on the housing ladder and everyone investing in the stock market. As a result, regulators are going light on the lenders and investment firms like AAT are minting it."

"Sounds good. Just remember who your partners are. You don't want to find yourself unable to pay those debts." Maish Cohen's voice went gravelly. Matt's face blanched at the thought of owing Maish one penny he couldn't pay. Maish was second in command in the mob. Alicia's father, while technically the head, deferred to him on most things.

"How can I forget?" Matt smiled and lifted his Coca Cola in a toast.

"Perhaps you would be wise to show your face? Ensure that JW doesn't forget who his partners are."

Matt paused. Maish never ordered anyone to do anything. He would only suggest. Only fools didn't follow his suggestions. "Let me think about it. We have a good thing going and I'm not sure I want to jinx it by changing anything."

Maish took a sip of his morning coffee and smiled. The grass was freshly cut and the lushness of the gardens was lost on him. "We'll see."

∞

New York, January, 2007

"So you finally got that killer bonus you've been working for."

"Yep. I don't know what to do next. JW is a good boss but my options are limited. I can't rise further where I am."

"Maybe start your own firm?"

"I don't have the contacts. It's all about clients and trust. I'm good, I know that, but the clients are loyal to JW."

"Maybe we can do something together. I've managed to cobble together six hundred fifty million dollars' worth of property in less than six years. Our equity position is acceptable and we may soon have enough to take on some of the more prestigious properties."

"I know, Dan, but that's your baby. I'll just get in the way."

"Never. You can run it all if you want. I have been enjoying myself putting it together. Running it is another story. It's hard work and the sooner we corporatize the team, the better."

"What is the average maturation date for your debt?"

"Just under two years, but that's because we keep refinancing. Everything is interest only and the banks can't get enough of it."

"What happens if you can't refinance?"

"It'll never happen. There's a wall of money globally, looking for places to invest. Where better than New York residential property?"

"The stats are good but you never know. I'll think about it. Just look into extending your refinance dates."

Daniel moved the duvet so he could see her face. They were propped up on their pillows, still recovering from the New Year Eve's party. JW gave his bonuses at the last possible moment and it was a shock to see the high seven digit cheque in the envelope. "I'll do that." His hand traced her body and turned her towards him. She smiled and closed her eyes when she kissed him.

∞

Matt landed in JFK and took a taxi to the Mandarin Oriental. He would surprise JW and see if there was anything he could do to assist. The market was red hot and he believed they needed to take more risk to capitalise on the opportunities. The next day, he walked in as though he had been there every day for the last ten years. It was ten in the morning and the office was hectic with activity.

"JW please."

"Do you have an appointment?"

"No."

"Then I think it will be difficult. Mr. Money's schedule is full."

"Just tell him Mr. Smit is here to see him."

"Okay, sir. Please take a seat and I'll let him know."

Matt didn't sit. Rather, he paced the foyer looking down the glass walls with their important-looking executives on telephones in front of three computer screens. The less important grunts would be in cloth-covered cubicles either out of sight or on the floors below. There was a bronze artwork from some unknown artist sitting prominently in the middle of the area between the elevators and the receptionist. Modern art hung on the wall. *May as well have been painted by toddlers*, he thought. There was an air of hushed energy as money was made with every telephone conversation, every click of a keyboard, and every smile of their executives.

"Good morning, Matt. You should've called. I only have a few minutes before I need to get back to my meetings."

"Morning, JW. I wanted to be dramatic. It gets boring sitting on the side-lines and I wanted to see what was going on."

"Follow me to my office. We can talk there." They walked to the end of the hall to a corner office, the glass providing a near panoramic view of neighbouring buildings, parks, and monuments. "A bit different from our last place."

"How's it going? It can't be easy."

"Better than I thought. There's a lot of sympathy for us and the government is determined not to let us sink into a recession. Money is easy. Keeping ahead of the pack is becoming more difficult."

"Can I help?"

JW paused, cautious. "We can always use help, but why now? You've been content being a silent partner and I've been appreciative of the way you've let me run things with a free hand."

"I have been looking at the sub-primes and began thinking that we aren't taking a large enough position. Bear Sterns is dominating this space. Maybe we could up our stake?"

"I understand your rationale, but we are restricted by our capital reserves and must maintain our other positions."

"I was thinking perhaps we could liquidate some of our positions in AAT and double down on sub-primes. It's easy money and allows us to crystallise the profits we have made in our bets on Amazon and Cisco."

"I'm constantly reviewing our value at risk and still believe it is worth sticking with those companies, along with the others. They have skyrocketed since we purchased their stock. Our investors are happy and we have a solid name. Remember, we're young. Give us time."

"I'm not looking to create a legacy," Matt said. "I want to hit this space as hard as we can and take as much as we can. If we play our cards right, we could double or triple our capital position within the next twelve months."

"Yes, possibly. But that would mean leveraging ourselves to the point where, if anything went wrong, we could go bust."

"I'm sure you have enough to live on if that happened."

JW was silent. "I can't be reckless with our investors' money. I have a responsibility."

"Let's not decide right now. Let's meet for dinner and discuss how it would be possible to ratchet up our exposure—and upside."

"Sounds like a plan. I'll see you at eight tonight if that is okay?"

"I'm at the Mandarin. I'll make reservations for a table there."

They shook and Matt left. JW watched him leave, feeling an unease he hadn't felt for some time. He turned his back and returned to his computer and preparation for his next teleconference meeting.

Matt walked slowly down the aisle of glass, taking in the pictures of family members on desks, reams of paper stacked on all surfaces, and how the carpet looked out of place with the rest of the décor. As he turned right, he froze. He smiled when the woman looked up, equally startled. He wiggled his fingers in an awkward wave and then braced himself as he knocked on her door.

"Matt, what a surprise." She kissed him on the cheek, her subtle perfume lingering briefly on his skin.

"The surprise is all mine. I didn't know you were working here."

"Six years in September."

"What do you do?"

"Nothing special. Mainly packaging financial products and selling them on."

"Sounds technical."

"It is."

Matt knew it was awkward but he persevered. "I'm in town for a few days. Are you free for drinks or maybe dinner sometime?"

"I'm married. I don't think it would be a good idea."

"It's just a drink. I'm not asking you to bear my children."

"More children. How's Alicia?"

Matt ran his tongue along his teeth and pursed his lips. "She's fine, thanks."

"Any more children?"

Another moment before he replied. "Two. Boy and girl. You?"

"Not yet. We're focussed on our careers and then, maybe, who knows?"

Matt's eyes slid down and to the left, looking at nothing. His face dropped slightly as he drifted somewhere else. It was only a moment, but it reminded Julia of that flash of sadness immediately after he had won all that money on the roulette table.

"Is everything okay?"

"Yeah. Everything's fine. I just wanted to meet up with JW and check on my investment."

"That's right, I remember. The New Year's Eve party in London. You were with JW then as well. Which fund did you invest in?"

"AAT."

"Funny, I haven't seen your name. I deal with investors all the time."

"I'm not that type of investor. I'm an owner with JW of the actual fund's management."

Julia took a while to digest that. "You're my boss?"

"I guess so, but I've always been a silent partner. Forty-nine percent. JW's your boss."

"Bizarre. I mean, good. I mean, it's good to see you." She became more flustered.

"Are you okay?"

"Yes. I'm late for a call to one of the investors. I need to go. Good seeing you." She closed the glass door as he shuffled out and returned to her computer.

That's weird, he thought. *First* JW *and now Jules.*

When he was gone, she called JW instead.

"I didn't know I had another boss."

"Sorry?"

"Matthijs Smit. Apparently he's your silent partner in AAT. Why didn't you tell us?"

He was silent for a moment. "Because he didn't want anyone to know. Does it make a difference?"

"It shouldn't, but I know him and I don't know if he's the best person to have as a partner."

JW wracked his brain, trying to understand how she knew Matt. He remembered introducing him to her at a New Year's Eve party in London. He made a mental note to find out. "Why's that?"

"He's…" she was going to say 'suicidal' or 'gambler' but chose, "a complicated person."

"I gathered that, but he invested and prompted me to build our second fund and it has been hugely successful."

"And now he's back. He probably wants to push for a bigger gamble, bigger returns?"

He paused again. "Possibly. We're meeting later tonight to discuss."

"You put me in charge of sub-prime and that's the only thing that could boost AAT's profitability. That means expanding my department's offering."

"Possibly."

"I want to be at that dinner to discuss the way forward."

"And if I say no?"

She wanted to say 'I quit' but opted for, "I will not be a happy bunny."

He laughed. "We wouldn't want that. Okay, we're meeting at his hotel tonight at eight. I'll ping you the details."

"Perfect. See you then." She hung up the phone. *Funny how when you're ready to leave, more goes your way*, she thought.

She left early to shower and change for the evening. Just seeing him rattled her. *What is it about him? His stupid blonde hair that can't be combed? His ridiculous walk that is devoid of any guilt or reason? I'm happily married and this guy comes back into my life. The man I was ready to live happily ever after with. The guy who turned his back on me at the first sign of his wife.*

"Dan, I'm home." Her voice thudded against the emptiness. "Dan?" She texted him on her Blackberry and got a reply within thirty seconds. *Out viewing potential properties. Back soon.* She texted her plans and got ready for her meeting. She wanted to look drop dead gorgeous. She thought about wearing the ruby but decided that was going too far. She settled on a suit, since it was a meeting. She would have to dazzle with her shoes and makeup. She saw how he still looked at her and wanted to remind him of what he was missing.

She arrived shortly after eight and was shown to his table. He was already there with JW.

"Julia, I'm glad you could make it." JW looked like he had come out of a magazine and not someone who had just finished fourteen hours at the office. "I understand you already know Matt?"

"She was my lady luck when I desperately needed some reversal of fortune."

"Sounds like a story."

"For another time. Welcome, Jules, you look wonderful."

"Thank you." She couldn't help but blush. He wasn't embarrassed about how he met her or that he knew her at all. *It's hard to be angry at him*, she thought.

"Shall we eat before we get into the details? The chef has a wonderful menu I have been eyeing. If you have the time, I think we can talk between courses."

They agreed and ordered. The pairing wines began as soon as the order was taken.

"Matt, I understand you want to boost sub-primes. That's my department, so you'll be dealing with me."

"This evening gets better and better." He smiled. He was drinking the champagne and not his usual cola.

"I just want to know how you want me to achieve this. There's a lot of competition in the marketplace."

"Nonsense. I'm sure you can source the tranches."

"I have an idea, but it's risky."

"I'm not adverse to risk."

"But our investors are," JW said.

"Yes, they are a nuisance at times," Matt said. "Don't you think it would be easier to get forgiveness than permission? When they're counting their money, they won't care how you made it."

"If we make it. If things go tits up, we're finished." JW hadn't touched his drink.

"But you're too smart to get caught without a chair when the music stops. Let's try it for six months. If it doesn't go as planned, you can deleverage the portfolio and go back to your strategy."

JW looked at Julia, who shrugged slightly. "That sounds reasonable. I just need to review our capital requirements and the degree to which we can leverage our position."

"Subject to what Julia finds, I can sign off on that plan."

"Then we are all best friends again and the meal won't be ruined by talking endlessly about business." Matt had finished his first glass and found it magically refilled.

"I'm not in yet," Julia said. "I'm just agreeing to see if we are legally allowed to do this."

"Then let's enjoy ourselves until we find out. Tomorrow will take care of itself."

∞

The next four months were the best time of Julia's professional life. She rubbed shoulders with the most powerful and influential people of Wall Street. She flew to London and Frankfurt to meet with pension fund managers and purchasers of AAT's product. She stood at the junction of need and want, marrying those with money with those without. Magically, it all worked.

"Jules, it looks like you are still my lady luck. I needed this and you delivered." Matt held a can of diet coke as he talked.

"Are you still here?"

"You know I am."

"I can't do this." She started walking past him.

"Do what?"

"This. Your compliments, fancy dinners, and big gestures." She brushed some hair from her eyes. "How's Alicia?"

"She's fine, thanks." He seemed to battle with something but decided against it, walking closer to her. "I have never known love before I met you." He said the words and stared at her.

"That is ridiculous. If it were true, I would be with you in Joburg right now. Instead, you went back to your wife and had more children. Where's the love? I didn't see you chase after me. I was a passing fancy for your gambling guilt."

Matt was silent, absorbing the anger, but happy to see that she cared enough to be angry with him. "I'm sorry. I loved you from the third day we spent together. I haven't stopped loving you. I'm with my wife because I am a coward. I say that with every humility. I know I can never have you or be with you, but I can tell you how I feel." He stood there, not moving, not reaching for her.

Julia waited for whatever else would come from his mouth. Hearing nothing, she turned and walked away.

There was nothing for her to say but it didn't stop her from shaking. On the hard wood floor, drops of milky coffee followed her to her office.

∞

"What do you mean we can't sell our paper?" JW was yelling at the phone when Julia walked in. She raised her eyebrows. She rarely saw him angry. Today, he was flushed and blotchy with rage. The phone slid to the edge of his desk when he slammed the handset down.

"Bad news?"

"Beyond bad. Bear Sterns just blew up two of its funds. I can't give away our paper and no one is answering my calls."

Julia was smart enough to be silent in moments like this.

"I need you to be brutal in how you handle this." His neck had expanded and the flesh pushed against his white collar. She could see him loosen his tie and unbutton the top two buttons.

"What are we talking about?"

"Liquidate everything to do with sub-prime. If we're lucky, we lose ten or twenty percent of our capital."

"If we're not?"

"We go bust." His voice was hoarse.

"I'm on it." She rose to leave and then turned. "Everything?"

"Everything. This is going toxic. We may only have a few hours."

She jogged back to her office. *I'll sell to the sovereign funds,* she thought. *Foreign funds believe in us and the United States and have the staying power to survive this cash flow crunch. They'll make money, we'll survive. Win-win.*

"Marlene, get me Helmut in Frankfurt and Tony in Athens. Also, line up telephone meetings with the heads of the top five oil-money funds and the three state funds we deal with in China. Yes, you heard correctly. Every twenty minutes starting at ten this morning. Just give me a heads up and ensure you're not getting them out of bed. Good, you got it. But first Helmut. Thanks."

We've got two hundred twenty-six billion dollars of this stuff, she thought. *I need to spread the risk onto people used to taking it. Ten to twenty billion each is not too much. At a thirty-five to one capital ratio, that's only around three hundred million per ten billion.* As she ran the numbers in her head, she laughed aloud when she realised that was the same pay-out ratio at a roulette table. *Matt's in the right game.*

Chapter Twelve

A New Beginning

Julia became suspicious when Marlene had difficulty confirming all of her telephone appointments. Helmut agreed to purchase thirty billion but demanded a heavy discount. She did the deal. Tony agreed to fifteen billion but with a slightly smaller discount. The Saudi Sovereign funds absorbed fifty billion with no discounts, as did the men from Qatar. That left eighty-one billion on the books and she still needed to paper the verbal agreements. She was on the phone to Japan when Matt burst into her office, looking more agitated than normal.

"I've tried, God knows I've tried, but I can't do it." He sat down in the chair across from her.

She mouthed *I'm on the phone* and ignored him, focussing on Mr. Nobuyuki. "Yes, sir, I am confident everything is fine. No, I'm not concerned about HSBC's ten billion dollar loss. No, I don't think we're about to crash. These securities are all triple A rated, guaranteed by AIG. There's no risk. I understand. Okay. I'll wait for your call. Thank you, Mr. Nobuyuki." She placed the phone back in its place, adjusted a pen that had skidded during their conversation, and put her hands in her lap. "Shit."

"I'm sorry if this is a bad time," Matt continued, oblivious to her plight, "but if I don't say this now, I'll regret it forever."

Julia looked up, as if seeing him for the first time. "What do you want? It's not a good time."

"I know. The company is in trouble, the world is going to hell, and I'm in love with you. There, I said it." He sat back in his chair, waiting for her reply.

"Matt, you don't love me. That's one. Two, the company will be fine. And three, the world is hell so there's no further journey to endure. If you don't have anything productive to say, please let me get on with what I need to do."

"This is important. I have done wrong by you and I want to fix things. I can't stop thinking about you..."

"That was over ten years ago. You're deranged. Go back to Alicia and leave me alone."

Matt was on his feet and came around her desk. "I need you, Jules."

"You need to see a shrink. Please leave."

He leaned over and grabbed her shoulders and kissed her. Instinctively, she pushed back her chair, trying to stand up. He held her next to her, kissing her neck and face.

"No!"

"Come on, you know I can't stand not being with you." His hands were holding her in an embrace, no longer gripping her shoulders. She went limp in response, not allowing him any emotion.

"It's time for you to leave."

"You know you want this." He pulled his face away to look at hers. She stared back defiantly.

"This is what you'll get." She grabbed his shoulders and pulled him towards her at the same time as lifting her knee with all her might. He crumpled to the floor and began coughing. Julia grabbed her cell phone and purse and walked out of her office. Despite the glass walls, she saw nothing but red.

∞

JW's usual mocha colouring was overcast with grey. His normally athletic gait was slow and ponderous. Even his suit looked rumpled. As he sat at the head of the boardroom table, each of the equity partners reported the health of their departments. It wasn't good news.

"We have heard that Bear Stearns will not survive. They were the single largest buyer of our paper. I have tried to sell directly to the end user clients from London to Tokyo but people have lost their appetite." Julia was equally exhausted. She had given up on sleep for the last month and did everything she could to save GVE and AAT and the equity stake she had earned over the years. Every bonus was rolled back into the company. Every extra penny she had was reinvested into the company. She felt like the Pope after he realised God was dead. Her voice made sounds but her body had become a shell.

"Has anyone heard anything else? What about Bernanke? Is he planning to do anything?" JW was irritated.

"It's not politically viable yet. The Dow Jones just hit an historic high of fourteen thousand. The public won't stand for it."

"Then we're on our own?" JW looked around the table at the multi-millionaires unable to come up with a solution. "I need to see Kilroy now. Let's reconvene this when we know something more." He got up without waiting for a reply and left the room. Julia was right behind him.

"JW."

"I'm late."

"Just a quick word." She had caught up to him and put her hand on his arm. It worked and he turned his head towards her.

"I don't think we'll be able to flog our paper. I didn't want to scare anyone in the room but I think we're in trouble."

"I know. I noticed the discounts you gave on your last selling spree. It ate into our capital reserves, impacting our other funds. We may need to liquidate those to support the damned toxic mortgage paper."

"I just hope you don't allow Matt to interfere in your business again. He's a gambler and this was always a big risk."

"I don't want to hear 'I told you so' right now. Just find a way to fix it." He had lost his look of invulnerability. "I don't need to tell you that we're in a world where we make money on the pennies in a trade. Until now, those gambles as you call them have been very profitable. We just need to weather this downturn." He turned away and kept walking. Julia let him.

We're going to go bust, she thought. *We're holding the wrong paper. No one wants it. We're going down.* Her body went cold then hot with adrenaline. Around her, colleagues busied themselves on their phones, determined to work the problem. *They haven't given up yet. At least that's a good sign.*

The next day, Julia learned her fate. JW was at the head of the table again surrounded by the executives of the fund. His body looked chiselled and his suit pressed to his body.

"I want all of you to know that I have taken decisive steps to ensure the continued survival of AAT and GVE. Due to recent events and the difficulties in the marketplace, I believe that if we don't act with certainty, we will fall by the wayside. As a company, we have responsibilities to our investors. Personally, I have responsibilities to you."

Julia noticed the slight movement of eyes as each person began to understand what was about to be said.

"I have been talking to the CEO of JPMorgan Chase and they have agreed to purchase us."

The table didn't erupt, but she felt a ripple of restlessness.

"What about our jobs?" One of the wet-eyed executives was the first to say what everyone was thinking.

"That will be up to them. Obviously we know our clients and I expect at least fifty percent of our staff to remain. But we don't really have a choice. The alternative is, if the market continues the way it is going, we do not have the staying power to survive. This way, your savings are not wiped out. You will take JPMorgan Chase stock in trade and have the comfort of being part of a bank too big to fail. Unfortunately, we don't have that designation. We can fail much more easily."

There was silence as his words were digested. Then a person started clapping slowly. Others joined in and eventually the entire table was standing and applauding JW. For his part, he bowed his head and then left the room.

Julia found herself clapping despite the certain knowledge that her investment in the firm was diminished. She was also likely to be one of the casualties of the impending merger. She returned to her desk and looked at the mass of toxic debt on the company books and wondered at the discipline of JW to cut his losses. She heard her door open as she rummaged through her desk drawer. She didn't look up until she heard his voice.

"Do you think I've done the right thing?"

"I think it was brave. I don't think I could have done it."

"I just need to know that you are happy with the decision."

"I know how precarious we are with all that toxic debt," she said. "I also know if the market returns to health, we'll be richer than ever. The bets were good, a little aggressive, but good."

"The problem is, I don't think this is a little blip. I'm beginning to think this is a major correction and is the result of governmental interventions and our own greed. We have brought this upon ourselves."

"Is everything okay, JW? We're in the business of making money, not saving the world. Greed is good."

He smiled at her attempts to cheer him up. "I guess I'm just feeling a bit beaten up. It was a difficult decision and I sometimes feel like others will resent me for making it for them."

"You have the majority of shares. We all know that. This is your firm."

"But still, it rankles. I wouldn't want my future decided for me."

"That's why you started your own firm. We are employees. You are the boss. You take the risk and you get the reward."

JW was looking at her, glassy-eyed. "Do you ever wonder if things would be different had we acted differently on that day?"

"Which day?" As she said it, her mind went to her kitchen six years ago. She had replayed it in her mind countless times, fingers tracing his flawless skin, body wanting him but mind overruling. "Ah, yes. I do remember."

He walked closer to her and took her hands. "I can't think of anything else. I haven't been able to think of anything but that kiss." He was dressed immaculately again, the crumpled look gone. His confidence was back, strong and defiant. She found herself taking a half step closer to him.

"I'd be lying if I said I didn't think about you. But you're my boss and I'm married. In a different life, different time…"

He didn't let her finish. He leaned in and stopped just in front of her face, waiting for her to close the gap. He waited for one second, eyes tracing her face. Two seconds, his eyes fixed on hers. Three seconds, and he saw her move towards him. Their lips touched gently, tentatively, fearing something even more than their physical touch.

"Let me love you," he finally said when he pulled away. "You know you feel the same way." He stood there, heart in hand, vulnerable.

Julia felt his intensity and found herself drawn to him. She kissed him and then drew herself back. "I need to go." She gathered her things and left for home. The office would need to take care of itself for a day without her.

The sun was shining and she decided to walk home. It was just under an hour's walk and she kept gym shoes in her bag for that purpose. *I look ridiculous*, she thought as she caught a glimpse of herself in a shop window. She was dressed in a black Gucci jacket and dress along with white sneakers. She smirked and carried on walking, over the Brooklyn Bridge to her home.

The day was glorious and she pushed images of Matt and JW out of her mind as she hopped up the front stairs to her Brownstone. It was different from living in London, but she had become used to the one way traffic, aggressive taxis, and flamboyant people of New York. She put her key in the lock and opened the door. The house was silent. It was her refuge from the chaos of work and the outside world. There, she was able to be herself and relax, unafraid of what someone might spring on her. No pension fund would try to outsmart her, and no scheming executive would try to increase his fiefdom in the office. Just peace and serenity.

She dropped her bag to the ground and kicked off her shoes. She started undressing as she walked up the stairs to her room, her stocking feet soundless against the cool hard wood. She was unbuttoning her shirt when she opened the door to the master bedroom. She stopped, frozen.

"Jules! I didn't think you would be home until later."

"Obviously." She said it like she had pieces of broken glass in her mouth.

"It's not what you think." He threw covers over another woman who got out and grabbed her clothes.

"You must be Ms. Patel?" Julia addressed the naked woman who also froze when addressed.

"Uh, yes. Oh, shit."

Julia stood without moving, hand still on her shirt button, watching the frenetic activity in front of her. The woman squeezed past her and disappeared down the stairs. Moments later, she heard the door open and close. Daniel sat in their bed like a deer caught in headlights.

"Do you love her?"

"Of course not, sweetheart."

"Don't call me that."

"It didn't mean anything. I love you and no one else. It was a mistake."

Julia raised her eyes, as amazed with her own lack of rage as the stupidity of what was unfolding in front of her. "I can't process this right now. I need to change. We'll talk later." She walked in a daze towards the en suite, closing the door behind her.

Once inside, she slid down onto the floor and began to cry softly. She didn't want to be heard. *I give up*, she thought. *I just don't know what they want from me anymore. Good wife, good employee, good girlfriend? I can't handle the one-way traffic any longer.* She reached the bath's taps and turned them on.

∞

She didn't talk to Daniel for the rest of the day because she didn't see him, nor did she want to. The next day, she went to work to find out the details of her new employment. Her first impulse was to cash in and check out. She learned that Matt had returned to South Africa, something about his wife and children according to her secretary. By the end of the day, she had decided.

"I need a break." She started talking the moment she opened his door. JW was seated at his desk.

"Is this anything to do with…"

"No," she cut him off. "Nothing. I just need time away."

"What are we talking about?"

"I don't know. I need time to think, to get my head around what I want to do."

"This isn't a good time, Jules. The merger is taking place at double quick time. Positions can't be held."

"I understand and I'm not asking you to. If it's okay with you, I'd like to cash in the value of my stock options and take a year off."

That got JW out of his chair. "What?"

"I need a break."

"Is there something I can do to make you feel more at home?"

That softened Julia and she put her hands on his chest briefly and then removed them. "No, thank you. It's been an accumulation of things and I realised if I didn't do something about it soon I would fall into a pattern that I would regret and then resent as time goes by."

"You'll be missed. I'll always have a place here for you when you return."

"I don't know if I'll return."

"When you return, I'll be here. Whether you want a job, that's your decision."

She felt her eyes moisten and she leaned in and kissed him softly on his cheek. "Thank you. You are a good man."

He nodded awkwardly but did nothing as she turned around and left his office. When she was gone, he sat back in his chair and felt the air leave his lungs. He felt heavier and discouraged. *Can't I catch a break?* He shook the thoughts out of his head and returned to his work.

When Julia returned to her home, she did so to collect some clothes and her passport. Her valuables were in a safety deposit box at Citibank's head office. It took only three hours to liquidate her stock options and transfer the cash to Julius Bär, a private bank with a branch in Monaco where she held her rainy day account. Her life was not in the United States, England, or South Africa. Her life was where she was, and she no longer wanted to be in any of those places.

When she left her home in Brooklyn, she also left a note on the fridge door. *How prosaic*, she thought with a grin. "I'll be back when I'm back. If you're here when I return, we'll talk."

She put her purse over her shoulder and pulled her carry-on luggage. She didn't take a computer or anything else. *Money and passport is all I need. Next stop, life.*

Chapter Thirteen

Life According to Matt

"I came as soon as I heard."

"I think it's too late."

"It can't be too late."

"It's too late." Maish's movements were slow. "The syndicate is not prepared to wait any longer."

"But I made them money. They got everything they invested back."

"You lost them a lot of money."

"That was profit. They got back their capital." Matt was sweating. Maish didn't look like he was going to budge.

"You know the rules, and this was clean capital. They can't replace that."

Matt was pacing, salty drops falling onto his shirt. "What are they going to do?"

"I don't know. Can you pay them back?"

"How can I repay one hundred million dollars in that sort of time? I'm good for it if you can wait a few years."

Maish sighed and poured another cup of coffee for himself. "Then we have a problem." He got up and left the room. The four men guarding him remained impassive.

Matt had arrived the night before, leaving New York the day after hearing about Bear Stearns. When he went home, no one was there. When he called Maish, he was told to visit him at his packing warehouse. Thinking nothing of it, he went there and was now being held within Maish's office.

The next person through the door was Ray.

"Hey, my boy, how's it going?" He acted as though they were going to a rugby game. Matt looked at him and saw the man who held his mother, wife, and children captive all those years ago. It was the moment when the solution he sought was a bullet in the head.

"What are they planning?"

"Can't say."

"Do you know where my family is? My mother?"

"Yes." Ray used his finger to dislodge something in his teeth.

"And?"

"I can't say."

"Should I be worried?"

"Can't say."

Matt was tired of the routine and turned his head to look out the window. The parking lot held a half dozen cars, probably workers who were maintaining the fruit packing equipment before the packers arrived in the morning. The site was clean and tidy with mountains of wooden pallets stacked near the loading docks.

Maish returned with a bald man carrying a black doctor's bag.

"Matty, it's time."

"For what?"

"For long overdue consequences." He motioned for Matt to stand up and ushered him through the door in the wall without windows. The four men went in before and after him, in case he tried to run. It was the last thing on Matt's mind.

"Where are you taking me?"

"You'll see."

"If you're going to kill me, just get it over with."

"I know you mean this. That's why I have something else in store for you. You see, we know you don't care if you live or die. We can inflict pain but we can't get our money back if you are dead."

"That sounds reasonable," Matt said, feeling slightly optimistic.

"Yes. We try to be reasonable." He didn't stop walking but indicated with his head to the four men. The bald man followed behind.

They reached a room that required them to climb some metal stairs, almost vertically like in a ship. The room was large and had a window that overlooked the warehouse floor. It was empty except for two metal chairs and two metal tables.

"Bring in the first one," Maish said to one of the four men. "You can sit over there," he said to Matt.

As he sat down, he had a feeling he would never leave that room, despite their assurances. He was concerned at how calm everyone was, including himself. When the door opened, his calm ceased.

"What is this!" he lunged forward. Arms he wasn't aware of restrained him and shoved him back in his chair. He felt the plastic slip ties go around his wrists, which were behind his back. They then did the same to each calf, attaching him to the chair. He struggled and then forced himself to be calm.

"As you said, we try to be reasonable. To date, this hasn't helped so we decided to think laterally. If you don't care about yourself, perhaps you care about someone else."

"Yes, but this is too low, even for you."

"Not at all. We only want to get your attention. Just imagine how hard it was for the syndicate to earn and save all that money, only for you to fuck it up as you usually do."

"You know what happened. It wasn't my fault. The market collapsed."

"It's no longer about blame. It's about ensuring others don't think they can get away with this type of shenanigan. When you made money, none of us cared.

When you lose us money, especially that much, we lose all sense of forgiveness."

"But Maish, this is wrong."

"Why?"

"She's my mother. You can't do this."

"I can and I will. Ray, help the doctor get Mrs. Smit comfortable."

His mother, usually so proud, held her head lower than usual. When she was sat down, she raised her eyes to her son and continued to say nothing. Matt could see the black pupils of her eyes. They looked the same as his did just before he pressed the gun's barrel to his temple. His body slumped, flesh feeling the cut of the plastic ties on his wrists. He wasn't close with his mother anymore but his childhood was good and the sight of her before him, humbled, made him cry.

"Stop your blubbering," Maish said. He motioned to one of the large men and Matt felt something hit him on the side of the head. "Not so hard, you idiot, we need him to be able to hear us. He is not the one who will suffer today, at least not physically."

"Sorry, sir." The man withdrew to block the door.

"What do you want from me? I don't have any money. I can't pay anything." Matt was blubbering again.

"Then consider this a reprieve," the older man said. "How many children do you have?"

Matt stopped crying, he face contorted with fear and rage. "You bastard. You fucking bastard!"

"I guess you haven't been around for a while so perhaps you've lost count." He turned to one of the men. "Andre, bring them in."

It took a few minutes but Alicia, followed by five children, filed in.

"There, you see? You have five children. How old are they?"

"Fuck you, asshole."

"The language," Maish said, feigning outrage. "Not in front of the children." He walked around Alicia, who was white with fear, shaking while clutching Jody, her youngest, to her chest. He put his hand on her face in a gentle caress, allowing it to move into her hair. His fingers ran the length of her hair as he closed his eyes and swayed. When the hair dropped and his hand was in the air, he brought it back, but this time onto the child. She instinctively pulled her away.

The room was silent except for the sobs now emanating from his mother. Matt had stopped crying and was simply watching in shocked horror. Maish walked slowly in front of the four standing children. He turned to Matt with a sudden grin, "you have enough children for your own Van Trapp family singalong! Come on, let's hear a song. I'd like to hear "Edelweiss" or "The Hills are Alive"."

Matt realised this was not about brinkmanship or instilling fear in him. His family was about to die and he would too after watching it. Seeing Maish begin to twirl was more frightening than the four silent men or the thought of execution. He had never seen Maish smile in his life. Matt knew he was one of the heads of the syndicate. He would never have had direct contact with him except for the fact Alicia was his niece—and that he reported to her father. Matt had never met the syndicate and only dealt with Maish. For all Matt knew, Maish was the syndicate and played a cover to deflect attention. What he was witnessing before him was not to be repeated—because he would never live to tell the tale.

When Maish finished his twirling and humming, he put his hand on the bald doctor's shoulder. "I think it's time to get ready. Andre, the rest of you, secure the kids and the mother." There were no more chairs so they all stood, hands tied behind their backs with the same plastic ties. Their ankles were also tied and they all swayed until they realised they could lean against the steel table behind them. The children began to cry.

"I think you've made your point," Matt said.

Maish turned and smiled. "Not at all, my boy. We are just getting started." He stepped back and appraised the sorry huddle of bodies. "Hardly heroic, but they'll do the trick." He nodded to the doctor. The bald man approached Alicia and took the toddler from her arms.

The crying stopped as the possibility of what was threatened became a reality.

"It is up to you, Matt. You decide who you want to die first. If you don't, I will kill your youngest. What's her name?"

Matt vomited, the sick covering his chest and legs with bits remaining on his lips. He was unable to wipe it clean and no one volunteered. "Jody," he whispered.

"Very good. Jody will die unless you choose another. This is fun, isn't it?"

Matt's mouth opened but nothing came out. Alicia began to scream but received a punch to the mouth from one of the men. Blood began to pool in her mouth. She spat it to the ground but didn't do a very good job of it. Most landed on her chest with strings of drool and blood remaining around her mouth. Matt's fear reached a breaking point as he realised Maish was prepared to hurt his niece. *Maish has snapped*, he thought.

"Me. Kill me." All eyes moved to the mother, white with despair. "I'm the oldest. I should go first."

"Excellent," Maish said, his mouth in a wide smile. "And how would you like to die?"

Matt's mother tried to be brave but he could see the stain around her midsection and guessed better. "A bullet to the head." She held his stare and then lowered her eyes. Everyone else had gone silent.

"That's not sporting at all. I have a better idea. Andre, take Mrs. Smit and put her on the table. There, that's good. Tie her arms and legs down. Excellent, yes. That'll do. Now, move the wife and children against the wall and our dear friend Matthijs closer so he can get a better view. Good. Now, doctor, I want this to be slow and painful. I want our friend to understand how much the syndicate is displeased."

"This is bullshit. Just kill us and be done with it. Torture doesn't get you anything. We don't have anything to give you."

Maish put his two hands on Matt's shoulders from behind and began to give him a massage. After a short while, he put his hands on Matt's hair, still massaging. It was a long minute before he walked around to face him. "I do this for my own pleasure. You wouldn't want to deprive a man of his pleasure, would you?"

Matt tried to understand how he was in this situation. He had known Maish for two decades and never saw a flicker of this side of him. "What happened to you? Who broke you?"

"I'm not broken, I'm the one who does the breaking. Doctor, if you please."

Matt's mother was as silent as she could be. The doctor started by cutting off her clothes. He then put heavy restraining straps across her shoulders, waist, and knees. Everyone watched in silence. Maish was the only one who paced. When he first cut the flesh, there was a high-pitched scream, then a whimper. He cut a shallow slice into the skin, not intending to sever any arteries or muscle. Matt watched as the doctor cut around the ankle and then up the shin, over the knee and up to the waist. He began to peel the skin back using a tool that firmly gripped it. When he had pulled back an inch of flesh, he fastened some thin medical cables with multiple rivets into the skin. The screaming was non-stop but Matt couldn't feel anything other than a numbing sensation of disbelief. He watched as the strap around the knees was removed and her legs were lifted to allow the skin to be torn off her. Two of the men held the cables firm as the doctor used his scalpel to separate the skin from the muscles beneath. Despite himself, Matt found himself amazed at how little blood there was. When they were done, the legs were returned and the strap removed. His mother had passed out and there was silence except for the sound of the metal cables against the steel table and the dragging of the pelt against the floor.

"Hang it up over there," Maish said. "Doctor, you are an artist. I have never seen it done with such precision. I bow to your talent." He bowed deeply and theatrically.

The doctor nodded and then began his flaying of the torso and arms. Matt watched his mother being disassembled in the most horrific fashion. He noted with horror that she was still breathing. *At least she was able to pass out. I'm sorry, Mom.* His thoughts turned on themselves and he struggled to figure out how to save his children. *All is lost.* When he lowered his head to look away, one of the men lifted his chin. When he refused to open his eyes, Maish threatened to replace his mother with Jody.

"Let her die, you sonofabitch," said Alicia, finally breaking her silence.

Maish turned slowly. "You're not immune from this, my dear. Your father can't protect you in here."

Alicia blinked slowly and then looked at Maish with her head bowed. "You will let us go if you know what's good for you."

He walked towards her and put his hand on her face, gently. Then let it drop slowly, allowing his hand to drag across her chest. "I can see why your husband would jump whenever you snapped your fingers." He glanced at Matt with disgust. "But I am not your husband and you do not make threats against me."

Alicia spit on his face. He didn't flinch but pulled a handkerchief from his pocket and wiped it away. "I didn't want to tell you this, as I don't like getting involved in family matters." He paused to ensure she was listening. "But your father passed away earlier this morning." He smiled. "It wasn't peaceful."

Alicia's confidence drained from her face and she began to shake. When the tears came, they were silent. There were no dramatics.

"Not so sure of yourself anymore? No more daddy to take care of your cheating husband? To make sure everyone licks your ass?" Tiring of her, he turned to the doctor and nodded towards the mother. "Take them out."

When the knife was inserted, Matt couldn't understand what they were doing. The skin was already off. His mother had suffered in the worst way imaginable. When the knife cut the cartilage, the sound was different from the silent cutting of flesh and muscle. When the bone was removed, it was accompanied by a deathly scream as the pain cut through all the adrenaline pumped into his mother's body.

Enough! he wanted to scream. *I'll do and say whatever you want, just end this barbarism.* Instead, he became calm on the outside. His serene face belied the rage beneath and his muscles relaxed against the otherwise straining plastic ties that kept him in place. Even his head rested lightly on his shoulders, neither drooping nor looking away. He watched with detached horror as the doctor dismantled what was once his mother. The blood had begun to flow when the bones were removed. Tourniquets were used at first but then abandoned as the arteries refused to be stopped. By the time they reached her hips, she was dead.

The doctor did not stop until every bone was removed. The second table held the bones in macabre fashion like a student studying anatomy. The skin was on the floor and the remaining muscle and organs were thrown down next to it.

"Are we boring you?" Maish noticed Matt's composure as he tried to provoke him by throwing the skin and muscle on the floor.

He gave no answer.

"I see you are taking another approach. You will find it will not help you or the ones you love."

Matt looked at Maish, blinking normally as though he was talking about the most recent turn of events at the local parent teacher association.

"Let's see how you fair as we begin with your family." He nodded to two of the four men. They took Alicia's arms and began to take her to the stainless steel table, now bloodied. The other two men took her baby and ushered the other children out of the room. "I can't stand the noise of screaming children," Maish said. He ignored Alicia's screams and clawing at the two men as she was moved and tied into place on the table. Her resistance was ineffective. The children didn't even cry as they were removed from the room.

Matt remained impassive and watched Alicia being put in place with a detachment that frightened even him. Something within him kept saying 'don't react'. He wasn't sure whether he was following the voice's suggestion or if he was saying the words himself in a state of shock. Was he acting in consequence or reacting to the events unfolding in front of him?

"You promised my father!" Alicia was fully tied in and unable to do much more than make noises.

"No, don't gag her. Let her speak," Maish said. The doctor put the cloth down.

"You said you wouldn't kill me. You promised him."

"Yes, I did. And I won't kill you."

That silenced her until she realised she was still on the table. "Then why am I here?"

Maish's forehead relaxed as he smiled. "Because I have been listening to you for my entire life and all I heard was bitching and complaining. You have never considered anyone else's feelings other than your own. You believed you could do it because your father was the head of our family."

"Uncle Maish, please don't." Her anger was gone and she had melted into the little girl she once was.

Maish paused as the image flickered in his memory but was then pushed aside. "Alicia, you could have been anything. Instead, you married that useless piece of rubbish who gambled and whored his way through life."

"Then why punish me?"

"Because you sided with him and because you are now a liability. He is the only one who can fix things." He looked at Matt, becoming increasingly angry at his lack of emotion.

"I don't understand." She was weeping, her body straining against the ties that held her in place.

"Enough talk. This is not about you." He nodded to the doctor, who pulled out an instrument a dentist might use. It was placed on Alicia's face and into her mouth, forcing her jaw apart. Her teeth were accessible and her tongue tried to understand its new environment, rapidly touching the metal and teeth. The result was audible noise but no more talking.

"That's better. And what do you have to say to your dear wife now?" He had walked from the table to Matt and put his hand on him.

Nothing came from Matt. Just the silent, doe-like gaze that followed Maish but gave no reaction to the torture of his wife.

"This is the mother of your children. Have you no sympathy for her? For your newly born child? Do you not fear for their safety?"

Nothing.

Disgusted, Maish turned his back to Matt and returned to his task. He tapped his left index finger while nodding to the doctor. The doctor nodded back and brought out two tools. One was a pair of pliers that locked and the other was the familiar scalpel. He took the pliers, clamped onto Alicia's left thumb, and pulled it straight. There was a feral groan from the patient but otherwise nothing. The scalpel was then inserted at the thumb's base and neatly cut the tendons and muscle holding it in place. It came off easily and was placed beside her. The doctor leaned down and brought out a small blow torch from his bag. He lit it and concentrated it on the stub that was once the thumb. The patient screamed and her body strained against the ties and then went limp.

"Matt? Are you there?" Maish waived his hand in front of Matt's face. He turned to the doctor. "Did anyone give him something?" When no one answered, Maish returned his attention to his niece. "Hold off on the adrenaline for now. Do the rest of them and then let's see where we are."

The doctor proceeded to remove each finger and thumb from both hands. They were cauterised using the blowtorch and there were no screams. She had passed out and had not awoken. Halfway through the toes, she awoke and more ties were applied as it looked like she would snap them. Each toe was dutifully removed and cauterised. She lost consciousness again.

"Beautiful," Maish said when the work was done. "A good reminder, wouldn't you say?" When he didn't receive a reply from Matt, he grew angry. "Wake her up," he snapped.

The doctor injected her with something that caused her to gasp and eyes open.

"Can you hear me?" Maish was standing over her.

"Uh-huh."

"I never wanted to do this to you, sweetheart. Your husband is not co-operating and I am forced to do this. I just wanted you to see me one last time." He leaned over and kissed her on the forehead. He turned away and left the room after nodding to the doctor.

His mother's remains continued to bleed onto the floor. He realised the floor was uneven when the blood never reached his feet, but felt terrible for even having such a thought. He was still watching events unfold without the slightest show of emotion. He had watched as her fingers and toes were removed. He saw Maish kiss her on the forehead and leave. He even thought there were tears in his eyes before he left the room. He saw the doctor use his scalpel on either side of her head before realising he was cutting off her ears. What re-mained were the holes. He found himself wondering whether they would insert something to break the inner workings of the ear or simply be satisfied with the mu-tilation of the outside.

This thought was put on hold as he saw the doctor stand up on top of the table and put a foot on either side of her head. The ceiling was just high enough for his bald head. He had something in his hands that looked like a plier but the handles were very long. He could see her eyes bulge and heard a scream that would haunt him until his dying day. The doctor instructed one of the men to hold her head still as it was shaking madly from side to side. He then inserted tongs into her mouth and grasped her tongue. He stood up straight and pulled with all his might. Matt could see the veins on the side of his neck. This continued for a number of minutes before the doctor instructed one of the men to change places with him. The man held the tong and applied pressure to the tongue but didn't pull with any great effort.

"Hold it steady," the doctor said. "Good, pull it that way. Good, now hold." He used the scalpel to cut the tongue while using the blowtorch to cauterise as he went. It didn't take long. "Well done. You can come down now."

The man came down and handed the tong and tongue to the doctor. It was placed beside the fingers and toes and ears. Alice sounded like she was drowning in her own blood and fluids so a tube was placed down her throat to allow her to breathe. The sound that came from the tube was fast and rough. She was hyperventilating.

"One more thing to do before I am done with you, little one." The doctor's voice was higher than normal and his attempt at a bedside manner made him even scarier. He pulled out his trusty scalpel and began to work on her eyes. He removed her eyelids and then tried to do something to the eyes themselves. "Stay still, damn it. It'll hurt more if you keep struggling."

Matt didn't see how that was possible but remained mute.

"That's enough," said a voice. It was Maish. He had returned and couldn't bear it any longer.

"But I still need to remove the eyes." The doctor looked like a child whose treat had been taken from him.

"That can wait." The aggravation was in his voice and his body. He looked at Matt. "Do you have anything to say?"

Matt was silent, outwardly serene.

"Damn you, man." He returned to Alicia, who was breathing heavily and staring at him through eyes without the reprieve of eyelids. "Do you want to live?"

She nodded her head, hair wet with tears, blood, and sweat.

"How do I know you won't talk?"

She tried to make her thoughts known to him with her facial expressions but the dental structure and lack of eyelids made that impossible.

He nodded anyway. "Yes, you're right. Because I will inflict on your children a punishment that will make yours look like a slap on the wrist." He looked at Matt and back to Alicia. "Do we understand each other?"

Matt remained in his stony silence. Alicia made motions of agreement.

"If you don't feel pain now, perhaps letting you live is a better punishment." Maish said this to both of them but it was directed at Matt. "I'm calling the police. You know what will happen if you mention me."

Matt felt a fist smash into the side of his head and everything went black. When he awoke, he was covered in blood and alone in the room with his mother's remains and wife. He then saw the pistols pointed at him and heard the shouting of police voices telling him to put the scalpel and blowtorch down. When he did so, he was tackled, handcuffed, and hauled away.

The next time he saw his wife was at the trial. The evidence all pointed to him losing his mind and killing his mother and wife in a most horrific fashion. The news was full of his murders and the judge was so disgusted he gave his sentence and stomped out of court.

Alicia was able to function without a tongue and her hearing was not totally lost. Her eyes worked but required specialist surgery to reaffix eyelids. She wasn't able to have her fingers or toes reattached but she was told that prosthetics were improving all the time and perhaps one day she would have functionality. Alicia testified against Matt at his trial, but the children did not.

When the bars closed behind him, Matt was alone in his cell. The warden deemed it wise to keep him isolated until they were able to assess him. The barbarity of his crimes meant that others would try to test him. Matt welcomed the isolation. The last few years had been a rollercoaster. *Losing my position at JW's firm, returning to South Africa to find myself the victim of Maish's madness, and now jail. What else could happen to me?* He thought about Julia and the summer dress she wore when he was going to propose to her. *Why did I ever marry Alicia? Why did I ever stay with her? Because her father was the head of the five families and because her father bankrolled my gambling,* he remembered.

"He won!" came a voice from another cell, three over from Matt's.

"Obama?"

"Yeah, just heard. First kefir president," said a guard who was kinder than most. "Congratulations."

"For what?"

"I don't know. You figure it out."

"Shuddup."

The guard had already returned to his post and ignored the chatter coming from the cells. He poured a coffee for himself and sat next to his colleague, who was watching the results of the election on the television.

"Who would've thought? It's 2008 and there's a black president in the oval office. Damn!"

"They said it wouldn't happen here and we got Mandela. They said it would be another hundred years before they got a black president there. Perhaps we just went through a time warp." He looked behind him comically and the two laughed.

"Anything else on TV?"

Matt sat on his cot, not feeling the scratchy wool blanket or the mosquitoes that filled his room. He had a window to the outside air but those bars couldn't keep the bugs out. His skin formed inflamed bumps where he was bitten. He didn't scratch or swat. The concrete walls were recently painted and the steel bars hurt his hands. After the guards had left, he punched the bars, leaving a bruise that he still felt. *I guess I should count myself lucky, not being put in the communal cells or even sharing a cell with another inmate.* He allowed himself to lie down on the cot. *That's because I'm white and I'd get my ass handed to me in general circulation. Better than any shit Maish would hand out to my kids or me out there.* Then he began to cry.

Chapter Fourteen

The Sun Always Rises... for Most

It was almost a decade before Matt received a visitor who wasn't a reporter or a young film student trying to find a subject for their documentary studies. When he heard who it was, he felt the first tinge of emotion since he had been sentenced all those years ago.

"Alicia?"

"It's me."

"I can't believe you're here."

Her head lowered slightly. She wasn't sure what she felt as he looked at her. They had been through hell together but he was not responsible for Maish.

Matt remained silent, waiting for her to open up.

"They managed to do something with the eyelids. And these," she waved her hands at him, "are prosthetics. I guess young American soldiers having their body parts blown off in war has some upside. I can even wear normal shoes again." The conversation was cordial, almost friendly. He could tell she was making an effort.

"You look good." He couldn't say much. He had stopped talking to people and kept his head down. He had been targeted a number of times and had developed a group of people who looked out for him. They thought he might be able to help them when they got out. It stopped him from getting raped and beaten. It also stopped him from smiling or talking like he used to. The cloud that visited him occasionally was now a permanent feature above him. The depression followed him, and he hoped someone would do him the favour of ending his misery. He wasn't suicidal but would welcome death if it came.

"Thanks." She looked down at the table, her hand dropping the electronic larynx she needed to speak. She was thankful he didn't mention it. *He didn't even look at it. He really saw just me*, she thought.

"Why now? It's been a long time."

She nodded. "Your son wants to see you."

"William?"

"No, Maritz."

Matt sat back, his dulled body trying to remember feelings. "I would like that very much."

"I wanted to see you before…" her voice trailed off. "Before anything happens."

"What can happen? I haven't seen my children for a decade. They think I murdered their grandmother and tried to kill you. He probably wants to spit in my face or tell me what a bastard I am."

"I don't think so," she said slowly. "I don't know exactly what he wants to say but he seems determined to do so face to face with you. He won't tell me what it is."

It was Matt's turn to sink into himself. "Whatever it is, I want to see my boy. Tell him I would love to talk to him."

Alicia stood. "I'll tell him." She started to leave before turning around. "Thank you, Matt. I know it hasn't been easy for you. It hasn't been easy for any of us." She smiled sadly and left. Matt felt acid bite at his chest.

It was nearly a month before Maritz came. On his way to the visitation cubicle, Matt became conscious of his baggy clothes and the way his feet slapped the floor like paddles. He sat down on his side of the glass barrier and picked up the phone. Maritz did the same. He could see the reaction in his son's face as he sat down. They were looking at each other but only saw themselves.

"Hi, son."

"Hello, father."

"I'm glad you decided to come. You have no idea how much I have looked forward to this day."

Silence. Matt looked at his younger self, marred by an event that could never be erased. *He hates me*, he thought. *He thinks I've done the things I'm in here for.*

His confidence began to drain into the muted floor. His hand gripped the telephone receiver, the only contact he'd had with his family in a decade.

"I just wanted to see if you are okay." The young man battled his own fears and looked his father in the eye. "I've heard bad things about these places."

"Ah, don't worry about that. I'm fine. Those are just stories. Don't mind them."

"I do mind them," Maritz said. "And I mind that you are here."

It was Matt's turn to wait. After a long moment, he asked, "Why?"

"Because you are innocent." The blue eyes looked at Matt with the certainty reserved for youth. Their effect was to electrify Matt's body and cause him to do something he hadn't done since the first day he arrived in jail. He cried.

"I'm sorry, son. I imagined a hundred scenarios but never this one."

"I know." He looked at his hands, then back at his father. "I couldn't keep living the lie. I didn't want you to suffer because of what that monster did to us that day. I don't want you protecting us by pretending to be a murderer."

Matt wiped his nose with his hand and then again with the back of his sleeve. "You're a good boy, but this is dangerous talk. You saw what they can do. If you talk, they'll hurt your mother and all your brothers and sisters. I love you for coming here and your brav-ery, but I can't watch you hurt yourself. These are bad men."

"I'm not afraid."

"You should be."

"I just wanted you to know that I know."

Matt nodded, eyes closed. He took a moment before he replied. "I love you, son. Come again soon."

"I love you too, Dad." He put his hand on the glass and Matt matched his on the other side. After nodding, he hung up and left. Matt kept his hand on the glass while he watched his son walk out of the visitor's room. It wasn't until the guard touched him on the shoulder that he finally moved.

∞

The following six months saw Maritz, William, and rest of his children visit often. Because of the number of visitors, the warden granted an exception and al-lowed them to meet in a room together. It was the first time Matt felt his children's hugs and tears and the feel-ing of love overwhelmed him.

"You have made me the happiest man on earth," he said as the tears wet his face. He was smiling genuinely and could feel a soul creeping back into his otherwise moribund body.

"It's okay, Daddy," Jody said, "we all know what happened." She was now twelve and wore braces. Her white blonde hair fell straight with her face cut out of the mop that formed on her head. She hugged her father as hard as she could.

Alicia stood aside as their children piled onto Matt. The older boys sat aside after the initial hugs and pats on their back but only after they each kissed him and felt their father's wet cheeks as he kissed them on the neck and forehead. The younger girls sat on his lap with their arms around his neck. He didn't want to let go of them either.

"Thank you." His voice caught. "Thank you for coming here. I know it isn't very nice."

"It's fine, Dad," Maritz said quickly.

"Yeah, and we wanted you to know that we're fighting for you to get out."

Matt's voice became cold, hard. "No. You must all listen to me. I love that you are here and I want you to visit me as many times as you can, but you must leave this alone. Those people are dangerous and wouldn't think twice about hurting you." He made sure he caught each child's eye before continuing. "And that would hurt me more than being in here."

Alicia put something to her eyes. He could see her sobbing quietly in the corner. No words were required.

"But Dad," William started, "this is unfair."

"Sometimes the best thing in life is to accept an unfair result." Matt's eyes stopped shedding tears and drank in the sight of his children. "We need to be thankful for what we have. We are alive and have each other. We still have a few Rand and I want you all to receive the best education in the world. You succeeding is the best revenge against the barbarism they committed against us."

The children were silent. William and Maritz didn't meet their father's gaze. The girls squeezed him tighter until he had to tap their arms to release his neck.

The buzzer sounded and their visit was over. When Matt returned to his cell, his body felt both exhilarated with the love of his children and worried at the anger displayed by his older boys. *It'll pass*, he thought.

New Year's Eve, 2019, was a good day for Matt. He had never loved Alicia in the past but had grown to admire her over the last year or so as she brought the children to him and reunited the family. Because he was white—representing less than two percent of the prison population—he was held in the hospital ward for his own safety. That, and a sizeable donation to the right people. It allowed him to hear the news and music from the guards. The music transported him to his days as a wild thing wagering all on the spin of a wheel, following his heart when he met Julia and the shock of seeing her again in London and then New York. She drifted in his memory like a silk scarf in the wind. She took form but never in a way that he could hold. When the music started, Alicia faded and all he could see was Julia's smile and graceful movements, with the ruby necklace around her neck.

He imagined where she was, a permanently rising star heading ever skyward. Perhaps still in New York or Paris? She loved art as much as business and wondered if she would find a balance between them.

His mind drifted to his children. To Maritz and the strong man he had become. To Jody, the flighty teenager giggling at boys' attention. Each of them had endured that day differently. Each had to grow up thinking their father did it until they remembered differently. *How is that possible?*

A nightstick on the bars woke him from his reverie.

"Smit, you need to come with me." The guard motioned with his head and Matt turned around and placed his arms behind his back. He was cuffed through the bars and the door was opened. The guard then secured Matt's feet in manacles attached to the handcuffs.

"Is there a problem?"

"The warden wants to see you."

The guard walked and Matt shuffled without speaking on the painted concrete floor. The optimistic music faded as they turned a corner and went through the endless doors and gates before they arrived at the warden's office. The door was open and Matt was ushered in. The guard closed the door behind him.

"Smit, I have some news that I thought would be best coming from me."

"Sir?"

"I'm going to tell you something and I need to know that you'll be okay."

"How can I do that until you tell me?"

"I'm just telling you that if you lose control, I'll have no choice but to put you in solitary until you calm down."

The warden's gravity began to dampen Matt's mood. *What can be so terrible?* To the warden he said, "Understood, sir."

The warden poured himself a glass of whiskey and didn't offer Matt any. He walked the length of the room and looked out the window. After a moment, he returned to the whiskey and poured one for Matt.

"Will you behave if I have your cuffs moved to the front? I have no intention of feeding you this like a baby."

Matt nodded. The warden nodded in turn to the guard who unlocked one cuff and allowed Matt to bring his hands in front of him. He then secured the cuffs again.

Matt accepted the drink warily and drank it in one shot. It was good. He hadn't had anything approaching this for longer than he could remember. He felt it warm him as he emptied the glass.

"Another?" The warden began filling the glass before the answer came. He filled the glass half full, emptying whatever was left in the bottle.

"Thank you, sir."

The warden was silent, watching Matt try to drink the whole amount in one go. Some spilled down the front of his chin and dripped to his chest. He watched it being absorbed into Matt's body. He could see his eyes change. He knew the alcohol would be effective on the prisoner after not having drunk anything in years. He prayed he had done enough. He remained silent for a long while.

"Smit, I just received news that your children have been killed. It's bad. Probably the worst most of the police have seen, apart from your murders."

The words were hazy as Matt's body became numb as the alcohol fought against the adrenaline and whatever else coursed through his veins. His mouth became dry and he felt his legs weaken. He decided to sit on the ground before he passed out.

"...like I said, they'll be doing a full investigation. Are you listening to me? They need your help to find who did this."

"How were they killed?"

"Weren't you listening? Just like you did to your mother, only worse. I don't know who you pissed off, but you can be sure they are some mean motherfuckers."

Maish, thought Matt. *Why? Why now?* "My wife?" He managed to ask.

"She's fine, but hospitalised. In stable condition. Shock."

"Can I see her?"

"I'm not sure if that's such a good idea."

"Goddamn it! I just lost every reason to live. Let me see her!" His rage was checked by the chains he wore. The warden didn't flinch. He was expecting worse.

"I'll do everything I can. As soon as she can come here, I'll arrange it. For now, I want you to stay calm. I'll get the doctor to give you something and I'll send down some more whiskey to your cell. Just don't let any of the other bastards know it's from me or I'll stick you in general population."

"Your secret is safe with me, sir." His head was spinning and he didn't have the ability to fight or argue with the warden. He needed to get out and be on his own. Anything the warden did to help him would be welcome. *He may be a tough sonofabitch, but that's one hell of a nice thing to do*, he thought. For a second he forgot about the deaths of his children and then felt even more guilty for his lapse of grief.

When his head hit his cot, he hoped it was all just some sick mind game being played by the warden, but news leaked out and he heard confirmation on the radio. Even the guards looked sympathetic. *They may be bastards*, he thought, *but even they understood the loss of five children.*

When Alicia arrived, she looked broken. She couldn't stand up. Her skin was sickly white, hair uncombed, and clothes hung loosely on her frame. As she sat at the cubicle opposite Matt, she wept. It took several minutes before she reached out and grabbed the telephone that connected them.

"They're all dead," she sobbed. Her head was down, almost touching the table where her elbows belonged. Matt could see grey roots at the top of her head where the hair parted to show some scalp. Even the hair that was there looked thinner, as though her body didn't have the strength to hold onto it.

"I heard," he whispered, tears flowing but still able to speak. "What happened?"

"Maritz. He wanted to avenge you and the family."

Matt let out a low groan. He shook his head, willing the words not to be true. "Why?"

"He remembered everything. He didn't say anything at first but started talking to the psychiatrist. That got him talking to William. The two of them remembered and compared what they knew. They had been planning something the moment they first came here to see you."

"What did they do?" He could barely ask the question. He had wanted to serve his time quietly knowing that everything was over. Now, all his sacrifice was wasted.

"They took the rifle, the one you keep in our room, and went to Maish's place. They waited outside the door and shot him when he came out. Unfortunately, they didn't kill him. Maish recovered and last week meted out his own revenge."

"How did it happen?"

She went quiet and swallowed back uncried tears. "I received five travelling trunks. In each trunk, there were three boxes. One contained the skin." She closed her mouth, trying to hold back vomit before continuing. "The other contained the bones. The third was the muscle and organs." She couldn't contain the sob that followed as the image returned to her mind.

Matt sat back and began to grieve. The phone fell from his hand, swinging from the cord where it met the table. His body became cold and shivered, and his eyes closed. Tears flowed as his body swayed. He didn't make a sound.

Alicia quietly watched him as she returned the phone to its cradle and left. She never saw him again. As she walked out of the prison, she waited for an oncoming gravel truck to pass. At the last second, she walked briskly in front of it. Her last conscious moment included the warmth of the sun on her face and the knowledge that the pain would end.

Every Beginning Has an End

On Wednesday, 13 August, 2036, Matt was released from prison. He never appealed his sentence after the death of his children, even after receiving numerous offers from King's Council barristers. He lost most of the extra weight he carried and appeared as a skeleton beneath his clothes. He walked with no purpose from the prison gates and entered the limousine where his solicitor was waiting for him.

"I'm glad to see you made it." His lawyer was dressed in the latest London fashion, a three-piece suit with tie and pin. He looked as though he hadn't a care in the world, his teeth gleamed and grey hair sat perfectly in place.

"Hi Percy."

"Don't be so glum, chum. You're out. Let's get you dressed in something better than that and have a good time. When's the last time you've been with a woman?"

"You mean ones who don't piss standing up?"

"Funny, yeah. I'm getting you cleaned up, suited and booted, and into the clubs. We are having some fun tonight!"

"I don't think I'm up for it."

"Look, we've been friends since we were knee-highs. You need someone to shake you up and get the blood flowing."

"Really, I'm not up for anything."

"Nothing? Okay, we'll sit tight and grab some cigars and go to Sun City. That always cheered you up."

Thinking about it caused Matt to feel a pain he hadn't thought about for a long time. That was where he met Julia. That was where he made that damn money. That was the cause of the gamble that got his family killed. "Not Sun City. I think I'd like to get out of South Africa for a while."

"Perfect. Where do you want to go?"

"Paris? New York? I don't know. Whatever I do, I need a passport."

"I'm getting that sorted. In the interim, stop being such a stick in the mud and let's meet some friends. We'll wipe that frown off your face. I've got someone in particular I want you to meet." He arched his eye. "You'll really like her."

Matt resigned himself to Percy's will and sat back in the leather seat. It was more luxurious than anything he' known for twenty-eight years. He closed his eyes and let the rest of the day wash over him.

∞

Six weeks later, he was well fed, well-friended, and ready to restart his life.

"You have all of the proceeds from you mother's and your wife's estates," Percy said. He couldn't help but repeat himself. He did it because he didn't think Matt was listening. "You have enough to live comfortably ever after. As your lawyer and friend, I am recommending you do just that."

"I think I'd like to be somewhere warmer than this. It's almost the end of September and winter isn't giving up. How about the US?" Matt was trying to be flippant but he knew exactly where he was heading.

"Anywhere that makes you happy, mate." He took another drink of his coffee before adding, "But I can't join you straight away."

"That's not a problem. I'm a big boy."

"You haven't been in circulation for a long time. You need a chaperone." He was smiling, partly in jest and partly because it was true.

"I'll keep you on speed dial. I've looked into flights and I can catch the red eye to New York on Saturday. I'll catch up with some of my old friends there."

"If they're still alive."

"Speaking of old friends, have you seen Maish lately?" Matt said it as calmly as possible. He had never spoken of it to anyone and, from what he could tell, no one knew what happened that day. *I need to visit that sonofabitch and settle an account with him for old time's sake,* he thought. *And I won't miss like my son did.*

"Maish? Haven't you heard? He died a couple of months ago, just before you got out. I think it was in his sleep, thankfully. I heard he had a couple of tarts with him but that never hit the news. You know how it is. Gotta keep up appearances. Is everything okay, Matt? What's wrong?"

The colour drained from his face. *I suffered like a tormented demon for the better part of three decades while he pegs out with prostitutes?* The idea of blowing his head off in revenge was the only thing keeping him alive since he heard the news of his children. He forced himself to eat the garbage the prison fed him instead of slashing his wrists. "I'm fine. Sorry, it's just a shock."

"I didn't know you two were so close. I know he was your wife's uncle and all, but he was a tough man to get to know."

"We were very close," Matt managed to whisper. "I just wanted to see him one last time."

"I understand. It's hard. You've been away so long, many of the old crowd are gone. The five families have now been reduced to three with Tony's son at the top. Who would've thought? He was such a dopey kid."

Matt began to piece together his life without the purpose that kept him going so long. "I need to get going. Sorry, I don't mean to be rude."

"No problem. Just remember I'm here for you." He got up and gave Matt a hug. It looked like he needed one.

∞

New York's JFK airport was like a fortress. Since the June Terror of '25, security had become almost unbearable. Matt didn't mind and allowed himself to be patted, scanned, interviewed, and released into the Big Apple. He went immediately to his old firm, only to find out it no longer existed. He tried to find JW but heard he was in China on business indefinitely. He tried to find Julia but no one remembered her or knew her whereabouts. Walking aimlessly in Central Park, he grabbed a hotdog and coffee and sat on the bench. People passed him without any thought of who he was or what he may have done. They barely gave him a second glance. Dog walkers, joggers, and cyclists passed in an endless parade of humanity. It inspired him that the future could be bright and depressed him that he had become so anonymous and irrelevant in the world. Even his enemies didn't care if he was alive or dead.

"Head's up!" He heard the voice just before a paper magazine hit him in the chest. He saw the kid who threw it shrug an apology before he disappeared around the corner. Matt looked at the garbage bin that was the target of the cyclist. Picking up the magazine, he caught a glimpse of an advertisement for Las Vegas.

"Maybe Fate is trying to tell me something," he said aloud. He smiled at the thought and threw it in the garbage. He finished his hot dog and sat watching the people go past.

A thought tickled at the back of his head as the hours wore on. It grew into an idea. He got up and hailed a taxi. After a short stop at his hotel, he was on his way to the airport. Next stop, Vegas. He had trusted his fate to luck before, and he would do it again.

The hot air hit him in the face like an old friend. It was less than a week since he left South Africa and he welcomed the intensity of the desert heat. It was a brief reunion as he sat inside the air conditioned Mercedes that took him from the airport to the Venetian resort and casino where he was staying.

The experience left him speechless. Prior to this, Sun City was the best he had experienced. He had been to Macau and even Vegas before but it never hit him like it did now.

"First time in Vegas, sir?" The concierge was trying to establish eye contact.

"Uh, no. It's just been a long time. I can't get over how clean and golden everything is."

"We try, sir. I have your key cards ready and Emmanuel will help you with your things. Please ask for me if you have any questions or need anything during your stay with us."

"I'm sure everything will be perfect." He meant it. It was a world he had forgotten about. A world of danger and chance where the spin of a wheel could change a life—for richer or poorer. "Which way to the tables?"

"This way, sir. Follow me." The young woman was no more than twenty-five years old and her uniform was tight in all the right places. Matt forgot to be unhappy as he followed her into the casino. "Just over here. The tables are to your left, slots in front, and the wheels over there." She smiled and walked away. *Have I become invisible?* He looked at himself in the mirror. *I'm not bad looking,* he thought. *But I'm old and irrelevant.*

He brushed off the doubt and walked to the cashier. "How do I buy chips?"

"Cash or credit card, sir."

"Do you accept American Express?"

"How much do you want?"

Matt thought carefully. "One hundred thousand please."

The woman on the other side of the bars looked up slowly. She was used to large numbers but also knew who demanded them. "I don't know you, sir. House rules demand amounts over fifty thousand to be approved by the pit boss."

"House rules? Since when?"

She shrugged. "Above my pay grade."

Matt looked around and found someone who looked like he was important. It wasn't the pit boss but he was directed to the man.

"Sure thing. Just regulations. Sorry about the hassle. What's your name? Smit? Where you from? South Africa is great. Been there with my family last year. Love Table Mountain in Cape Town. Family loved the… oh, yeah. No problem. Here we are. Mary? You have my approval to advance as much as Mr. Smit's card allows. No problem. Ok, that's signed. Mr. Smit, good to have met you and enjoy your time. If there is anything you need, you just ask me. I'll find one of our hostesses and ask her to watch out for you."

Matt barely had time to talk. The man had taken him from where he was found to the cashier, approved everything, and disappeared before he could do more than utter 'thanks'. *Things run differently here than Sun City*, he thought.

"I'll carry your chips for you, sir." A young man appeared behind him. Possibly Mexican-American, he was smiling and holding out his hand. He was immaculately dressed with polished shoes and perfect hair.

"Thank you, my friend. I want to look around first if that's okay? I want to get a feeling for the joint."

"No problem, sir. I'll be right behind you."

Matt walked past the slots. *Suckers*, he thought. But he knew he had been lucky on those in the past. *Maybe I'll try them later*. He walked past the craps and blackjack tables and found what he was looking for.

"Thank you. I think I'll try this table." The young man nodded and placed the box of chips on the table and left. Within a few moments, a young woman in her early thirties arrived and asked Matt if he wanted a drink. "Coke please, lots of ice." She disappeared to get it.

There were four other players on the table and Matt decided to watch for a while. The croupier noticed the stack of chips and nodded at its owner. The other players recognised his presence with a sidelong glance but little else. He settled into his chair and began removing his chips from his plastic box. He lined up the thousand dollar chips into five stacks of ten and the remaining ten thousand dollar chips in one stack. He put them all close to the table's edge immediately in front of him.

The croupier was around fifty years old. She looked like she could have been Mexican or Aboriginal or Spanish. Her hair would have been raven-black when she was young. It wasn't as polished anymore but still healthy. It was cut short, just above the shoulders, but held itself in a shape that indicated a lot of attention by its master. Her face was wide with quick eyes and red lipstick. He noticed her smile because of her lips. *A kind face*, he thought. *Not a mean croupier. I think I'll give it a try.*

Matt rearranged his blazer he had worn since New York and began to think he should have freshened up before coming to the floor. He put his hands around the ten thousand dollar chips, feeling the toothed edges, when he froze. His thought he saw someone, but he couldn't be sure. They had disappeared. He sat back in his chair and watched the wheel go around.

The croupier was smiling sympathetically as she took the bets off the table. No winners. Two players left and a Chinese man joined the table. He sat next to Matt. They didn't speak but nodded at each other. When the man and the other players placed their bets, the croupier spun the wheel. Matt pushed ten thousand dollars on his usual numbers, twenty-nine and the neighbours. The croupier shot him a sharp look but didn't stop the bet. The man next to him turned and smiled in appreciation and then returned his gaze on the wheel.

"Twenty-eight. We have a winner." She placed her crystal marker on the number and removed the other chips. She had to place the marker on top of Matt's chips, as was customary. She counted out his winnings and smiled.

People walking past noticed the win and gathered to watch what happened next. Matt took all his winnings and placed them back on the same numbers. He hadn't touched the pile of chips next to him and worked with only the winning chips. The others on the table chose other numbers. The wheel was spun and landed on his numbers again. He didn't cheer or make any noise. He just drank his Coke and watched the chips increase in front of him. The croupier exchanged his lower value chips for ones more suitable for his gambling style.

More people gathered as the he put all his winnings on the same numbers. When the croupier spun the wheel, he took all of the chips next to the wall and put them on eleven and its neighbours.

"Ten. We have a winner." She gave Matt a curious look and the pit boss appeared next to her. He had a word with her and she was replaced after she paid out the winnings.

"I'm out," Matt said. "For you," he flung a chip at the woman. The young man appeared and escorted his chips to the cashier.

"Congratulations, Mr. Smit. You have had quite a day." The same pit boss from earlier came over to talk to him as he walked.

"Just luck. Some days are better than others."

"Can we convince you to stay a bit longer?"

"I saw someone I need to find. I'll be back later."

"Of course. Thank you, sir." The man looked like he had swallowed a wasp but was determined to maintain his composure. He disappeared and Matt handed the chips to the cashier.

"I'd like to hold this to my credit, if you don't mind? I'll be back." He smiled and tipped the young man a thousand dollar chip and then went to his room.

The Venetian has every extravagance a gambler and his family could want, he thought. I used to go to Sun City to get away from the family. Over here, they expect you to bring them with you. The thought clouded his win and he looked for a way to distract himself. He saw a sign for an exhibition on post-modern impressionist art and decided to try it out.

He covered the distance from the casino to the gallery with urgency in his step. The endless hallways were in gold with polished marbled floors inlaid with more marble to create a dizzying array of designs that was as garish as it was exquisite. *Too much*, he thought. *But what would be right?* In the end, he accepted his surroundings and eventually found the entrance to the exhibit. It required him to go through a security screening of the same calibre as the airport. *Things have really changed,* he thought.

He enjoyed the finer things in life and enjoyed the opulence of his surroundings. The paintings seemed to be the perfect touch—having museum quality art in a hotel.

"Are you looking for anything in particular?" He couldn't identify the speaker.

"Excuse me?" He turned around and saw nothing.

"Down here."

"Ah, sorry. I was in my own world." The voice belonged to a dwarf in a tuxedo. Matt tried to hide his embarrassment at overlooking him. "How can they have an exhibition like this in a casino? It belongs in the Guggenheim."

"It's here for the wedding."

"Sorry?" Matt began to sense this was not an ordinary exhibition.

"Mr. and Mrs. Großfreund."

"Never heard of them."

The dwarf seemed thunderstruck. "I'm sorry to sound rude, but what planet are you from? Mr. Großfreund is one of the richest men in the world and he owns most of the Venetian."

"You mean this exhibit is part of his wedding?"

"Yes, sir. And it really is sensational. It includes his own private collection but most of it is on loan from the Guggenheim itself. I understand he is a big donor there as well."

And you talk too much, Matt thought. "Where is the lucky couple?"

"They're around somewhere. I just saw them a moment ago. There they are. He's the tall one and she's the one with the stunning ruby necklace."

Chapter Sixteen

Julia's Story

Freedom is doing what I want, when I want, and with whom I want. And how I want, she added coyly to her diary. She sat in her parents' home with a diary on her lap. *What am I? Fifteen years old? My name isn't Bridget,* she thought and then laughed out loud. Her room was exactly as she left it when she went to Oxford. She visited often but it remained as a shrine so that her parents could remember her as they wanted to, frozen in a moment of pink flowers and big dreams. She put down her diary and moved to her computer.

She opened Google and tried their new maps function. Her objective was not to run, but to decide what she really wanted. Faced with that decision, she realised she didn't actually know.

"What are you looking at? Is it okay for me to come in?" Her mother peeked her head around the door jam, enjoying every moment of Julia's time at home. No mention was made of Daniel or her job or anything that would make Julia uncomfortable.

"Just surfing the net, trying to see what I should do next."

"What about going back to school? You were so good at it. Get another degree, become a professor or do something academic."

"I am attracted to that but I want more from life."

"More money?"

"No, but also a bit yes."

"A baby?" Her eyes shone when she thought of a grandchild.

"Oh, no. Never."

"It's not that bad, you know."

"For me, it is. I'm not ready."

"Then what about travel? Take some time off. You haven't had a vacation since your gap year."

"I'd like that. But where?"

"What do you want to do? Sunbathe or explore?"

"Nothing. I actually don't want an agenda or destination."

"Then you may as well step outside your front door and start walking. It's as good a place as any other." Her mother was speaking facetiously but meant every word.

"Profound. I'm thinking of changing my life's direction."

"Your father and I enjoyed travelling Europe when we were younger. Museums, cafés, and meeting other young people made us feel alive."

"I'm not eighteen anymore." She closed her laptop and swung her legs off her bed. "I'm thirty-one years old. I should be inventing things, writing books, making a difference."

Her mother smiled and sat down next to her. "Try making yourself happy first. The other things will follow." She put her hand on her daughter's shoulder. "Are you okay?"

Julia had realised the fundamental truth of her situation. *I'm not happy*, she thought. Images of the three men who affected her most flashed through her mind. *Matt should have been the one*, she fumed. *Daniel could have been the one. And JW was the one I wanted.* She felt a bolt of electricity as she said the words to herself. Before now, these were images and thoughts she was afraid to articulate. Now, sitting in her old room, contemplating divorce and resetting her life, she realised her underlying emotions. "I think everything has happened too easily for me," she said to her mother.

"It is the curse of all beautiful women," her mother replied, kissing Julia's head. "Embrace it and make it work for you. We are dealt our cards from a stacked deck. Men control the world, but we can control them."

"You're the best mom in the world, you know?" She hugged her mother but didn't agree with her message at all. *I don't want to define myself as the wife or partner of a man, controlling him or otherwise. I need my own identity if I am going to be happy.* It wasn't a conversation she wanted to have with her mother. She needed to figure it out for herself first.

"I just want you to be happy. Everything else comes second."

"I wish I had your clarity."

"It comes with having children."

"I'm not having children."

Her mother shrugged and patted Julia on her leg as she got up. "Can't fault a mother for trying. Whatever you decide to do, your father and I are a hundred percent behind you."

"Thanks, Mom." Everything was making Julia cry lately. She wiped a tear from her eye and smiled back.

Lacking any better plan, she pointed her parent's spare car towards France and started driving. She left the day after her conversation with her mother, deciding to take the car across the channel and then follow her nose. She marvelled at the simplicity of driving her car onto a train in Folkestone and waiting during the half hour crossing. When she drove out of the train carriage, she was in France. The rest was simply following the navigation system on the car's dashboard and paying tolls. The roads were better than England's and she enjoyed the food in the rest stops. Her language was rusty but she didn't have plans to discuss the meaning of life anyway. She was passing through, planning to try the wine and cheese along the way. When she was tired of a place, she would get in the car and drive until she found something more interesting. She saw her exit and flicked the lever on the side of the steering column without thinking. It took just over twelve hours of driving from her parents to Bordeaux.

At first, the signs for Paris excited her, but the thought of a big city drained her energy. She was alone and didn't want to be reminded of her time together with Daniel in the city of lights. She loved their walks along the Champs-Élysées, her hand in his, being part of the crowds, doing nothing but living in the moment. It hurt her to think of those times. They were perfect in a perfect setting. She didn't want to relive that or change it. She wanted something new.

She had read about Bordeaux and booked a room online in a central hotel. By the time she reached it, her eyes felt like stones and her body ached. The suburbs of Bordeaux looked like slums compared to the pictures she had seen online. Perhaps it was exhaustion from the drive or disappointment in her own expectations but she began to swear at herself and the shitty city planners who allowed such utilitarian dwellings to tarnish such a gem of a city. When she reached the core, she wasn't disappointed. *It's like a miniature Paris*, she thought with a smile. The architecture, grand sweeping road system, and waterway captured how her imagination envisioned it. The navigation system delivered her to her hotel and she was able to find parking on the street until the morning. The attendant warned her that she needed to move her car in the morning or else she would get a ticket.

"Is there a parking lot nearby?"

"Of course." He drew a map on some spare paper and gave it to her.

"Thanks. I don't want to worry about things like parking. I don't want to get into my car again until I am ready to leave."

"I am sure you will enjoy your stay. If there is anything we can do to make it more enjoyable, please let us know. The gym is always open; just use the key card. The pool is open from six in the morning to ten at night. The concierge can arrange any tickets you need or information required."

"I'm sure it will be magical. Can you take my things to my room while I park my car?"

"Of course."

The sun had gone down and the lights were out in full force. People walked slowly along the cobbled walkways and pedestrian roads, many hand in hand. The carpark was newly painted and the tires made an embarrassing amount of noise as she turned and twisted her way downwards until she found an available spot. Driving with a right-hand drive car didn't seem to make a difference and very few people took a second look.

When she returned to her room, the bed's duvet and pillows were bursting with feathers and she sunk into them with a sigh she had been holding in for twelve years. Some thoughts flittered through her mind but were blanketed with a deep sleep. Only her shoes were off.

∞

There are two things a red-blooded Frenchman finds irresistible. First, it is a woman sitting alone at a table drinking wine. Second, it is the same woman saying no to their advances. Combined, the woman finds herself a magnet to all self-respecting men who are determined to uphold the stereotype of the French lover. To Julia, her rediscovered desirability was both flattering and exhausting. It was healthy to feel wanted but it bordered on harassment after the first week. She decided to do something about it.

Her solution was a women she met while eating breakfast. They shared the only remaining English newspaper before joining each other for coffee. By the time their breakfast was finished, Julia realised her solution was sitting in front of her.

"What are your plans for today?"

"Nothing much. I am meeting with some vintners around eleven but then playing things by ear."

"Mind if I join you?"

"It'll be boring. Business stuff."

Realising she was crossing a line, Julia decided to tell Adele her reasoning. "I understand. I must be sounding a bit crazy, but I have been here a week and I am finding myself the recipient of a lot of unwanted attention."

"Ahh," she said, sitting back with a smile. "Understood. You are looking for a shield."

"Two women may get a comment, but men will leave them alone. A single woman seems to mean an invitation to sit down and chat them up."

"Okay. I could use the company as well. I don't have the same problem as you," she said as she raised her eyebrows and looked Julia up and down with a knowing nod, "but it can't hurt to try it and see."

"Excellent. Then it's a plan." Not having any direction, every opportunity became an adventure.

"I've got some errands to attend to but if you want to meet here around half ten we can go together to my meetings. The harvest is soon and they want to presell their wine. It's the best time to be in Bordeaux." She got up, tucked her handbag under her arm, and drifted out of the room.

Classy, she thought. *This could be fun.* She checked her watch. Two hours until she needed to meet up. She got up and decided to take a walk along the streets. Every street had its own character jumbled up in eighteenth century grandeur. Thanks to a concerted effort, UNESCO designated central Bordeaux a world heritage site. The city resonated with Julia and she felt drawn to walk the ancient streets, mindful not to be longer than two hours. She decided to walk around the nearest large city blocks.

In front of the hotel balanced a statue of a narrow face, layered to give different personalities from different perspectives. She revolved around it as a moon does a planet. She lost herself in the pride of construction and the dirt on the windows of unoccupied spaces. Her concentric circles took her further from the hotel, further from the two blocks she limited herself to until she was walking along the waterfront.

"The water is deep enough for cruise ships to dock," said a voice from behind her. She startled and turned around.

"Excuse me?"

"The water we are walking along. Historically, the Danish and English ships were filled with casks of wine but now cruise ships come. Despite English embargoes and wartime rhetoric, wine from the region always found its way to the English great houses."

"I'm sorry. I don't want to disturb your walk. I was reading the history on the phone," Julia said.

"No problem. I am a guide. I can show you."

"I really can't. I need to get back to my friend shortly."

"Then let me talk while you walk. I can walk next to you and you can listen if you want."

She smiled. He was young, around twenty-one, tall, and good looking. He had friendly eyes and his hair was slightly messy. "It's a free country, I think. I can't stop you."

He smiled and walked next to her. "The name Bordeaux was derived from the simplicity of its location— literally along the water. The original French was *au bord de l'eau*." He shrugged.

They walked in silence for a moment and she noticed four other young men approach them from the other direction. They waved at her and the man beside her waved back. They decided to join their friend and all six of them walked along the waterway. Julia noticed that the shops hadn't opened yet.

"Sorry, I didn't catch your name," she said to her tour guide.

"Marcel."

"I'm Julia. Nice to meet you. I need to go now but hopefully we are able to meet up again." She smiled and turned to go.

The other young men stood in her way. When she turned to go through a gap, they moved and blocked her again. Marcel said nothing. He was staring at her hungrily.

"Come on, guys, that's enough. I get the joke, very funny, but I would like to go."

One of the bigger men put his hand on her arm. She pulled away. She lunged backwards only to find herself in the arms of Marcel, who held her gently but firmly. She tried to break lose but his grip was firm. She kicked with her leg but that only got some laughs. They grabbed her legs and took her away from the main walkway, behind one of the merchant buildings.

"You American?"

"No, she's British."

"That'll do."

They had switched to French, but the sentences were short and easy for her to understand. She knew what they wanted and she couldn't fight five young men. She felt Marcel hold her arms. Her torso twisted wildly, legs kicking at anything they could connect with. Two men grabbed her legs. She writhed and began screaming. One of the men put his hand over her mouth. She bit him hard. *You bastards may take me but not without a fight*, she thought. She refused to say anything, jaw set shut as she breathed heavily through her nose.

She heard the ripping of fabric as they tore the shirt off her back, exposing her nakedness. She felt their hands grabbing at her, squeezing so hard it brought tears to her eyes. She felt them pull at her jeans. They were tight and they needed to unbutton them first. Their hands were rough and their breath still stank of a night of heavy drinking. Her eyes were closed by now, wishing for anything, praying for something to stop what seemed inevitable. She felt the top button separate, then the zipper, then the jeans against her flesh as they were pulled off. There was a jumble of voices, each wanting to be the first. She felt Marcel letting go of her arms, only to be replaced by another. He stood in front of her and prepared himself. She went limp and wished she was dead.

As she waited, the microseconds extended forever. *What are they waiting for?* Her mind could see herself from above with the hyenas surrounding her, waiting to devour their prey. She held her eyes shut and prayed to God to help her. *If you exist, please help me. Please. Make them stop and I'll be your servant. Do this for me and I'll be yours. Help me. Please.* The tears flowed down her cheeks and she began to sob, as much in shame for praying as what was about to happen. All her mind could repeat was *I'm sorry. I'm sorry. Please help me. Help. Please.* Time had stopped and she separated from her body, the pain no longer in her arms or the bruises that would surely appear on her legs. She didn't want to think what diseases these swine carried with them. She resigned herself to what was about to happen and then let go.

At that moment, her arms were released. She didn't move for fear of what might happen. Her legs were also released and she lay still, terrified of what they were planning. When a cool hand touched her face, she opened her eyes and saw Adele. She took off her jacket and placed it over Julia's naked body. There was a man there as well, with something in his hand. A crowbar or hammer, she couldn't tell. The man turned away to give her privacy. She felt Adele take her in her arms as she curled into the smallest ball she could. She began to cry. The tears were blinding and Adele let them come, making soothing sounds while rubbing her back.

When the crying finally stopped, Julia wiped her eyes and nodded to Adele.

"I'm okay. Thanks."

"You don't look okay."

"Where did you come from? What happened?"

"You never showed and I had an appointment with a wine merchant close to here. I saw you engulfed by those men but I was too far away. I ran as soon as I saw what they were about to do to you and began yelling. One of the men working on the quay saw me and came running."

Julia's tears returned.

"I pointed to the men and you and he hit the man who looked like the leader just before… just in time. The others fled. He'll testify to the police. He knows two of the boys' families. They won't be doing this to anyone else."

Julia tried to speak but it was too hard. Snot flowed as fast as tears as she gulped for air. When she was finally able to speak, she wiped her nose and eyes with Adele's jacket and looked at her squarely in the face. "You are the angel I was praying for. I was so scared, I'd never felt anything like it before. And I prayed to God to help me."

"Shhh. I'm just glad I was around."

"No, you are proof. I demanded proof and one was provided." Her eyes sparkled with tears and realisation, then she crumpled again. "I'm so ashamed."

"You have nothing to be ashamed about. Let's get you back to the hotel. Everything'll be alright." Then, gently, like a parent dressing their new born, Adele helped Julia back into her jeans and jacket. They stood up and hugged and wept.

Chapter Seventeen

Nineteen Years Later

"I have seen enough of life to know I have everything I could ever need right here."

"But don't you tire of the poverty and the disease? Surely you'd be happy back home."

"Mom, this is my home now. You should come and see it. It is wonderful and safe." Julia had tried to convince her parents to join her in India but their fear of the unknown was too great.

"I haven't seen you for over a year and I miss you." Her mother knew how to pour on the guilt.

"We can talk via our phones or the computer. It's almost like we're in the same room."

"But I can't hug a computer or give my daughter a cup of tea through a monitor."

Julia sighed. "I can't fly to see you even if I wanted to. Ever since the June Terror, flights have been extremely restricted, especially in this neck of the woods.

Only government business or very connected people can fly right now. Unless I buy or charter a plane, I couldn't get to you if I wanted."

"Then how do you expect us to visit you?"

"I would charter a plane for you." *Damn her logic*, Julia thought. Then she added, "It's too expensive from here."

"It sounds like you're making excuses." The voice carried an edge. "Just tell me the truth: You can't be bothered to visit your parents."

"I'll come but I can't just now. I'll check into the flights and see what I can do. I have responsibilities here."

"That's why you have people helping you. You're not running the ashram yourself, are you?"

"No, but I started it to help people, especially myself. I want others to share in the peace I have found. Since last year, we have had more heads of companies join than ever before."

"Midlife crisis. They're reassessing why they didn't die, that's all."

"Mother, you know it's serious. And I'm middle-aged now."

"Which makes me old and wise. You should listen to me more."

"I did and I do. I followed my heart and soul to set this up. Corporatizing it just made sense. It allowed me to bring in the clients who could pay for it and make it the success it is. It also allowed me to provide a facility that brought in the most enlightened and deserving teachers."

"Aren't they called yogis?"

"We aren't restricted to yoga. We provide an environment for many masters in order that seekers hopefully find something from their journey."

"You mean happy clappy?"

That made Julia laugh. It wasn't meant to be mean. Her mother was sympathetic but wanted her daughter next to her. If that meant denigrating her work, then that was what she would do. "Sometimes. At least they're happy."

"Then why do you need to stick around?"

"They look up to me. I have become something of a spiritual leader myself somehow."

"Okay, enough about this nonsense. I have accepted that you aren't going to give me a grandchild. When are you going to find a man to make you happy?"

This was another subject her mother never relented on. Julia never divorced Daniel and this fact grated on her mother. She didn't need to know about the men in Julia's life but she was right in one respect: she didn't have anyone special. "Since when do I need to have a man to make me happy? I'm content by myself."

"Phfff. Nonsense. If you're going to talk this nonsense, then find another man who is content. Together you can make each other happy. I've never heard such nonsense in my life. Content. So what? You're not unhappy but you're not happy either."

She's got a point, Julia thought. She waited a moment as she inhaled deeply and exhaled slowly. "I will find the right person when I am ready."

"You're fifty years old. When do you expect to be ready? And when are you going to finally get rid of that no good husband of yours? So long as you are bound to him, even if just by a piece of paper, you're not ready to give yourself to another."

"Is this what I should expect when I come home?"

"No," her mother said, smiling. "When you come home, I'll feed you tea and scones and we can walk next to the swans and talk about anything you want. But so long as I have to talk to you through this damn computer," her voice assuming a mock sense of hurt, "I'll do it straight."

"I love you, Mom. I gotta go. Give Dad a kiss for me."

"Love you too, sweetheart. Take care of yourself and call me tomorrow."

Julia ended the call. *I need to meditate after that call*, she thought with a smile. As it happened, she went for breakfast instead.

Over her Vedic breakfast of toasted farina cooked with carrots, peas, and ghee, she closed her eyes and savoured the hints of cumin and ginger. She felt as much as heard someone sit next to her. She felt a warmth of fresh food waft towards her in the disturbed air. She heard the placement of the food on the table. But she felt the entire table shift as something big sat down. The bench was attached to the eating surface, picnic table style, so it was impossible to be fully oblivious to a new person joining. Many ashrams sat and ate on the floor. Julia didn't like it so she introduced tables.

When she opened her eyes, she felt a shock of electricity from a pair of blue eyes staring at her. It was a man with hair so black it shone blue, despite his age. *Hair dye*, she couldn't help but think. The face was square, solid, and serious. He looked comfortable with power and held responsibility easily on his shoulders. He was a big man, at least six foot four, she guessed, but it was difficult to tell sitting down. He was not skinny or fat but seemed just right.

"Hello," she said. "I haven't seen you here before. Have you just arrived?"

"Yes, last night. I hope you don't mind me joining you but I recognised you from your photos. If you don't mind me saying, they don't do you justice."

Julia blushed involuntarily. *You're not fifteen years old. Get a hold of yourself, girl*, she thought. "Are you taking one of our courses?" She decided to ignore the compliment.

"Yes. You're difficult to find and hard to get to, especially after what happened last year. Flying has become more arduous for all but the most determined."

"How long do you plan to stay with us?"

"I'm not entirely certain. I have been looking at places like this but couldn't decide on one. I read the

New Yorker's review on you and decided to come here."

"Hmm. Michael was kind in that article. He stayed for a month."

"I hope to stay for at least three."

"Have you always studied yoga and meditation?"

"Never. Can't even touch my toes."

She laughed. "Don't worry. This heat and diet will get you limbered up. Just don't push things. Everything will come eventually."

"And go."

"Excuse me?"

"And go. Everything will come and go eventually. That's why I'm here, actually. I've reached that time in my life where everything is downhill from here."

Julia tried not to smile. She had been dealing with people going through midlife crises since starting her ashram, but this person looked more like someone taking out insurance. *He is inoculating himself*, she thought. *Very interesting*. "So you want to deal with things before they become a problem, or are you already struggling with something in particular?" It was personal and unlike her to ask, but she found herself wanting to talk to this man. She found herself drawn to him in a way she hadn't felt for a long time. Her mind was a stew of conflicting thoughts.

He smiled and she knew she was in trouble. It was the smile of someone who could see the world as it was and still wake up in the morning with hope. It was the smile of someone she could imagine waking up next to. "No more than anyone else, I guess," he said. "I reached a point in my life where a weekend retreat in the mountains wasn't enough. My day job had taken away all my freedom while I told myself I was doing it to be free. One day I woke up and my status quo wasn't enough. It was shortly after reading about you and your ashram in that article. I knew for me to have more, I needed to make do with less."

Julia felt her insides grow warm as he spoke. She didn't break his stare and her food went uneaten, as did his. "What about your wife or partner? What do they say about your plans?" *Please don't be married and* PLEASE *don't be gay*, she thought. She found herself wanting to touch his hands as he spoke. If it were anyone else, she would have already. It was who she had become. But she hesitated with him. His hands were large and moved like an orchestra of digits. His palm had deep lines but there were no scars. *He deals with paper*, she thought. *He must go to the gym to keep that physique.* She stole glances of his shoulders under his linen shirt. They held in place like mountains overlooking a plain. His torso was broad and erect. Neither his back nor shoulders slumped.

As she measured and appraised him, he was silent. "My wife died last year in the explosions," he said finally. His face lost its confident smile and a grey curtain closed over it. His blue eyes lowered to his food.

"I'm sorry."

"Me too. She was my inspiration and hope. It's been tough."

Shit. How can I compete with a ghost? she thought. *What the hell am I thinking? He's a client, a guest. I can't be thinking like this. And yet I am.* She finally put her hands on his. "Take the time. Meditate and pray and keep in touch. I'm here."

"Thanks." He squeezed her hands and silently ate his breakfast. "By the way, do you ever change the breakfast? Do you think we'll get some bacon and eggs?"

Julia laughed. *He's going to be trouble*, she thought.

The days passed slowly at first and she found herself distracted by his presence. Then her rhythm returned and she found herself resuming her role as the prime mover of her ashram. She wanted the outside world to join her but only on her terms. She charged a lot for her western students; so much so that her local swamis and gurus could stay for free. It was a symbiotic relationship, similar to the corporate philanthropy championed by Gates. Hers was a spiritualism that was not divorced from the corporate realities of the day. Money was required to buy food and pay utility bills. That didn't change. Modern day princes and princesses were required to support the enterprise through their patronage in the form of exorbitant fees. Julia didn't think twice about it as these same people often paid upwards of five thousand dollars per night at a hotel.

Their problem was not money, but time, and her job was to improve the quality of what time they had left.

"I've seen the way everyone looks at you." The man started talking without warning. Julia turned around and smiled at him in his yoga outfit. "Have you taken the name Swami or anything like it?"

She blushed. *Why do I keep blushing around him?* "Not at all. Some people like to take the title and many people call me alternatively Guru or Swami out of respect. But I'm just a person who is trying to do my best in contacting myself and anything else that might be out there."

"Do you believe in all of this stuff?"

"I wouldn't have been doing it for twenty years if I didn't."

"Do you ever see yourself doing anything else?"

"I have stopped planning. It is part of the philosophy that drove me to start this place. It is simple. I try to reduce my wants to less than my needs. The result is contentedness."

"But not happiness."

"Have you been speaking to my mother?" She was smiling broadly, her lips red from healthy living, teeth white and straight from winning the genetic lottery. Her hair was still blonde but grey was beginning to creep in.

"Should I?"

"She'd love you." She regretted saying it as soon as it left her lips. *Flirting. Definitely flirting. Not allowed. Stop it, Julia.*

"Then maybe I will."

Was he flirting back? "My name is Julia," she said, holding her hand out. "But you probably already knew that."

"John." His hand held hers. She could feel the pads of his fingers against her flesh, warm and comforting. He held her hand a moment longer than a handshake required.

"How are you finding it here? Are you able to touch your toes yet?"

"Three weeks and I can now almost touch my toes."

"That will change. Not all people are flexible. It doesn't matter. Just do your best and open yourself to yourself. There are no right answers."

"Except your philosophy," he said. "That sounds pretty right to me."

She blushed again. *How is this possible? I never blush*, she thought. "Let me know how it goes for you. I used to live the corporate life and I loved it. I never saw myself leaving it. But I've never been more content than I've been here."

"What made you take such a radical change of direction?"

Julia paused, thinking of how to respond. "I had a religious experience. I decided to pursue it and here I am."

"Here you are," he repeated. He was looking at her with just a hint of an upturn of the corners of his mouth. "I've got to go to my meditation class. Would you like to have some tea with me some time?"

Her body felt like it was punched with an invisible ball of electricity that filled her from her fingertips to her toes. "Yes, that would be nice. Classes go until nine, as you know, so it would need to be after that."

"Or first thing in the morning."

Her body shuddered with a bolt of adrenaline at the image that accompanied the words. *Or both*, she thought. "See you tonight." She turned to go before she lost her ability to speak. *What's happening to me? You're supposed to be centred and serene and you are falling apart like a schoolgirl*. Then she smiled. *Maybe I wasn't ready to feel like that until now.*

Two weeks later, they moved in together. Three months after that, he proposed.

"Why would you want to marry me?" she asked. "Don't men in your situation want some twenty some-thing?"

"Is that a no?"

"It's a why."

"Because I thought I would never fall in love again. Because you give me hope again. Because I can't see myself living apart from you."

Julia felt her cheeks burning from the blood rushing into them. "Don't you want children?"

"I don't have children now; why would that change?"

"You just met me. You don't know me. I could be a crazy person."

"I love you. I know what I want and I don't want to lose you, crazy or otherwise."

"This is crazy." She found herself fiddling with her hands. *This is the type of thing Matt would have done. What skeletons does John have? Is he married?* Then she remembered. "I'm married already."

John paused, not expecting that. "And you didn't think that was something I should have known?"

"I left him twenty years ago."

"Religious experience?"

"No, him in bed with his agent."

"Ah."

"I never got around to filing the papers and then I ended up here and it just didn't seem to matter."

"Until now."

"Until now." She held his hands and felt his warmth. "Are you angry with me?"

"No, but you haven't answered my question."

Julia leaned forward and kissed him slowly, letting it linger as she moved herself onto his lap. Then she whispered, "Yes" into his ear.

∞

The weather of Surrey was colder than Kerala and she felt the rain cut into her. They had rented a car and she drove, knowing the way. John sat serenely in the passenger seat, looking into the distance. His private plane flew them to Gatwick and he wanted a limousine to deliver them to her parents but she didn't want to overwhelm them. Her parent's home was nestled amidst a tangle of rhododendrons, their blossoms long gone. A little gate glided open when they pressed the buzzer and the home became visible as they made their way up the short curved drive.

"Are you ready for this?" Her face was nervous and excited. She wore a scarf around her neck, which made her look very glamorous in John's eyes.

"Don't you think you should have told them about me first?"

"It would ruin the surprise."

"Some surprises backfire."

"Don't be a sourpuss. Let's go."

They rang the bell, Julia standing directly in front of the door with John behind, a good six inches taller. He put his hand lightly on her waist.

When the door opened, her mother let out the anticipated cry-scream of joy at seeing her little girl. They hugged and cried before John was even noticed.

"Hello, I'm John." He extended his hand to Julia's mother.

"Hello. Nice to meet you. Julia, it's bad enough not telling me you were coming. It's worse manners not telling me you were bringing a friend." She tried to scowl but was too happy. She called into the space behind her. "Rupe, you're never going to guess who's at the door!" She then ushered Julia and John into the house.

Her father came around the corner, slightly stooped and wearing a navy sweater. They hugged with wet eyes before settling into the lounge for tea and biscuits.

"How did you manage to make it here?" Her mother said. "I thought you said there were no flights."

"There weren't. John brought me on his plane." That spoke volumes for her parents. First, he was rich, otherwise how would he have his own plane. Second, he was tall and dark and handsome and was sitting close to their daughter. It could only mean that they were romantically involved. Third, he must be a good man because he brought their daughter home to them.

They chatted for a while, and Julia's parents showed wonderment, respect, and a little fear for the gulf of wealth that separated them. Neither Julia nor her parents were poor but John was rich. Very rich. He knew it and they learned it quickly without him having to say a word. Julia never asked him about his business or wealth other than what pleasantries demanded. She knew he was involved in a hedge fund he started with the help of his father. She knew he grew it into one of the five largest financial management firms in North America. She could do the math but never made much of a comment other than the bare minimum. It is one of the things he loved most about her.

"There is something I wanted to tell you," she said eventually during a lull in the conversation. "John and I are getting married and we would love your blessing."

"Ahh, that's wonderful sweetheart." Her mother got up to give her another hug. Her father stood up and gave a firm handshake to John.

"I know about Daniel," John said. The room fell silent.

"Then you know there is some outstanding paperwork that needs to be done." Rupert didn't say 'divorce' as it wasn't a marriage in his mind.

"I know that she needs to get divorced. None of that matters to me. I wanted to meet you both, get your blessing, and the rest will take care of itself. In the meantime, I get to learn who Julia is. She is the best thing that has ever happened to me."

Julia's mother was crying again and Rupert gave John a hug. It was the only way they could express their blessing.

Chapter Eighteen

Daniel's Story

Deedee was her nickname but the only one he knew. She was Ms. Patel to others. Her parents originally came from India but she was born in New York. Regardless, she suffered in New York after the attacks in 2001 because people thought she was Muslim. She was educated as a solicitor and opened her own real estate agency. Her firm was just her and a handful of like-minded, driven souls who saw opportunity in the commission-rich world of selling property. Her strategy was to focus on high-end properties and ignore the meat-and-potatoes of most agents' world. "If you are going to be an insect, at least fly around a full honey-pot," she would say.

She sold the brownstone to Daniel and Julia Stone in early 2001. Julia was still finishing her studies in London and Daniel had come to New York to find them a new home and explore the idea of building a property portfolio that would support them as a plan B—in the same way he had created a portfolio in London.

They hit it off immediately, but everything was kept professional. It was always easier to work with someone you liked. She had many contacts and he had none. She was selling a product and he was keen to buy. It was a perfect professional match. Within a few years, she had sold twenty three million dollars of property to him by introducing him to financial advisors and taking a commission from them as well. It was only when the market became overheated that she was able to get him the type of funding necessary to build his portfolio into the hundreds of millions of dollars.

The first time she allowed herself to cross that invisible social line was shortly after they signed up on a hundred and seventeen million dollar office building. They got one hundred and five percent funding, which paid for her commission and all the other transaction costs. Daniel got the debt and the building. His strategy was to buy and hold and let the building work its way out of debt over twenty-five years or longer.

"To New York City! Whoohoo!" She raised the open champagne bottle over her head and did a little dance.

"I just called Julia. She can't come. Something at work."

"That's okay. I could party by myself I'm so happy!"

"Let me take you for a nice meal, at least, to say thank you. I could never have done this without you. Your contacts in the property market, banks and everything has made all of this possible."

"True," she was twirling. "That's why you pay me the big bucks."

He watched her metallic black hair straighten as she turned. She wore a form fitting skirt with top that followed her curves and cut a professional figure. She was smart, attractive, and well dressed. Watching her let loose in her professional clothes was strangely unsettling for Daniel. It was like watching your kindergarten teacher get drunk. It didn't sit right in his mind. He took a sip from his drink.

"Come on, dance with me. You deserve it." She had put on a CD of heavy metal ballads. The beat was slow and the vocals sweeping, then grew in intensity as the chorus kicked in. It made him want to bob his head and let go. She grabbed him and handed him the champagne bottle. He took a swig and used it as a microphone as he sang along. She took it from his hands and took another long drink and leaned into him to share the mic with him. They sang as though they were on a stage in front of thousands instead of her office after everyone had gone home. Somewhere between Ozzy Osborne's "Mamma I'm Coming Home" and Scorpion's "Wind of Change", they dropped the bottle and stopped singing. Their fingers entwined and pulled together.

"I'm married. I can't do this," Daniel said.

"It's okay. I don't mind."

"I love my wife."

"Then what are you doing here?"

"I need to go." He pulled away from her but one hand still held her fingers. The music pulsed against his chest.

"I know." She walked a step forward. "You need to go. But you're here right now. And you want to be, don't you?"

Daniel could feel himself gulp. He loved Julia but she was so busy in her life. *Why didn't you just come here tonight? Why are you always at your damned office? This is a big deal and I'm here by myself with a horny agent.* His mind clicked and decided he could do this. *Just this one time. It was a massive deal. It means nothing.*

When he returned home, it was late and he reeked of booze. Deedee had poured a bottle over them in bed. She was wild and fun and reckless. Images replayed in his head.

"You're home! Finally. I was going to send out a rescue team."

"Sorry. I got carried away with the guys. We were celebrating."

"I can see and smell. Throw your clothes straight in the wash. Your suit'll need to go to the dry cleaners. It's full of booze." She started undressing him. "And grab a shower. I want to give you my own congratulations." She kissed him long and slow with no doubt what his reward was going to be. He gulped and went to the shower.

∞

The first time was the most difficult. He was wracked with guilt and his body bristled at attention, listening for any clues that Julia knew. When the first week went by, he realised he got away with it. He still thought nonstop about that evening at Deedee's office. They had met on numerous times since that time as reams of paper still needed to be signed prior to the conveyance of the property. Each time she looked better than the last, making him crazy with desire. She could see that he wanted her and did nothing to force his hand. She didn't flirt or wink or anything other than her job. She knew he was hers, like a fish on a line. She just needed to wait before reeling him in.

Daniel immersed himself in the increased administrative load the new property demanded of him. He had taken space in his new building to expand his own staff he now employed to assist in the daily operations. But his objective was to continue to grow his portfolio and this required viewing properties, and there was no one better than Deedee Patel.

The second time was shortly after hurricane Katrina hit New Orleans. The hundred billion dollar disaster killed thousands and wiped out tens of thousands more.

One person's disaster was another's opportunity. An insurance firm went bust from the claims against it. As part of its liquidation sale, Daniel was able to purchase its Dallas headquarters and New York office building. Julia was travelling on business and Deedee found herself celebrating with Daniel again. After that, it became a regular thing until they were discovered in 2007 by Julia.

"Deedee, Daniel. I just wanted to see how you were after, you know, that."

"More than a little embarrassed."

"She left me."

"Wh--?"

"Julia has left me. I tried to follow her but she's done with me."

"I'm sorry. I never meant for this to happen."

"I'm not. If I was happy, this would never have happened. You know that and I know that. It was just a matter of time. Besides, who screws their mistress in their own home?"

Silence greeted this confession.

"Hello? Deedee?"

"Yes, I'm still here."

"Did you hear me? We can be together without running around. We can be honest about how we feel about each other."

"Look, I've gotta go. I'll call you later."

Daniel's head fell back. He put the phone in his shirt pocket and returned to his computer screen. After ten minutes of staring, he pulled the phone out and called Deedee again.

"Look, whatever is going on at a personal level, we need to look at the options available to us. The stock market is all over the place and I think we should figure a way to ride the wave."

Daniel couldn't see her expression and just heard silence. "Okay, good idea," she said finally. "I'll work something up and we can meet with some of the financial firms. They must be looking to raise cash at fire sale prices."

"Amen. When the streets run red with blood, we need to be there buying." He could see himself reaching a level that was unthinkable a decade ago. He could see himself owning over a billion dollars of property. "This is an opportunity of a lifetime. How often does the market go into the crapper? At least every ten or fifteen years. If this is as big as people are suggesting, this is a once in a generation opportunity. We need to leverage up until we can't breathe."

"And let the magic of amortisation do the rest," she finished. They were in sync when it came to property deals.

"See you tomorrow?"

"Can't wait."

The next day came and went. They met and had sex and talked business, and did it again the next day. They repeated this as often as their schedules allowed.

"Let's move in together." Daniel said, cup mid-way between the table and his lips. He was relaxed, enjoying the day. They had been in contact with AIG and were looking at opportunities they couldn't imagine only twelve months earlier.

She put her cup down slowly. It made a slight clink sound as it settled into its saucer. Her eyes lowered and she brought her hands to her lap. "I don't think that would be a good idea."

"Why not? You're not married. We get along great. It would allow us to see more of each other." He listed the benefits on his fingers as he talked.

"Daniel, I don't want to have this conversation."

"Why?" He was becoming agitated.

"I think we should go home."

"What have I said? I love you and I think we should live together. I thought that's what you wanted."

"I don't think this is working."

Daniel stopped moving, freezing even his ability to blink. His head moved slightly forward and backwards as though it was held by a strong rubber band from the back. Each time he moved, it looked as though he was about to say something. When nothing came out, his head went back, recalculated something inside and then went forward. Nothing came out.

Deedee stood up. "I'm sorry. It was never supposed to be serious. It was fun, you know. I loved it. And you're so cute and loveable. But I'm not looking for that type of relationship." She started to walk away. He reached out and grabbed her wrist.

"Don't leave me."

"I was never with you." His fingers relaxed and she left.

As he watched her walk away, he felt a crumbling in his chest. He began to feel himself swallowing and it hurt. His head was under pressure as he scanned the surrounding tables to see if they were reacting to his devastation. No one took the slightest notice of him. He put his cup down, slipped cash under the saucer, and left.

∞

"I don't know where she is. I haven't seen or heard from her since she left two months ago."

"I know we haven't spent much time together but you and Julia were close. You're probably the only person she really respects. There must be somewhere."

"There's always the tried and true: home. Have you tried her parents?"

"Yeah. They either don't know or aren't telling."

The voice softened. "Listen Dan, I know these things are tough. I'm here if you want to get in touch. My door is always open. But I got to go to a meeting. I'm already late."

"Thanks JW. It means a lot that you took my call." Daniel put the phone down and turned on CNN to watch the latest financial panic unfold. *You need to either buy so much they can't let you fail or sell everything now*, he thought. *This doesn't feel good.* He steeled himself and picked up the phone again. "JW? Yeah, Dan again. Sorry, I know you're on your way out. Any chance of us grabbing lunch sometime this week? Yes? Excellent. See you then."

JW and Daniel met that Thursday at Trinity Place, a fine dining restaurant set in an old vault dating back to 1904.

"This is the coolest place I've ever seen." Daniel couldn't help but gawk at the steel vault door, the copper covered walls, and heavy leather bench seats that lined the inside of the old vault. White tablecloths and fine crystal sat in perfect juxtaposition to the harshness of its surroundings.

"It is one of my favourite places."

The waitress came over and sat them, got their first drinks, and took their order.

"So you wanted to talk?" JW unbuttoned his jacket but left his vest together. He was always immaculately dressed in tailored suits. "How can I help?"

"I've heard about the funds you deal with and was wondering if I could dump my property portfolio into one of them." He had heard that Wall Street financiers didn't like small talk so he jumped right in.

"Our firm has dealt with a lot of these things, but the market is unsettled. I don't know if it still has the appetite for this."

"I'm no expert, not like you, but I thought that AIG provided insurance for these portfolios, making them investment quality. If AIG provided the wrap, we could sell them to anyone."

"If investors were buying. Last year, I would have broken your hand off. Today, I'm not so sure."

Daniel wasn't certain if this was posturing or the truth. It made him nervous nonetheless. "Would you be willing to take a look?"

"Our minimum tranche size is fifty million but, in reality, we like to be working with larger numbers. At least one hundred fifty plus."

"I've got just over a billion in assets with just shy of a billion in debt. I'd be prepared to put the whole shooting match into a wrapped fund. I'd like to cash out."

JW sat up a bit taller. The deal size was right, his firm's commission would be healthy, and he would be helping his protégé indirectly. "I'll take a look at it. If it is a fit, we'll do it. I can't guarantee anything and you'll need to take a haircut on your side."

"How much?"

"To make it attractive, we'll shave ten percent from the gross value. Investment funds will feel they are getting it cheap and snap it up. Do you have more than ten percent equity to give away?"

Daniel took a sip of his drink that arrived silently while they talked. "Not much more, but I'm looking to cash out in a timely manner. If you are saying this is the price for me to exit, then that's what it is. Julia trusted you. I trust you." *I'll be left with less than twenty million after all the effort and risk,* he thought. *But quitting while you are ahead is not the same as quitting.*

JW was putting his drink down as the food came. They both sat back and adjusted their napkins on their laps and waited for the waitress to go. "Send over the details and I'll have a look. I'll be able to give you an answer within a couple of days. If everything is a go, we should be able to turn this around in three months."

Daniel reached across the table and put his hand out. JW shook it and they shifted their minds and conversation away from business. The subject neither of them touched was the one both of them thought about the most. Where was Julia?

∞

Why do you care where she is? Good riddance. Find some nice girl and start living your life. Forget about the past and look to the future. The words scrolled through his mind.

"Hello, Daniel. It's been so long." Julia's mother didn't register surprise or anger at his unannounced presence.

"Nice to see you after such a long time, Penny." He leaned in and gave her two kisses, one on each cheek.

"She's not here."

"I figured that. I just wanted to see if you knew where she was." He stood on the threshold, trying not to look as foolish as he felt. Noticing this, Penny opened the door and ushered him into the lounge.

"Settle in and I'll make us some tea. Rupert isn't here so you'll have to make do with me, I'm afraid." Daniel didn't answer and she turned around to see him crying. Not knowing what to do and not liking the display, she stood next to him and patted his shoulder. "There, there. Whatever it is, it will be okay."

"It won't be. I've been a terrible husband and a terrible person and she won't even see me or talk to me. She just disappeared."

Penny went into the kitchen to make the tea. When she returned with snacks, Daniel had composed himself and she felt better.

"I know I don't need to say this but I am her mother. I'm going to side with her on anything. And you were unfaithful." She paused, surprised at her own frankness. "I don't understand why you even care. You're free now to pursue whomever you wish." She took a sip of her tea. *Surreal*, she thought then smiled.

"I was an idiot. I love Julia. I've always loved her, from the moment I met her…"

Pathetic, she thought. *What kind of men do they make nowadays?*

"…I lost my way. I haven't been with anyone else. The woman seduced me and I couldn't help myself.

Then it became easier because Julia was working all the time…"

Who does he think I am? His mate? If I were a man, I'd kick him out on his backside. Where is Rupert when you need him? She dunked a digestive biscuit into her tea and sucked the juice from it before eating the soggy mixture.

"I never meant for her to find out. I thought it would end and that would be it. I need your daughter. I know I'm pathetic but if that's what I need to do to demonstrate my love, then that's what I'll do. Just tell me where she is."

Penny looked at him. *He still is my daughter's husband, however distasteful,* she thought. "Perhaps she doesn't want to be found."

"Perhaps she is in danger. Perhaps she needs me."

"She's safe."

"Then you know where she is?"

"No, but I get messages."

"Just tell me where and I'll find her."

"That's probably what she doesn't want. Look, you've got to pull yourself together. Julia has gone to develop herself without you. This may mean that you hurt her so deeply she needs to heal herself first or she simply doesn't care. Either way, it's up to her to decide if and when she sees you."

"I can see you disapprove of me."

"I can't approve of what you've done. Until that point, I thought you were a perfectly respectable man."

"Thank you for that."

Penny smirked but said nothing. They sat in silence as finished their tea. Within five minutes, Daniel picked himself off the sofa and disappeared out the front door.

Chapter Nineteen

A New Man?

"So let me understand this correctly, Mr. Stone. You underwent some supervening event shortly after your wife left you. You divested yourself of all your holdings, amidst the largest collapse of market confidence for nearly a century, and now are volunteering your time at a homeless shelter."

"I am building a homeless shelter. I have been working with the local councils and government to deliver a more effective solution to those who don't want solutions. Homelessness is not a choice but an abrogation of it. They want out for as many reasons as there are people. I want to help those who still want to help themselves."

"But forgive me for the timing of all this. You come out of the one of the worst crashes having made more money than you imagined possible. My sources indicate something north of two hundred million dollars after tax in your pocket. That's not too shabby."

"Just lucky. I couldn't have timed it. No one could. My wife left me, my life fell apart, and I wanted out. That's when I decided to return to the UK. It was either that or take a step off the top of one of my skyscrapers." *And I didn't expect to receive one tenth of that,* Daniel thought. *Sometimes fate smiles on you.*

"You say that but it doesn't change the fact that the Securities Exchange Commission in the United States is investigating those transactions, as is the Secretary of State for Business, Innovation, and Skills in the United Kingdom."

"I have the most reputable advisors and they all assure me that these are just formalities. I had a public holding company. It was a requirement of my fundraising efforts. No breaches of any kind were found. I think we have exhausted this. Can we move on?"

The reporter squirmed in his chair. The interview wasn't going as he had expected. "Yesterday you put your name forward to run as the conservative candidate for your constituency in Surrey. You've never been in politics before this. You've lived a large portion of your adult life in New York. People are talking about smoky back-room politics."

"That couldn't be further from the truth. I have always been a keen supporter of the conservative party and I have regularly donated throughout my life. When

I didn't have much, my donations were modest. Recently, I had more to give."

"And you have been given one of the safest seats in all of the country. Many say they could run an Orangutan and get it elected."

"I have noticed my hair turning orange," Daniel said, smiling. "Seriously, I am proud to have been selected and I look forward to the race and serving my constituents if I am elected."

"Moving on." The reporter flipped the page of his note pad. "We have seen violence and uncertainty on all fronts over the last decade. The entire European project seems uncertain. How do you see yourself contributing to this?"

"Martin, I'm trying to serve my electorate. I am going to represent their interests. I don't think they want me to chase ghosts of the European past. They are interested in good homes, secure jobs, and safe streets. We are just over ten years since those bombings in London. Britain has resoundingly voted to leave the European Union. It's nearly 2017. Yes, there is uncertainty, but that's why the electorate wants a leader who is independent and knows how things work. I have always worked for myself. My opponent has never had an actual job. She has been a politician or bureaucrat of one form or another since she graduated from her political studies degree. Many of the politicians of this country should be voted in on the basis of ability, not just how long they have waited in the political queue."

"Mr. Stone, thank you." The lights went dark and the production team began talking amongst themselves. Daniel shook the reporter's hand and left.

The election went as expected. Daniel won comfortably and found himself in the government's cabinet. His donations got him there and now it was up to him to keep the position. He performed better than the critics anticipated and soon found himself being passed from one cabinet post to another as he gained seniority. In the next election, his party was pushed into opposition. He bided his time as a new party leader was elected and eventually won power in the next election. This time, Daniel became home secretary. Soon, he was being tipped to be in the running for the highest office in the land. That opportunity presented itself when they were voted out of office during the next election. There was another party leadership bid and he won it. It wasn't until 2027 that he won the coveted position of prime minister.

It was thirty-seven days into his new job when the call came. Julia was back and needed to see him.

"Julia." He spoke the word the way an atheist would pray to God. "Please, sit down. It's been so long." The understatement was too much for her. She burst out laughing.

She was sitting forward and had waited for the attendants to leave and the door was closed. "Daniel, first I need to say sorry. I'm sorry for being a bitch and leaving you without ever calling or writing." As she spoke, she took in the room, the furnishing, and the magnitude of whom she was addressing. *Just my husband*, she thought. *The man I need to divorce.*

Daniel didn't sit. He paced. "Why now? Why wait all those years and appear at this moment?"

"I'm not after anything. You don't have to worry about me at all."

"You want a divorce."

She paused. "Yes. How did you know?"

"The benefits of MI5. I've known where you've been ever since I became an MP."

"Then why didn't you come after me?"

"Because you seemed content. I didn't want to hurt you or do anything that might distract from your plans. If you weren't so full of your own self-righteous anger, you would see that. I rearranged my entire life for you. From the beginning, I made sure our UK properties were convenient for you, then I abandoned my life's work to follow you to New York. I created a sustainable and successful business there but you couldn't have cared less. You never came to my big days or celebrated my victories…"

"No, that's what Deedee was for."

"That's what she became, but not originally. I loved you. I love you, always will. But you hurt me deeper than my betrayal could have hurt you. I realised during these years that you probably never loved me. It was always a one-way street. Your way or the highway."

Julia never expected this conversation. She remained silent.

"While you hummed and clapped in the jungles of India, screwing the students you saw fit to grace with your body, I dealt with the reality of our marriage. I looked in the mirror and didn't like what I saw. I made myself a better person. Because of you, ironically. But I am now that better person without you."

"You sound bitter."

"Yes and no. I used my weaknesses to make me strong. Your absence created a mystery around me. Young voters thought I was cool. Old voters respected my commitment to you. The security services confirmed I hadn't killed you—which is why I know about your ashram happy clappy place—and the newspapers made me into a cross between a stoic and a rock star. By the way, we're fairly rich. The papers loved my contradictions even though most politicians get crucified by money. Somehow, your absence became part of my persona."

"That's great. You made lemonade from lemons."

"And now you expect to shit on my sandwich and have me call it peanut butter. You can't just do whatever the hell you want. There are other people in this world. It is not all about Julia Frist. This time it's about Daniel Stone." He opened a bottle of his private stock scotch and poured himself a large shot.

"I understand you are angry. I am sorry about everything you said. You're right. I just..." She stopped.

...never even factored you into my thinking, she wanted to say. "How can I make this work for you?"

Daniel poured himself another half glass and sat next to Julia. He wasn't overweight but was breathing heavily. His eyes lacked their usual lightness and his hair had already gone largely grey. When they locked onto hers, he held them for a long moment before continuing. "I want you to disappear to under whatever rock you came from. I don't want you getting married and I won't grant a divorce. Yes, you can force me but I think you owe me on this."

She sat speechless. The stench of the peaty scotch was overwhelming. She found herself looking at his fine tailoring and polished looks and realised this wasn't the same Daniel she left twenty years earlier. He had evolved into someone, something, else. John may be rich, but Daniel was the head of state with an army and an entire infrastructure of security behind him. If he didn't want something done, it wouldn't be.

She took his glass without speaking. He let her. She raised it to her lips and drank it all. She resisted the initial urge to vomit and then stood and began to leave. At the door, she turned and said, "How long?"

"Until I am voted out."

Daniel Stone, prime minister of the United Kingdom, enjoyed an unusual popularity that lasted a decade, equalling only a handful of past prime ministers who managed to stay in power that long. He stepped down after a general election defeat in which the conservatives were swept from power in May 2036.

In June, he granted her a divorce. In August, John and Julia made their announcement that they were getting married in the Venetian, Las Vegas, in October.

Chapter Twenty

The Establishment Man

"Mr. Carter, it is a pleasure to finally meet you."

"Thank you. Please, sit down."

"I was surprised to receive your phone call."

"You shouldn't have been. We've been watching you these last few years."

"We?"

"You have done well since Goldman's," he said, ignoring the question.

"Thank you, sir."

"I also understand you are finding yourself in a bit of a squeeze."

"Where'd you hear that?"

"Here, there. You know."

"We're fine."

"I'm sure. I just wanted to put an idea out there for your consideration. I am not trying to interfere, but I am concerned about where things are heading, especially your firm."

"Sir?"

"It's no secret that you're over-committed, over-leveraged, and vulnerable. Perhaps you survive, perhaps not. I think you've played an excellent game for over a decade but you may have found yourself in a position where the next move is a gamble and not an investment."

JW was quiet. He agreed but wasn't going to talk down his own firm. If there is one thing more important than money in the bank, it is the perception that you have money in the bank. Credibility was everything.

"I'm here to offer you a helping hand," Carter said. "If you want it."

"I'm listening."

"I have been spending a lot of time with people who are much smarter than me on these matters. They all agree that we are heading for a massive market correction. Depending on when and how, it could affect the fabric of society."

"In other words, a crash."

"Possibly, but nothing is ever certain and so much depends on the public's trust." Carter reached for some water and filled his glass, then JW's. "I want to be your friend if you'll let me, and part of that is warning you of dangers before they are a threat to you."

JW was wary but the stature of Carter was beyond reproach. He was among the ten richest men in America. He sat on government advisory boards that swayed the president and influenced global leaders. When he said he wanted to be your friend, you listened. "Thank you very much, sir. I'm not sure why I am deserving of this honour."

"You are the future of money and this country. I would hate for you to stumble on something beyond your control."

"I try, but I'm not sure what danger you are referring to."

"You are over exposed to the subprime disaster coming down the pike. If you don't insulate yourself, you could be caught without a chair when the music stops."

"That's true of any number of investments we hold."

"But subprime and various derivative papers you hold represent too much of your portfolio. You put your head above the parapet on this one and I think it's going to get shot off by the marketplace."

JW agreed but wasn't about to say so. "What do you propose?"

"Merge with a bank that is too big to fail. It will mean eating a little humble pie but you will survive."

"I don't think it's that bad yet."

"Believe me, it is. Take the offer. It's a bank we control and can help you restore your own finances once the dust settles."

"You keep saying 'we'. I don't think it's a mistake. Who is part of your group, Mr. Carter?"

It was Carter's turn to be silent. He had been granted a certain latitude by his Order but was not allowed to explicitly talk about them. He knew he needed to say something that made sense to his target. "We are a group of concerned citizens. My friends are camera shy and don't wish to be known directly. We try to ensure the stability of the world's economies and, at the same time, ensure that we are able to act as meaningful players in the game."

"Sounds very Orwellian," JW said with a smile. "If it wasn't you, I would dismiss it out of hand. As it is, I will take your suggestions. Can you make the necessary introductions? I can't guarantee that I'll say yes, but I'm prepared to talk and analyse the proposal."

"I wouldn't respect you if you didn't." Carter stood and the meeting was over. They shook hands and JW left with a distinct feeling that he had just gone down the rabbit hole.

∞

JW merged his firm in time. Julia left, as did Matt, the former for reason, the latter for none. Matt was always a wild card and acted as though the merger was the end of his life.

"You'll be given the same or better than what you currently have in equity. You're no worse off." JW set out the plans to Matt the best he could.

"I'll become a pebble on their behemoth beach. They need you, so you'll be fine. I don't want to merge. Can't we get them to buy us out instead? I need the cash."

"There is no cash in deals like this. They buy our paper with theirs. We then gamble that their paper is more credible than ours when the system crashes."

"But according to this deal, I can't sell my paper for two years." Matt looked anxious, almost manic.

"What's the problem? We've done well together. We've made a lot of money. We've joined the billion-aire's club."

"On paper."

"What else is there?"

"Cash. Real money."

"We'll convert soon enough."

"Not soon enough for me."

"We don't have a choice."

"I know. Do the deal. I've gotta go back to Joburg. This is bad news for me."

"Matt, you're the only person I know who would look at a billion dollars of paper from a bank like JPMorgan Chase as bad news. Listen to me carefully. If we don't do this deal, our shares in AAT and GVE will be worthless. We have no choice."

"I know. I don't have to like it."

JW put his hand out, as there was no use for any more conversation. They shook and Matt disappeared.

A couple of months later, Daniel contacted him, asking to be bailed out. It represented an opportunity for JW to see what Mr. Carter meant.

"You want to bail out a friend of yours?" Mr. Carter had poured his water and was leaning back in his chair. They had become friendly and tried to meet up at least once a month since their first meeting.

"It makes financial sense. It is a lot of property and should pay its way easily. The guy wants out."

"What kind of person is he?"

"Daniel? He's the wife of one of my most trusted employees."

"Why not lend it to her instead?"

"She quit. Not sure where she disappeared to. We wouldn't be having this discussion if it was her asking."

"Do you trust this Daniel?"

"I think so. He's ambitious. He's originally from the UK and just wants to cash out. I think he's got some emotional problems with his wife."

"That's okay. I like motivated sellers." A thought crossed Carter's mind. "Do you think he'd be prepared to try a creative buyout structure?"

"I think he'd take anything we give him."

"Perfect. There's a project I've been working on. It's an alternative currency based primarily to assist central banks. I am trying to figure a way to apply this to end users. The lot size is large enough, over a billion, so that is in our favour."

"What are you thinking?" JW liked anything that sounded like an alternative currency. He wanted to position himself to take advantage of Carter's inside knowledge.

"There are instruments designed to bolster countries' currencies in times of crisis. You have probably heard about the special drawing rights we used in England in the sixties. Essentially, it's a note based on a basket of currencies. We would issue it from the International Monetary Fund. Considering how desperate the current financial system is, I am wondering whether we could use some of these SDRs to underwrite the buyout of your friend's portfolio."

"You are talking about a test case. I love it." JW really loved it. This represented an entirely new universe of funding opportunities if it worked.

"Exactly, but we need to ensure that this Daniel character understands what's at stake. My friends have larger objectives and wouldn't mind helping a like-minded person in a time of need. The payback would be that he would need to help us as well."

"What are you thinking?"

"We use the SDRs to underwrite the purchase of Daniel's property portfolio. Make him rich. Then back him to become, I don't know, say prime minister in the UK—or at least a senior cabinet minister. Subject to all the usual background checks, naturally."

JW coughed and started laughing. "Daniel Stone as PM? I'm sure he'll go for it. He has the ambition for it. But it would take a long time."

"We've got all the time in the world. We will do our part and he will need to do his. Just remind him that we can make him poor just as easily as making him rich. He must decide carefully."

"Sounds doable, sir."

"And another thing, JW. I don't need to meet with him. You deal with him and manage him as you would any other asset. We are investing in him and expect a return in due course."

"Understood, sir."

∞

Everything went to plan. Daniel was ecstatic but understood his obligations. He moved back to London and began laying the groundwork for the next phase of his life. What wasn't expected was the freak accident that killed Carter in a hunting expedition in British Columbia, Canada. It cut the steel cable of certainty that JW had in his new reality of high finance, society, and his visions of the future.

As he watched the coffin lowered into the ground, he thought of Julia and the way she looked at the Ambassador's residence in London at the Millennium Eve party. She was still young and he could feel the heat of her body when he stood next to her. *I can't remember how my date looked or even her name*, he thought and then smiled despite the funeral. *And she wore a ruby necklace. It was striking and out of place, yet belonged on her. It glowed warm in the light of her sparkling eyes. Why didn't I do more to pursue her?* He could barely hear the voice of the pastor as Carter's body reached its final resting place. A hand gripped his and a head leaned on his shoulder. It belonged to Shelly but he knew it wouldn't last. She was no Julia. After the ceremony, he dropped her off and went to his favourite watering hole.

"I'm fifty-two years old and unmarried," said. "Maybe I should have settled down and had some kids."

"You don't like kids."

"I don't dislike kids. I just didn't want any of my own."

"Same thing. You've chosen your life, now live it. You've done things most people could only imagine, been to places they can only dream of, and will do things most people can only read about."

"However much I love flattery, I don't need the pep talk. I'm just feeling lonely. I have no one to share my accomplishments with, no one who knew me when I was young and physically fit and not some old greying money man. I want to be with someone who I don't need to talk to and who will understand anyway."

"Sounds like you should get a dog. Have another drink." Paul pulled a bottle from below the counter and poured. Paul Wilson was Australian but he married a

Chinese New Yorker so he could stay in the United States. He studied philosophy in Melbourne but spent all of his time trying to keep his pub alive. It represented his life's savings and passion. It allowed him to have conversations with big shots like JW.

"Are you happy, Paul? Marriage agrees with you?"

"My marriage is perfect. There were no delusions. We've been together for ten years and I actually like her. I never would have thought it. She grew on me and now I can't see myself living with anyone else."

"I'm still not convinced. I'm lonely as hell but can get any woman who's looking. If not, I can always pay for it. You know what they say…"

"Yeah, yeah. But it's not the same. For me, I'm a one woman man. She's maddening at times and she can't stand me at times but it provides a sort of continuity for my life."

"Good for you. Maybe she's got a sister?"

"Don't even joke about it. Just say the word."

That got JW smiling. "I'll get back to you." He had enough therapy and allowed himself to slip off his stool and out the door.

When he got home, he had a visitor. His building had a porter and the best security. Yet, when his elevator door opened, there were four large men in suits with ear pieces. They stood stock still, one of them with his back to the door.

"Excuse me, but you're blocking my door." He had a few drinks but was otherwise fine.

"I understand, Mr. Money, but there has been a change of plans. My boss is in your apartment and I need to frisk you before you can go in."

"Inside my apartment?" JW was getting angry but quickly quieted himself. He had no chance against four men.

"Yes, sir. Just raise your arms and I'll pat you down." He ran his hands over JW's body and up to his crotch. He then took a metal detector wand and waved it all over his body. It beeped and he took out his change, phone, pen, and whatever else caused a blip. "Thank you, sir. You can go in."

The door was already open. *If they wanted me dead, they would have already done it. No running from these guys,* he thought. *Whoever they are.*

"Hello, Mr. Money." An ancient man sat in an over-stuffed leather armchair. JW walked towards him incredulously.

"Mr. Rock? It can't be."

"It is."

"This is an honour." JW looked around at the two bodyguards who stood behind Mr. Rock. "But a little confusing. The last time I looked, this was my place."

"I know. Sorry about that. Security is impossible and I didn't want to advertise our meeting."

JW sat down cautiously, opposite the legendary billionaire investor. "I didn't know we had a meeting scheduled." He looked at the old man and couldn't believe it was really him. His name adorned the largest monuments and rang throughout the last century of finance and industry like none other. He was a legend.

"We didn't." He nodded to his security guards, who moved away and stood next to the apartment's front door, out of earshot. "I have a proposal that could only be asked in person."

"Sounds interesting."

"It is. I have been hearing a lot about you from our mutual friend Mr. Carter. He said you are trustworthy and mentally agile. I wanted to meet you and see if that is true."

"It is impossible to say anything to compliments as high as that from such a man as Mr. Carter. He was a gentleman and a friend. I will miss him."

Rock paused and watched JW's reactions. It seemed to help him decide something that was turning over in his mind. "Do you think you might be able to replace him?"

"No one can replace Mr. Carter. I can try to help if you feel I can be of assistance."

"No, nothing like that. I am here to invite you to join a group. It is a secretive group and is not something that can be spoken of outside our membership."

"But you're speaking it to me."

"Because I know you'll accept."

"If I didn't?"

Rock's face darkened. "You will."

"I'm listening."

"We are concerned citizens trying to make the world a better place. Our group includes eleven members. One of them was Mr. Carter. We have been watching you and your name came up as a suitable replacement. It's a job like none other. There is no salary or secretaries. It is done entirely on your own time, but it affects the world in a way you couldn't imagine."

"I have a pretty good imagination. I'm guessing it is full of powerful men like yourself who represent a significant percentage of the world's productive output. You have influence in government and private industry. If I understand correctly, your group wants to make the world a better place. Because it's secret, I can only assume your methods are not entirely in line with conventional means. It also means that if I decline, I am likely not to show up to work tomorrow. Am I correct?"

Rock laughed. "You make us sound like monsters. Hardly. We are no more monsters than the members of the Pentagon or some of the ultra-secretive defence firms. We are secretive for a reason. To be effective, we mustn't be influenced. We must determine our ideal and follow our goal with a single mindedness that is only possible in small groups."

"You didn't answer my question."

"You know the answer. Now, before we continue, I need to know yours."

∞

A few years later, Rock, too, passed on. His mantle was transferred to his son. No member objected as it was expected.

Junior reduced his voice to a whisper. "I know what you mean, but I've been living it my whole life. Even since my father passed away, I am beginning to see how much goes on that was planned by the Order ten, twenty, even thirty years ago. It plants the seeds and they oversee it, trimming and fertilising as required."

"I was sorry to see your father go. I don't know if you knew but he was the one who recruited me. He was a good man." JW took a sip from his drink.

"Thanks. I'm just glad that none of us got caught up in those terrorist attacks last year. There are eleven of us. You would have thought one would have been on a plane that day."

"When was the last time you flew commercial?"

Junior laughed. "You're right. I keep forgetting about that. I just associate the day with so many deaths—my mind didn't distinguish what types of planes."

"Speaking of which, do you think we should be expanding our core group? It seems so ridiculously small to be effective."

He shrugged. "Most decisions are straight forward. We don't need the administrative staff. We just make requests of the government organisations. Why replicate the IMF's or the various central banks' work?"

"But aren't we relying on our financial influence too much? Aren't we vulnerable?"

"My father grappled with this but came to the conclusion that anonymity was better than efficiency. As soon as people know who you are, you lose a lot of your ability to decide and act."

"I'll defer to Mr. Rock's wisdom. Your family has been involved in this longer than anyone."

"Only Roth's family has been longer. Now that the old man has passed, we are dealing with his son Momo. But we all get along well. Take, for example, your friend Daniel. He was an investment that took twenty years to materialise. Now, he is the PM and is eminently pliable. I would say we have the ear of eighty percent of the world's most powerful men through each country's presidents and administrators."

"I don't doubt it. I just find it funny how things make sense now. I used to break my head trying to understand why a country acted in certain ways, especially when it wasn't logical or fully in their interests. Now I know."

"I think what we do is in the interest of the countries. They just don't know it yet."

"Historically, people got their heads cut off for saying less," JW joked. But he meant it. Anonymity was the only thing keeping them alive.

"We are close to implementing an alternate currency, the SDRs. Daniel was the first to use it in private commercial terms. We have expanded this into the developing world economies and even the Russians have taken to it. It may still take a generation before it is fully in place. By then, we will have achieved one of the greatest objectives of the Order."

"To world peace."

They clinked glasses and turned their discussion to the latest Wimbledon scores.

Chapter Twenty-One

Venetian Ever After

Matt felt a cold sweat take over his body. It was the same necklace he bought in his manic moment forty years ago. When he saw her face, the years melted away and he was back in Sun City. The gold of the Venetian became a distant glow and the little man in a tuxedo faded. It was as though he was looking through a tube in which everything else became blurred lines and he was alone with Julia. He found himself walking in her direction. She was busy with a large man next to her. He was built like an aging athlete with shoulders that filled his suit and a bald head. His clothes looked crisp and new, both comfortable and fashionable. He wore them effortlessly. It was hard to tell his age, but neither of them were young any longer. *When did I get old?* he thought. *I feel like I did when I first saw her.* She was also beginning to look older, but the smile she wore made her look twenty years younger than her sixty years. *Why did she wait until now to marry? She would've been snapped up in a heartbeat by anyone.* His mouth became dry as he got closer. He could see the engagement ring sparkling on her finger and her refined skin that had aged so well. Even her wrinkles were cute. The man next to her looked like he was the proudest man on the planet. "He should be," he said to himself.

"Excuse me?"

Matt snapped back into the present as the tuxedoed dwarf began speaking.

"Excuse me, sir?"

"Sorry, I was in a different world. I didn't know you were still there."

"I can't allow you to wander just anywhere. The exhibit is over there. This is for wedding guests only." The little man was getting more excited as the betrothed drew near. He wanted them to see him doing an outstanding job.

"I'm sorry but I know the bride."

"Oh," he drew back. "I had no idea. Your name isn't on the register."

"It was a last minute thing. A bit of a surprise."

"Well, then I'll leave you to it. Enjoy the rest of your day." He almost bowed and left.

Where do they find these people? Matt thought. *He didn't verify what I said and believed the first thing that came out of my mouth. I could be a stalker for all he knew.* His thoughts were interrupted by a hand on his arm.

"Matt? Is that you? I can't believe it! John, this is the man I was telling you about. Matt, this is John, my fiancé."

The words hit him like a wave of cold water. He wanted to hear her voice and take her away with him but didn't like the words "John" or "fiancé". He stared at her for a long moment, shaking John's hand and seeing her lips move. Her eyes danced and smile entranced but he couldn't hear her. He could see the girl next to the roulette table, his lady luck. His love, were it not for Alicia and her family. *If only I wasn't such a coward and followed my heart instead of my fear*, he thought.

"Julia, I can't believe it. You look exactly as you did when I last saw you. Oh, and congratulations. Quite the venue."

"It is out of this world. John thought of it. You two would get along well." She gushed as she held onto John's arm. He stood tall and made himself big, like a warrior meeting a rival in the forest. The only thing missing from the scene was a mane or the beating of his chest. He stood silently nodding, polite but not enthused at the intrusion to his wedding by Julia's old flame.

"You're a lucky man," Matt said and meant it. He didn't mention the necklace, as he wanted to see her wearing it. If John knew its origin, he would probably make such a fuss she would be forced to throw it away.

"What are you doing here?" she asked. Then, conscious of how it sounded, she added, "You know what I mean. I haven't heard from you for almost thirty years. That's a long time in anyone's book." She was saying the words but all anger against him was gone. She was seeing him for who he was, the man with the hurt eyes and the undying love that he bore for her. Or at least, that was what Matt thought he saw.

"It's a long story. Perhaps you've got a few minutes?"

Noticing Julia's hesitation, John interrupted. "That's fine with me, sweetheart. I have some things to attend to and we can catch up in a bit."

Julia's body language was grateful but she was careful with her words. "Are you sure?"

"One hundred percent. The ceremony isn't for at least another five hours."

"Are you sure you don't mind?" she asked again, knowing in her heart she shouldn't leave John's side.

"Your bridesmaids should be keeping you occupied in any event, not your future husband. Go and enjoy yourself and I'll see you at seven. Matt, it was good to meet you. If you are able to make the wedding, it would be an honour for us to have you."

"I will do my best to be there. Thank you."

John gave Julia a quick kiss and strode off. She looked at his figure, hoping she wasn't being insensitive. She knew she was. *If I'm thinking about it, then I've done it,* she thought. *What the hell is Matt doing here? Why didn't he find me in India? Why now?*

She hesitated when he offered her his arm but found her arm already linked in his as they began walking slowly. He didn't speak and she enjoyed the quiet of his older self. *He was always shy*, she thought. *I forgot how much I liked it.* His eyes would look at her and then dart away. She ignored it but noticed his every glance. She saw him looking at her hands and legs, but always returning to the face. She saw him glance at her breasts but realised it could be the necklace. Every time she wore that ruby on her chest, she felt young and invulnerable. She felt the exuberance of that day and the insanity of her decisions. She smiled at herself and her put-on maturity, just nineteen at the time. He was her first real love and he haunted her. She knew he wasn't the right person for her, but the scar was deep and would never heal. His being there caused her to feel the scar begin to bleed.

"Are you happy?" The question broke their silence but was one that Julia didn't expect.

"Yes, very. John is a wonderful man."

He paused. "That's good. You deserve a good man."

"Thank you. It means a lot coming from you. How's Alicia?" She didn't want to ask and it grated on her as it left her lips.

He paused again. "She's dead."

"Oh my god, I'm sorry."

"It's okay. It's been a while."

"Your children?" She wanted to move on and talk about more pleasant subjects.

Matt stopped and his head was bowed. She had to look to realise he was crying.

"What's wrong?"

"They're dead. All dead."

"I'm so sorry. I didn't know."

"How could you? It's not your fault." He found a seat and she sat next to him, her hand gently on his leg.

"He killed them all."

"Murdered?"

"Every one of them. He's the reason I couldn't be with you and he still did that to me."

Her head shook involuntarily. "You chose Alicia over me."

"No. I had no choice." He wiped his face. "You don't understand."

"Then tell me." It was a hole in her life she wanted filled. *Not the best timing,* she thought, *but if I don't do this now, I'll never know.*

"I was desperate and married into one of those families you don't divorce, if you know what I mean."

Julia shook her head, not understanding.

"Remember when you asked me what I got up to? You said that it was the type of thing the mafia did? I dismissed it at the time, but the reality is, I married into one of the five families that controlled crime in South Africa. The police looked the other way as long as civilians weren't hurt. The families dealt with everything from gambling to prostitution to drugs. We controlled the black areas and white areas. Even the securities commission got its cut when we dabbled in stocks and bonds. It worked and everyone was happy."

"Then?"

"Then I overreached. I got into some trouble with the families and I went to one of the friendlier competitors for a loan. When my money had almost run out, that was shortly before I met you. You saved me. Fate brought me to you and I fell in love with you."

When he said that, she felt a bolt of hot adrenaline fill her. She began to sweat lightly and her fingers tingled.

"And I think you fell in love with me." He stopped and blew his nose and wiped his forehead with the same tissue. "But I couldn't put you in that type of danger. Alicia's father was the head of the most powerful of the five families. They tolerated my affair with you. They all had someone on the side. But they wouldn't tolerate me breaking up my family. Alicia knew this better than I did. When she drove past us that day with her uncle Maish, she was reminding me of a warning I received earlier that day."

"Which was?"

"If I tried to break my marriage, you would be buried in the back yard of our first house."

Julia's mouth dropped and then closed. Her eyes began to dart, taking in more of her surroundings to remind her she was safe. "I had no idea," she whispered.

"I know, and I didn't want to hurt you any more than I had. I wanted to let you go."

"If it helps you, I don't think I ever let you go." She put her hand on his and allowed him to look into her eyes, no longer hiding her hurt from those memories.

He closed his eyes, nodding. *I can't tell her about jail*, he thought. "When I saw you with JW, I was jealous."

"It was a job and I loved it." *And I should have loved* JW, she thought. She was now firmly back in the past, oblivious of her impending nuptials.

"You were spectacular at it."

"I was OK." She blushed.

"I should have taken my chance with you then," he said. "It's too late now."

"Things are never too late." She was talking like she had in her ashram, not realising how it could be construed by Matt.

"Perhaps." He stood up and gave her his hand. She took it and stood. They resumed walking. "When I don't know what to do, I let fate decide."

"I remember. But I think you were suicidal and just lucky."

"Not at all. Fate wanted me to meet you and you me—twice. Our lives have both been enriched as a result."

"True," she said slowly. "But there's nothing to decide. I've made my decision."

Matt linked her arm in his again and began walking out of the exhibition. "Most of you has but not all. I would like to see whether fate agrees."

"What do you want to do? Get a gun and play Russian roulette?" She laughed but realized that could be exactly what he was planning.

"Close, but this isn't dangerous. It's only money. Let's play a game of chance." He led her to the casino and the cashier, where he took out all his money in chips. He instructed them to deliver the chips to the main roulette table.

"Matt, this isn't necessary. I'm certain that I'll marry John."

"Perhaps, but I told myself if I ever saw you again, I wouldn't leave anything unsaid." He stopped and turned to her, arms on hers, and looked into her eyes. "Julia, I love you and always have. I always will. I did wrong by you and I am sorry. I am doing this because I think you still love me as well."

Julia was speechless, half glancing over her shoulder to see if any of John's friends were near. She was relieved not to recognise anyone around them.

"You were my lady luck and the love of my life. Come with me and let's live happily ever after."

"We don't live in a fairy tale. I love John." *And I love you,* she said to herself. "We can't be together. Too much has happened."

"Nothing has happened to stop us being together. I know that and I'm going to let fate decide."

At the roulette table, a clear plastic box of chips was waiting for him under the watchful eye of the cashier's porter. He nodded and left Matt with his chips when he was certain he had completed his duty.

"This is crazy talk, Matt. I'm not listening to you." She pulled her arm from his and began to walk away.

"I'm playing this round, Julia, whether you are here or not. The outcome will be the same."

He watched her dress disappear out of the casino. He burned into his memory the shape of her back as it became her hips, then legs, then feet. When she was gone and he was alone, he made his request to the gods of Fate.

I love her. She loves me. I am asking you to decide what I should do, he thought to himself. He said the words in his mind, seeing the spelling of each word like subtitles. *If I shouldn't be with her, I'll win this bet.*

He squared himself with the table and waited for the croupier to spin the wheel. At the right moment, he put everything on number twenty-nine. The other members of the table let out a collective gasp and the croupier sought out the eyes of the pit boss, who was already on his way over after the cashier porter informed him Matt was at the table.

Willing himself to lose, Matt replayed the five spins of the revolver and the five spins of the roulette table forty-one years earlier. He could feel the cold, unyielding steel against his temple and the pressure against his finger as he pulled the trigger. He forgot to cock the hammer and it took much more effort on the first pull than he anticipated. He was careful to keep the barrel to his temple in case he grazed his skull and ended up a vegetable instead of dead. The hammer fell and fate decided. He lived. Four more times the hammer fell and he continued to breathe. Then came the roulette table and he realised why he was alive—to meet Julia.

He knew she had left but also knew she would be back. *A roulette wheel has thirty-eight pockets, giving me a two point six percent chance that she doesn't want me,* he thought. *This is a no brainer. She loves me and wants me. I'm ninety-seven percent sure.*

Images of Maish butchering his mother, wife, and children flashed across his mind. It caused a shadow to cover his face for anyone watching. He felt the jailhouse bars against the insides of his hands. The repainted bars uneven with the old paint and rust that battled the South African air. He could feel the cement under his feet as the wheel turned. He could see JW's face when they shook hands for the first time, and then the last, his face uncomprehending Matt's anxiety. And he saw Julia's eyes, letting him look deep into her soul just minutes earlier. *There can be only one outcome,* he thought. He began smiling with the thought of taking Julia from this new man in her life, however rich and powerful he was. They could go to Canada or Europe or wherever she wanted. They were rich enough.

"We have a winner!" The voice of the croupier was hoarse with disbelief. Her usual impassive announcements were silenced with the magnitude of Matt's bet. It gave her a taste of the fear and excitement of placing a reckless bet that couldn't possibly win, but did.

Matt didn't hear it at first as he was lost in his thoughts, certain that it would be any number but his.

"Twenty-nine. Sir, congratulations." The croupier counted out the winnings and was removed by the pit boss. The familiar black silk cloth emerged and was draped over the table.

"Sir?"

"Uh, yes?" Matt couldn't believe his luck but was determined to honour the Fates.

"Congratulations, sir." The pit boss began to drone on about the table, the odds, and how they could help make his stay more enjoyable. Matt had heard it all before and was numb with disappointment.

Matt thanked the pit boss and croupier with a ten thousand dollar chip each and left the casino for the concierge desk.

"Can I help you, Mr. Smit?"

"Yes, I'd like to check out please."

"Is everything okay?" The man looked genuinely concerned, especially after hearing about his luck at the tables.

"Everything is fine. Something came up and I need to leave. I'm really sorry."

"Shall we wire your winnings somewhere or would you like to keep it here for your next visit?"

"I'll give you my bank details shortly. Can you arrange a car for me?"

"Certainly. Are you going to the airport?"

"No. I'd like to drive myself. Get me something comfortable."

"Certainly, sir."

He left the Venetian and didn't make it to the wedding.

Chapter Twenty-Two

Road Trip

M. I. A. M. I.

Matt punched the name into the on-board navigator. He didn't want an auto-drive car. He wanted to steer and brake and be part of the trip. His first impulse was to get as far from Julia as he could. As he had no destination, it didn't matter where he went. He decided to go as far east as possible.

The first tank of gas came and went. His mind was numb with fate's decision. As the black road unfurled in front of him, he settled into a radio station only to have it become fuzzy after an hour as he drove out of range. He found another, then another. He would pause at truck stops to refuel but refused to stop. He drove through the night and most of the next day. As he reached the outskirts of Dallas, his car died.

He wasn't even angry. It felt like fate giving him another kick in the backside. *What do you want from me?* He kicked the side of the driver's door as he closed it. He found a spot off the shoulder and waited for the new rental car to be delivered.

It took nearly three hours for the new Lincoln to arrive. *Brand spanking new,* he thought. He inhaled the new car smell and smiled. He started driving but then got off on the next exit. *Maybe the Fates don't want me to go east*, he thought. *I'll go north as far as possible and then decide what I'll do next.* He used the facilities of the local truck stop before getting back on the northern interstate towards Canada.

"I feel free already," he said aloud. It felt better saying the words.

The steering wheel felt different from his first car. It was a little looser. The car's suspension was set to comfort and he floated on the highway. The states began to pass. Oklahoma, Kansas, Nebraska, South Dakota, and then North Dakota. It was a blur of nothingness as he kept himself occupied by staying between the lines of the interstate. His mind entered a meditative state of alert driving and non-thinking. His adrenaline barely took him through the first state, but his numbness kept him going. When he reached the Canadian border, he had no idea where he was going.

"Passport please." She read *Republique D'Afrique du Sud* and then *Republic of South Africa.* "You're a long way from home." The officer looked back at Matt's face then to her monitor that showed the Texas licence plate. "Going anywhere in particular?"

Matt didn't have the energy to be nervous or concerned. "Just driving. No direction."

The officer didn't hesitate long before instructing him to pull over. "Just park over there where my colleague will have a word with you."

That doesn't sound good, he thought. He drove forward, then pulled left under the roof of the inspection area. *I hope Percy got me a clean passport. If there is any mention of my record, I'm finished. But, then, I wouldn't have been allowed into the* US *either*. Matt forced himself to relax.

"Please step out of the car, sir."

He did.

"I am doing a routine search. Nothing to be worried about. When I'm done, we'll give you your passport and you can carry on."

Matt stood there, not caring. After a short while, he began to notice the cold.

The officer swabbed the steering wheel, door handles, and window sills. He popped the trunk of the car and opened the area where the spare tire sat. Each seat was examined before he turned around slowly.

"Where are you from?"

"Johannesburg, South Africa."

"I mean, where did you come from in the US?"

"Las Vegas."

"With a Texas plate?"

"My car died in Dallas."

"Why are you driving all this way? Do you have friends in Manitoba?"

"No, I just wanted to drive."

"You don't have a destination?"

Matt thought quickly. Despite his apathy, he realised this could go in the wrong direction. He was an ex-con. Once they found that out, if they found that out, he would be treated differently. He hadn't done anything wrong but he was doing it in the wrong way. He wracked his brain to figure out why he would want to come to Manitoba.

"Polar bears."

"Pardon me?"

"I wanted to see the polar bears. I don't like flying and thought I could see something I couldn't see in Africa."

"You're going to Churchill?" The officer's face still harboured doubt.

"Yes, sir."

"Then where are your things?"

"I travel light. I can purchase most things cheaper than lugging them around."

The officer paused and then popped the hood of the car. He shone his flashlight into the corners before closing it. "Just a minute." He left Matt and went inside.

Other drivers turned their heads to look at him, wondering what crime he may have committed. Faces that said they were glad it wasn't them. Others seemed to hide their own secrets and were pleased not to get caught.

"Thank you, Mr. Smit. Sorry for the delay." The officer was walking towards him with Matt's passport. He offered his hand and Matt shook it.

"Not a problem. Have a good day." He got back into his car and pulled onto the highway. The car had cooled off but became warm soon enough. It was around ten in the morning and the sun was massive in the blue sky. It created a glare that his sunglasses couldn't overcome. *Maybe the polar bears are just what I need*, he thought. He looked on his phone and saw his new destination. Churchill, due north.

There were no more states to enumerate, just this big massive piece of land called Manitoba. The route seemed easy enough and he drove on. As he approached Winnipeg, the temperature began to drop significantly. The sun had disappeared and the sky became an indeterminate grey.

Snow began to fall. He had seen snow in New York and his travels but from the safety of a taxi or limousine or aircraft. Now he was driving in it. The thick flakes melted when they hit his windshield. *Not that bad*, he thought. *Quite an adventure.*

The snow continued to melt but fell harder. Apart from the reality of the windshield, the scene looked like being on a cake as the baker dusted it with icing sugar. Soon Matt noticed the white forming on the ground. The roads were kept clear by the traffic and it wasn't until he was at the northern edge of Winnipeg when he realised the snow wasn't stopping.

"I'm in a new car with all the safety features. I'll be fine." He spoke to himself in encouragement. He enjoyed the challenge of the elements. He refuelled just before he crossed the perimeter highway that circled the city. He loaded up on coffee, chocolates, and other snacks he thought he would need. *I can always sleep in the car*, he thought. *How bad can it be? Just not sure how I'm going to make my way all the way to Churchill.* He was becoming determined to reach his new destination.

The sky was low and the clouds heavy. Matt enjoyed the sense of danger and pushed on. The roads were less travelled and soon the only thing keeping them clear was the wind, which was picking up. The flakes no longer melted on the windshield.

A couple of hours north of Winnipeg, he noticed a lone figure standing at the side of the road. *What's the worst that can happen?* He stopped and offered him a lift.

"Where you heading?" He was driving to forget and wondered why he didn't pick up anyone before this.

"North."

"Hop in."

He put his bag in the back seat and joined Matt in the front.

"Is that all you got?" Matt noticed a single bag and couldn't help but ask.

"Yep."

The hitchhiker was late middle aged, bearded, and wearing a heavy coat. There wasn't much more Matt could see from where he was seated. He knew that the guy would be dead if someone didn't pick him up soon.

"Waiting long?"

"Yeah. Not too many people pick up hitchhikers these days. Thanks." He shrugged and tried to smile. The cold must have frozen most of his face but Matt understood the gesture.

"I'll let you warm up before I start talking at you too much," Matt said. The new guy didn't respond. "I've got a thermos of coffee in the back if you want something to drink. There's probably a sandwich and some chocolate if you'd like."

"You sure?"

"I wouldn't offer if I wasn't. Help yourself."

He did. He poured a coffee for Matt, black, and one for himself. A few minutes later, he began thawing out and took off his coat and put it in the back seat. He then unbuttoned his heavy flannel jacket, which he left on, and rubbed his hands on the sweater underneath to warm himself. Matt was surprised his guest wasn't smelly.

"Do you smoke?" Matt asked.

"When I have the chance. What do you have?"

"Just tobacco," Matt said, realising how it could have been misconstrued.

"Works for me. I only smoke tobacco."

"Sorry, I didn't mean anything by it. I was just trying to be friendly."

"I've got cigars on me if you like but you may not be too keen on smelling up your new car."

"It's a rental."

That got him interested. "Where you heading?" he asked.

"North sounds good to me. I've been driving since Dallas. Need a change of scenery. I looked on a map and saw Churchill and thought northern Canada was as good a destination as any. You know, polar bears and all that."

He smiled. "Running or rough patch?"

"One hell of a rough patch. Just need to clear my head."

"You know you can't drive to Churchill?"

"Uh, yeah, I figured that out when I passed Winnipeg and picked up a map. My phone said there was a road but I now know better. Who would've thought?"

He was silent for a bit. "I'm heading to Churchill too. My plan was to grab the train from Thompson. If you still want to go, that's really your only option unless you want to fly. But you don't seem like you're in any great hurry."

Matt smiled. "Sounds like a plan."

"You driving through the night?"

"Was planning to but I think Thompson's only around seven more hours. That should get us in just before midnight."

"Assuming the weather co-operates," the hitchhiker added.

It didn't. Three hours out of Winnipeg and two hours after picking up his new travelling companion, the wind picked up even further and the snow on the fields started blowing across the road.

"This is beautiful," Matt said. "It's like something out of a National Geographic landscape. The grand expanse of white with a setting sun is amazing." They followed the black tarmac, his eyes glued to the road.

The snow had stopped falling but the stuff on the ground was being driven onto the road, clawing back at civilisation. Snow fingers thudded against the tires as they drove. He slowed down, turned on the lights, and watched the snowflakes begin again.

"I never thought about the weather," Matt said as much to himself as his companion. "Who the hell thinks about the weather? That's what good cars are for." By the time he accepted the reality, light panic set it. There weren't many towns along the highway. He kept his eyes peeled and gripped the wheel.

"Don't white knuckle it," the man said.

"Huh?"

"Relax your hands on the wheel. Slow down and let the car drive. We'll be okay."

"Easy for you to say. I've never seen snow like this, let alone driven in it."

"Do you want me to drive?"

Matt hesitated. He didn't know this guy from Adam, but he seemed like a survivor. *Not many people would try hitchhiking in this type of weather*, he thought.

"What do I do?" Matt decided that this guy's survival skills were worth more than his spotty driving ability. *Besides,* he thought, *my nerves are shot and all the romance of clearing my head and driving north has reached its limit.*

"Okay," he said. "Take your foot off the gas, but don't hit the brake. The last thing we want is to start spinning at this speed."

That just made Matt more nervous. He hadn't considered the risk of spinning out. He allowed the car to drift to a halt. When they were stationary, his hands were cemented to the wheel. He managed to pry one hand off and put the car into park. He pried off the other and sat back in his seat, sweating. He welcomed the blast of cold air when he opened the door to switch seats.

"You okay?" said the man as they settled into their new positions.

"Yeah, thanks. I owe you one."

"No, I owe you for picking me up. Sit back, have some of your chocolate, and I'll get us to the next town. I think it's Grand Rapids. It's not glamorous but I'm pretty sure they'll have some sort of hotel."

Matt sank into his chair and watched the snow in the headlights. The sun was down and it felt like they were driving at warp speed, stars racing towards them, blackness all around. The warmth of the heating and the exhaustion of non-stop driving sent him to sleep quickly.

When he awoke, they were stationary. The snow was still falling, heavier than before. There was a glow of lights off a white building next to them. His companion parked right in front of the hotel entrance and left the engine running as he went inside. When he returned, he was smiling and held up a set of keys.

"They only had one room but it has two beds. I figured that would be okay. I don't think we have too many options. The restaurant is open for another hour or so. That should get us enough time to unpack and grab a bite before everything shuts down."

"Thanks," Matt said. "What do I owe you?"

"Nothing. My treat."

Matt thought it odd for a hitchhiker to have enough money to pay for a room. The thought passed as he looked forward to getting out of the wintery hellscape and for the sun to rise again. He grabbed his suitcase and emptied the car of anything that might explode when frozen and joined him in the small, dingy room.

Calling the establishment a hotel was being kind; it was a motor inn. It was of wood construction, built some seven decades ago, with a steep roof and aluminium front doors. But it was shelter from the cold and Matt was thankful. The beds were lumpy and the covers had an odour that fell somewhere between urine and vomit despite clearly being heavily bleached and washed. Matt didn't care. It was warm and the heaters were sufficient to keep the cold outside. They ate some semblance of food in the restaurant and had a few drinks in the motel's bar. The people were friendly and couldn't have been more helpful with directions, stories, and sympathy at their plight. *Under different circumstances*, Matt thought, *I could see myself liking this place.*

The next morning Matt woke to the glow of the radio's red clock. It was almost eight and still dark outside. His travelling companion was still snoring. He had a shower, shaved, and readied himself for the rest of the journey to Thompson.

"How's the weather looking today?" he asked the waitress as she poured his first coffee.

"Look out the window, hon."

"Is that normal?" he asked.

"Normal enough. Looks like a big one. I don't think anyone's going anywhere for a few days."

"I'm sorry?"

"You haven't heard? Biggest storm of the season blowing in. You were lucky to get here when you did last night. We're expecting up to fourteen inches but the wind'll continue for a few days. It'll take a good day or so after it stops before the roads open up."

He put his coffee down. He wasn't in a great hurry, but neither was he expecting this.

"Have you decided what you want yet?"

"I'll have the special. Sunny side up with brown toast, please." *No sense in starving if I'm going to be stuck here*, he thought. *But what am I going to do for the next few days?* At that point, the hitchhiker joined Matt.

"Hear the news?" He grabbed a chair and sat across from him.

"Yup. Not too great."

"Oh well, can't complain. We're in a decent place with hot food and all the amenities. Could be a lot worse."

"Not much," Matt grumbled. He had been in worse places—jail, for one—but the idea of willingly submitting oneself to this type of life grated on him.

"Believe me, this is heaven. And from what I can surmise from you and your situation, this may be just what you need."

Matt tried to smile. The guy was just too damn optimistic. "Not sure if you're qualified to say that," he said. The hitchhiker was at least twenty years Matt's junior.

"You'd be surprised. Let's grab some grub and I'll tell you a story that'll make you happy to be alive."

They finished breakfast and, having nowhere else to go, positioned themselves in the motel bar. It was next to the breakfast room and had a large television on the far wall with the only comfortable armchairs in the whole place. It was early and they figured they'd be undisturbed there. The waitress saw them move spots and offered a carafe of coffee.

As the hitchhiker started talking, Matt realised he was listening to a person who had lived a life, one who knew powerful people and had equally powerful enemies. *You can judge the measure of a man by his enemies,* Matt thought.

The man's name was Jack. He told Matt about his first love and his first betrayal by the CIA. It involved his parents who, he discovered, were CIA spies. He told him about his second love and second betrayal, this time by the girl. He told him about a secret global organisation called the Order of Prime, whom he blamed for the death of his parents, and his third betrayal, this time by his biological father.

By the time the story was over, the bar table between them was littered with glasses, mugs, and snacks. Outside, the wind continued to howl and the sun had set hours ago. Other stranded travellers had come and gone and would likely return for an evening of drinking but, for the most part, they had been alone. They were alone when he finished his story.

"That was twenty years ago," Jack said.

"That's one hell of a story," Matt said. He rarely interrupted him except to order food or drink or visit the men's room.

"It was a scary time," he said.

"Why me? After all this time, why let me in on your secret?"

"Most of what I told you has already come to pass and the key players are all dead. I just needed to tell it. I can't explain it better than that. It's like an itch that has been gathering inside me. I'm not a religious man but I've been told that confession is good for the soul. Not just for absolution, but for the act of letting it go."

"Do you feel better?"

"Strangely, yes. I've been on the run so long it has become second nature to me."

"And the authorities?"

"They're not looking for me anymore. In many ways, there's no reason for me to be on the run. I've dropped off the grid and stayed there. I figured out how to manage funds without tripping any red flags. I have a network of people I can rely on when I need to."

"How did you find those people? How do you know you can trust them?"

"I have a good feeling about these things. If I feel comfortable, I tell them my story."

"And in return," Matt said, "they tell you theirs?"

"Something like that."

"And then what happens?"

"We shake hands and if we can help each other, we do."

Matt was silent. It was an invitation. He'd never offered an explanation about how he got there and he was never asked. The storm was still blowing. They were still stuck.

"Maybe we should have a drink," Matt said.

"Sounds like a good idea," he said. "Scotch?"

"Beer please," Matt said.

They got their drinks, ordered some burgers and fries, and Matt told Jack why he was heading to Churchill.

Chapter Twenty-Three

A Game

They were both drunk by the time all the stories were told. Matt told Jack about Maish and his jail time. He told him about JW and Daniel and John Großfreund. And Julia. He cried at times and Jack let him, not doing more than putting a sympathetic hand on his shoulder. They were still drinking when last call came, and they crashed fully dressed onto their beds when they were kicked out of the bar. It was ten before their eyes cracked open. The windows were white with snow, the sunlight blocked by three inches or more.

Jack recovered first and, after showering, went downstairs. Matt came an hour later.

"I didn't tell you my whole story," Jack said. They were half way through their trucker breakfasts and he started talking as though last night was still in session.

"You don't need to," Matt said. "We've said enough."

"But I think you will want to hear what I am about to say." Jack was serious. His eyes blazed, despite the hangover.

"Okay, we're not going anywhere."

Jack told him the rest of his story. About his revenge against the Order of Prime. About the planes and the quarter million deaths. About his way home, capture, escape, and subsequent revenge against all people involved in that way of life. Matt grew quiet as he realised he was sitting across from one of history's most wanted men. It put his own failings in perspective.

"You can't be that man," Matt said finally. "He must be dead or hiding. No way it's you."

Jack nodded. "Perhaps. I just told you my story because I recognised who you were. I thought I knew it yesterday but was only able to confirm it this morning."

Matt felt a warm shot of adrenalin that made his hands tingle and then palms sweat.

"You're JW's old partner. The one who's real name is Jefferson Washington Money."

Matt smiled. "JW was always embarrassed of his last name. I guess it had something to do with his profession."

"JW is now one of the Order's members," Jack said without smiling.

"JW? He's a black guy. I would have thought your conspiracy guys were all white."

This time Jack laughed. "You're a funny guy, Matt. The Order has Chinese, Indian, and Black people, as well as the usual suspects."

"Like Roth and Rock?"

"They are the pillars of the organisation."

"Okay, so what?"

"You are the first person I have met who is wholly oblivious to the power of the people around him. There is another person you know who is a decision making member of the Order."

"I hate to disappoint you, but I've been out of circulation for a lifetime. I'm just happy to be walking around. Hell, part of me wants to top myself because I'm walking around."

Jack ignored him. "John, your girl's fiancé."

"Husband."

"Right, husband by now."

"So? Who cares? I don't plan to do anything against them."

"And Daniel? What are the odds that you are involved with two members and a puppet?"

"Puppet? I must be getting slower by the minute."

"Daniel was the prime minister of the UK. He was put in place by the Order. It's not unusual. The Order backs most of the main leaders and all of those who remain in power. The question I'd like to know is whether Julia is involved."

Matt stopped taking this lightly. He was seated across from one of the greatest killers (*or liars*, he thought) in recent history. "Julia is innocent."

"Most likely. She was off saving the world in Kerala when she got caught up in John's web. Not her fault." Jack drifted into his own thoughts for a moment. "But do you think she can be trusted?"

"What is this? Look, I don't care what you do or to whom. I don't care if you are just lying to me. I'll assume you're lying because no sane person confesses this to a stranger. Just leave her alone, and me as well." Matt grabbed his things and moved away from the table.

Jack got up slowly and joined him. "No one is going anywhere. We may as well talk this through."

Matt looked at the front door. It was also caked from the outside with snow. *Why would anyone live here?* he thought. "What's there to talk about?"

"I have come to believe that nothing happens by chance. I had already given up trying to avenge my parents or even my own circumstances. But then you come into my life and you have direct contact with two out of eleven of the most dangerous people on the planet."

"Excluding yourself," Matt said, not smiling.

"I'm no angel but I didn't ask to live this life. It was thrown at me and I'm doing what I need to do. The question is what you will do."

I'm a coward, he wanted to say. *I turned my back on Julia twice when I had the chance. I paid for it by watching the butchering of my mother and wife and then my children. For what? To play investment banker for some Mafioso wannabees?* What he did say was, "I won't do anything or say anything to anyone about you. You can count on me."

"That's not what I'm after. I trust you. I don't know exactly why, but I do. I want you to help me, not cover for me."

"I'm not the best when it comes to heroics."

"You don't need to."

"Then what do you need?"

"Your help."

"For what?"

"When you kill a president, another takes his place. When you kill an Einstein, it ends there. Many imitators and smart men will try to fill the void but will fail. Eventually, another great mind will be born. Hopefully it isn't killed through apathy or neglect. When you kill a Hitler or Stalin or Mao, it ends there. Many bad men will step forward to fill the void, but few are as effective."

Matt listened the best he could. Depression was starting to take hold and it was all he could do to keep it at bay. Jack's voice droned on in his ear.

"Bureaucracies cannot be killed. They are the structure and people fill the void. We are replaceable, cogs in the master scheme. They are tinkered with, adjusted, and occasionally evolve. Revolutions don't kill them.

Ancient Rome or Xian or Babylon were run by its systems of politics and power; money is integral to the form of the structure. People are merely the blood that flows through its veins, the cogs that turn the wheels.

"Occasionally, there are men who understand the system, who are aware of the structure and who are able to manipulate it without becoming part of it. Those men sit on the top and turn external valves that increase or decrease the flow of its parts; they encourage or discourage evolution of the design. Those men and women are like Einstein, only without the genetic material. They are a creation of chance combined with wisdom handed down. It is learned and it is privileged. Kill them and they, like the Einsteins, Hitlers, and Maos, are not easily replaced.

"They may become as gods, part of history and lore. Their influence would be discussed in hushed tones and written tomes. But they would be dead. They would be the blind watchmaker, the indifferent god who winds its wares and walks away. We endure and persevere within the construct and within the rules laid out by it. It would remain cruel and harsh but it would be fairer."

Matt listened and drank his Coke. "So what are you saying? There are a handful of people it pays to kill because they can't be replaced?"

"Exactly," Jack said. "That is why the Order of Prime and its successor organisations and members must die."

Matt almost spat out the Coke he had in his mouth. He looked left and right. "Are you crazy? You can't just talk about killing people without getting arrested— or worse."

"I'm still here. Everything we do is monitored. The question is whether that monitoring is effective or efficient. By the time anyone discovers our conversations, we will be gone. Yes, we should be having this stark naked in a hurricane, but that isn't so practical."

"I think I'm just going to change your name to Satan."

Jack laughed. "I like your sense of humour. It's a credit to you considering your own journey. I wasn't looking for anyone, partly because I don't trust anyone. Then, when I was ready to return to the world, heart at peace and no revenge on my mind, you come into my life. This isn't just a coincidence."

"Are you superstitious?"

"No, I just don't believe things happen by coincidence. We are all connected, if only through national security cameras and recorders. We can be better than simply puppets. We can be men and women, unique and free. We can choose to serve, but I want that to be a choice made freely."

"Don't you think it's too late to be a revolutionary? Isn't that treason?"

"I don't believe so, but I also don't want to be caught and found out. That's why I took the battery out of your phone and left it in the car."

"I don't have a phone," Matt lied.

"Then whose was it?"

"I don't know."

"Better that I did it then. It's in the car if you need it."

"You're really starting to concern me."

"I think you can handle much more than what I've been talking about."

"Why are you so confident about me?"

"Because I read your file."

Matt paused. "File?"

"I have one on every connection to the deciding members of the Order. It's encrypted but I accessed it this morning. That's why I know you're tougher than you make out. You watched your mother flayed, dismembered, and packed up and never ratted out the person. That couldn't have been easy."

Matt was feeling ill. The image always made his stomach turn.

"Your children were found in similar ways and yet you never pointed the finger at the culprit, preferring to stay in prison. I thought about that and then realised you wanted to kill him yourself. Did you do manage to do it?"

Matt's mouth became gooey with a thick saliva under his tongue and dry on the roof. He tried to swallow and almost choked. He took another slug of Coke before speaking. "He died a few days before I was let out."

Jack slapped his knee. "I knew it. You have exactly what it takes mentally but you need help to carry out the plan."

Matt was silent.

"I can be that man. I can make your plans come true." Jack's eyes glowed as he spoke.

Matt's head was bowed, deep in thought. "You want to chase puppet masters, yes?"

"I want to cut their threads."

He paused and smiled. He couldn't help it. "I don't know what decision is the right one. You also said that everything is connected and that there is no such thing as coincidence, yes?"

"I did."

"Then I suggest we try something I use when I don't know what to do."

"Sounds like a good idea. I'm game."

"Find me two revolvers and two bullets. We'll let fate settle this."

"Russian roulette? Are you crazy?" Jack was looking at the man from South Africa and wondering if he made a mistake.

"No crazier than anything you've just told me." Matt leaned back and drank his Coke. *If this idiot actually finds the revolvers, I'll be amazed*, he thought. *Especially in this weather.*

"I'll be right back. Don't move." Jack got up and went to the front desk. He talked with the woman for a while and then was directed to the kitchen. In the back, he was introduced to Zayne, the owner of the hotel and head cook. He lived in an apartment attached to the building.

"How can I help you?"

"First, I wanted to say that you have a great hotel. My friend and I have been enjoying your food and comfort of your bar. We keep commenting on how lucky we have been to have reached your place and not to get stuck in the storm."

"Thank you. Thank you very much." He took off his hat and shook Jack's hand. His face was reddish purple with broken veins on his nose. His hair was matted from the sweat under his cap. What hair remained was long but he was otherwise bald.

"I'm really sorry to ask this but my friend is a gun nut and wanted to show me a few things with a revolver. I told him everything will be closed due to the storm. Then I thought perhaps you might know of a shop that sold them."

"No. Nothing in town. Everything's shut. Sorry."

"Okay. Just thought I'd ask. If you think of anything, I'd appreciate it."

"I do have a few revolvers myself, if that helps. I'd need to know what you guys are up to. I can't just give it to you." His eyes looked more alive when the guns were discussed.

"I understand. I'm sure my friend won't mind having you take part in whatever we do."

The owner's eyes began to dart with excitement. "Sounds good. When do you want them?"

"After you're finished in the kitchen. We'll be in the lounge."

"See you then."

Jack shook hands and returned to Matt.

"Found two revolvers. They are the owner's so he'll need to play along or at least watch. Is that a problem?"

Shit, Matt thought. *Oh well, if that's how it's going to be... Fate will have its say.* "Great. We'll get ourselves ready," he said.

∞

"Zayne's got them in his apartment. He's waiting for us."

"So you want to do this?"

"No, but I need you and this is one way to determine this once and for all. No police, no complaining, just a test and an answer."

"I thought I was the crazy one."

"Life is about risk and decisions. You told me how you decided your fate in South Africa. I believe you. This is what you need."

"What if you die?"

"It'll be too late to worry about it. Now let's go."

There was a walkway between the kitchen and Zayne's apartment. It was more of a shelter than a part of the hotel but at least they didn't need to go into the storm itself.

"Welcome to my humble abode." Zayne was waiting like the good host and opened the door the moment they knocked. The apartment wasn't large but had a good sized lounge with two overstuffed sofas, a glass magazine table and a massive television mounted on the wall with speakers and stereo system below. Wires led everywhere and game consoles were sitting next to the TV remote control.

"Thanks, Zayne. I know this is crazy."

"Hey, no probs. I know the South Africans are as crazy as the Yanks with their guns."

Jack and Matt smiled.

"I've got drinks in the fridge and snacks on the table, but let me show you the toys." He skipped to his bedroom and was back within seconds. In his hands were two revolvers. One was a .357 Magnum and the other a .38 Special. He checked each one to ensure it was unloaded before handing them over, first to Jack and then Matt.

"This looks the business. Where do you want to sit?" Matt was weighing the larger gun in his hand.

"Let's sit in the kitchen. Less chance of us falling over."

"So what is it you want to know about these guns?" Zayne was keen to involve himself in the conversation.

"We want to play a game." Matt said it deadpan as he looked at Zayne.

Zayne, in return, smiled. "I'm all for a game."

"Russian roulette." Matt was deadly serious.

The owner's smile slowly disappeared and he became excited. "Are you serious? Don't shit with me. Are you really serious? I'm in!" He thumped his chest and howled. "Yeah! I want in."

"We're serious," Matt said.

"So am I. Do you know how long I've wanted to play this? Everyone talks about it but no one does it. I'm in." He sat at the kitchen table and produced two types of bullets, one for each revolver.

Matt looked at Jack for guidance. The other shrugged and they both sat down.

"What are the rules?"

"We're not doing anything stupid like putting in multiple bullets. One is enough. That gives us a one in six chance of blowing our brains out."

"Okay, but what's at stake?"

"You don't need to play, Zayne. We need to make a decision and this is the way I have done it in the past. I'm letting the Fates decide."

"Cool!"

Matt rolled his eyes. *I'm sixty-seven years old and I'm going to be found dead next to some nutter who lives in an ice box.* Then he thought about Julia and what got him where he was and he refocussed.

"Choose the revolver you like," Jack said. "I'll take the one you don't want."

"I'll take the .357," Matt said. "I like the weight and the cylinder spins like a charm."

"I keep them both in perfect working order."

"I can see that. Nicely done."

"Can I play?" Zayne looked at them like a younger brother wanting to join a ball game.

"After us. If we're both still alive and you want to play, it's your life."

"Cool."

Zayne gave each of them the correct bullet for their gun. Each of them double-checked the calibre by looking at the back of the bullet. Convinced, they put the bullet in the cylinder and spun it as hard as they could. They snapped it into place at the same time and held the end of the barrel to their head, just behind the eyes.

"We can call this off if you want," Matt said. He was beginning to sweat. The adrenaline was kicking in and his hand began to shake slightly.

"Not at all. We made an agreement and I'm seeing this through."

"You guys are fucking nuts! I can't believe you're doing it."

They ignored Zayne.

"On three… two… one…" they both pulled their trigger. Both hammers fell and slammed into the firing pin. The firing pin was punched out with enough force to ignite the small explosive force inside the primer. But both pins punched into empty holes. Click click.

Jack was shaking convulsively by now, as was Matt. They slammed their revolvers onto the table and tried not to vomit. Jack was finding it hard to see.

Matt's eyes glimmered brighter and then a cloud passed over them as they realised he was still alive.

"Holy shit! Holy shit!" Zayne had kicked back his chair when the hammers fell. "I never thought you'd actually do it!" He was pacing his apartment, swearing and whooping. "I need to do it."

"Just wait," Matt said. "There's a second part to it."

Jack's head snapped towards him. "I wasn't told of that. You're changing the rules because you didn't get the result you wanted. We had a deal." He was seeing fine now.

"Part one is for us to pull the trigger on ourselves. Part two is for us to pull the trigger on the other party. We'd do it the same way, on three."

"This is crazy shit! I love it!" Zayne was yelling. He couldn't be quieted. "I'll do it."

"No. It's between Jack and me."

"I'll take his place," Zayne said. "I've always wanted to do this. I'm just watching and my body is buzzing. This is better than anything I've taken. Better by a long shot. Let me do the next round."

Jack was silent. He did what he had agreed to. He wasn't suicidal. This next round was just that. "I'm okay with Zayne taking my place." His voice was hoarse from the adrenaline. *Fate.*

"I'm okay with that if Zayne is," Matt said. "You okay? This is serious."

"I'm okay." Zayne took the .38 and pointed it at Matt. Matt did the same to Zayne. Neither cylinder was spun.

"On three… two… one…" they both pulled their trigger. Both hammers fell and slammed into the firing pin. The firing pin was punched out with enough force to ignite the small explosive force inside the primer. Both pins punched into waiting primers. Bang Bang.

Chapter Twenty-Four

Oh Shit

Jack had been watching the two men holding their guns. Matt's hand was definitely shaking more than Zayne's. The sweat was running freely from Matt's forehead down into his eyes. Jack could see Matt squint to counter the salty sting on his vision. Zayne was frighteningly calm considering the stakes. His eyes were cool, calm, and inviting of the rush.

When the bullets flew, Jack's body jumped and his chair kicked back behind him as he stood. The blasts were eardrum breaking in the small confined space of the kitchen. In one instant, he saw both guns drop to the table and fall off. Zayne's head snapped back as a hole ripped through him from the eye socket and out the back. Jack didn't have time to comment or think about the size of the hole other than to know Zayne was dead. His peripheral vision saw Matt fly back at the same time but he didn't see any blood against the wall behind him. He ran over to see if he was hit and then saw the blood.

"Matt! What the hell!" Jack threw the table aside to get to his new friend faster. He grabbed the unconscious head and searched for the source of the wound. The blood was pouring from a graze that ran alongside the side of his head from the eye socket past the ear. The ear was badly damaged but he otherwise was in one piece. "You lucky son of a bitch!" He put him down and ran to the bathroom. Zayne was bleeding out badly and there was blood everywhere. *One thing at a time,* he thought. *Triage.*

"Shit, this is the worst stocked bathroom cabinet I've ever seen." Jack was talking to himself but didn't care. He needed to think and talking helped him focus and fight off the shock. "Bandages? Towel? Okay. Spray on deodorant? Might work. Kitchen. Find something there." He grabbed some Band-Aids and a towel as well as the deodorant. In the kitchen, he looked for anything that would help cauterise the wound. *If I was Rambo, I'd use the gunpowder from the shell*, he thought.

He knew that corn starch or sugar or even cayenne pepper would work. He found corn starch and cayenne. "I'll use them both," he said aloud. "Sorry my friend. This is going to hurt."

He found some bottled water and poured it out slowly over the wound, exposing it and letting the water push the hair out of the way. He then used the spray deodorant up close against the length of the wound. Matt remained unconscious. He poured the entire contents of the corn starch on the wound and then the cayenne on top of it. He looked at the Band-Aids but couldn't figure out how to make them stick. He used the towel to wrap Matt's head. He then undid his belt and used that against the towel to apply pressure.

"Not pretty but it should do the job." He went to Zayne but there was no pulse. "Poor bastard. Sorry to have dragged you into this."

He picked up the phone to call the emergency services and then heard the howling of the wind. There would be no rescue, no police, no nothing until everything opened up.

"What did you make me do? I thought my running days were over. I just needed to get to Churchill and I was to live happily ever after. Now I've got a dead body, a gunshot wound, and all of our DNA and fingerprints at the scene." He looked at the pool of blood. "So what am I supposed to do now?"

He heard a groan and some movement from Matt. He rushed next to him. "Take it easy, you'll be okay." He was careful not to move the head bandage as he helped an increasingly conscious Matt sit up against the wall.

"Y… Wh.. K…" He was moving his lips but little sound was coming out.

"What's that? Keep silent. Conserve your energy." Matt refused to relax and pulled Jack's ear next to his mouth. He was only able to manage a whisper but Jack heard him loud and clear.

"You win. Let's kill 'em all."

ABOUT THE AUTHOR

Baron was born in Canada.
He currently lives in South East England,
somewhere near the Surrey/Sussex borders.
Sightings vary.

If you'd like to follow Baron and receive free samples of his
future writing before it is published, please visit
www.baronalexanderbooks.com